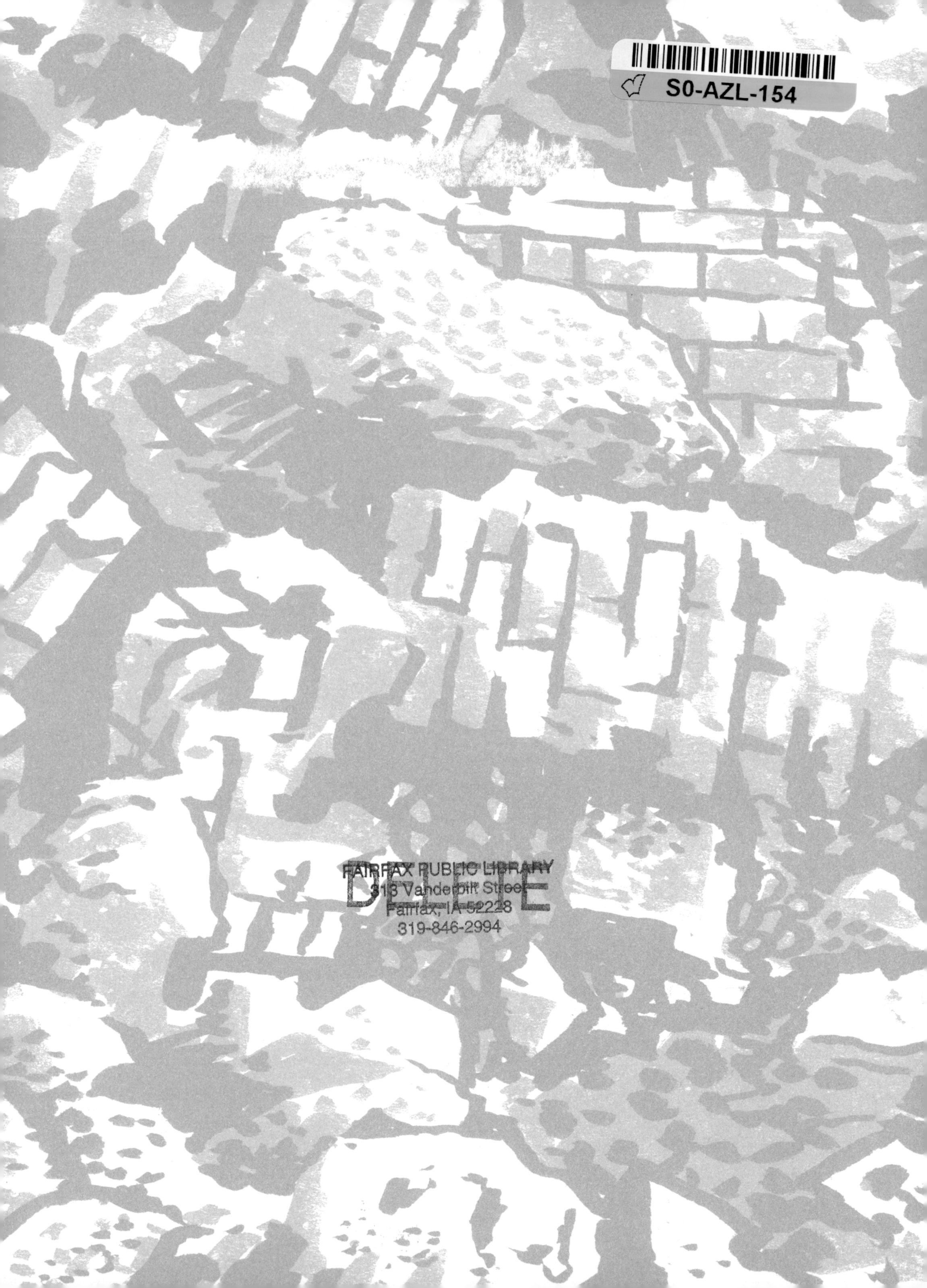

For Amy

Kingdom © Nobrow 2018.

This is a first edition published in 2018
by Nobrow Ltd. 27 Westgate Street, London E8 3RL.

Text and illustrations © Jon McNaught 2018.
Jon McNaught has asserted his right under the Copyright,
Designs and Patents Act, 1988, to be identified
as the Author and Illustrator of this Work.

Published in the US by Nobrow (US) Inc.
Printed in Poland on FSC® certified paper.

MIX
Paper from
responsible sources
FSC® C001693

ISBN: 978-1-910620-24-3
Order from www.nobrow.net

Fx: 09-19

KINGDOM

Jon McNaught

NOBROW

London | New York

To the Sea

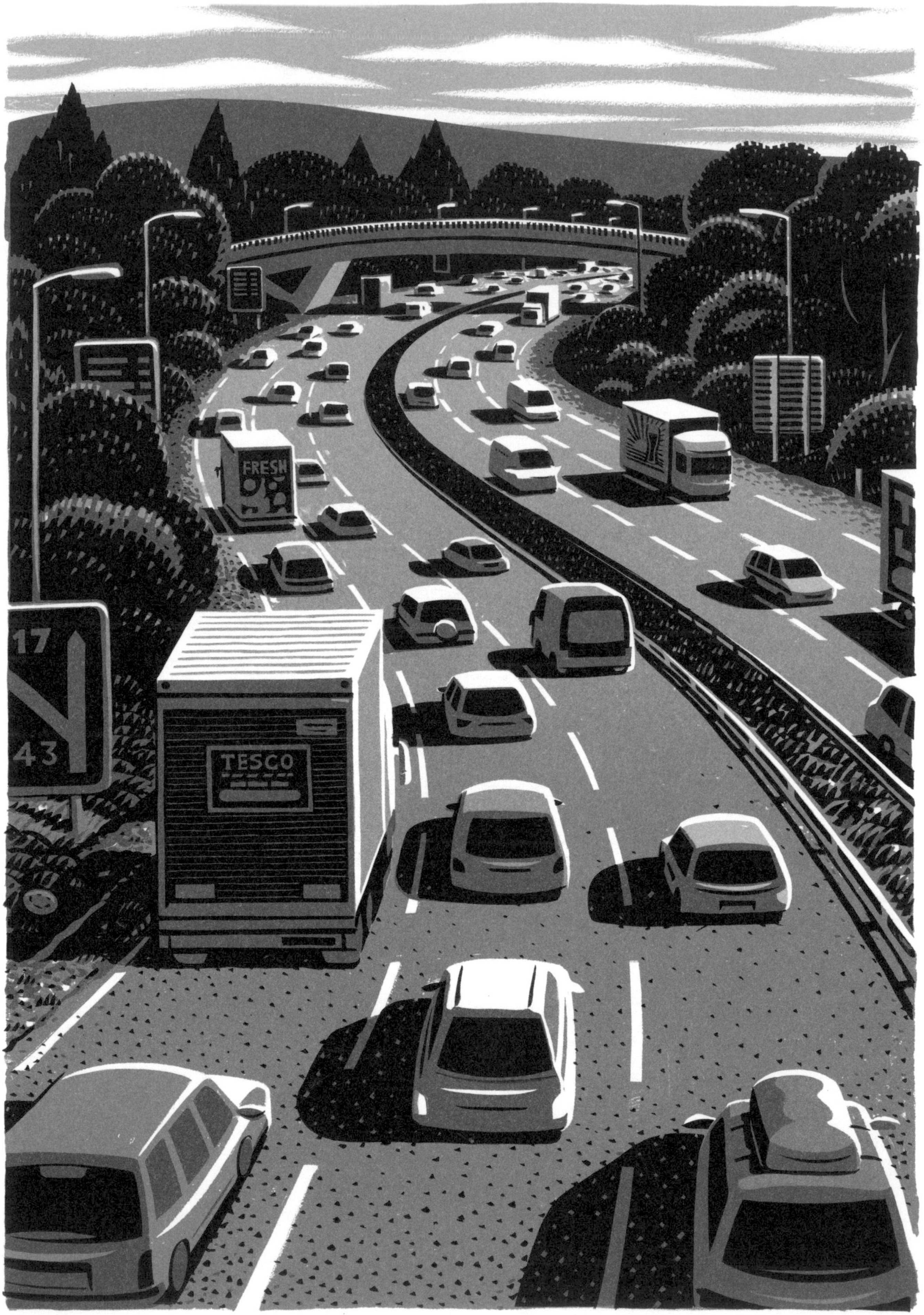
17
43
FRESH
TESCO

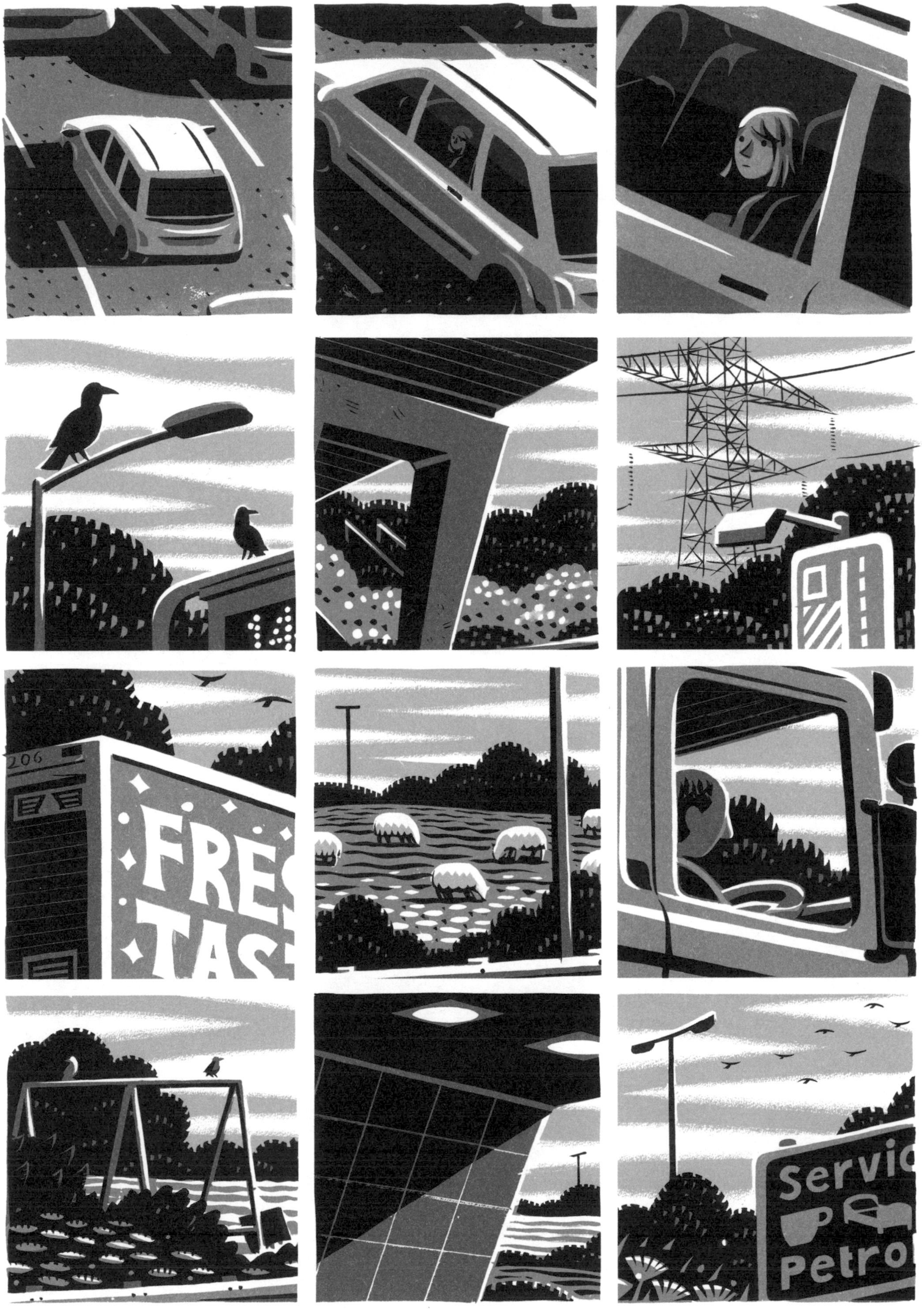
206
FRE
TA
Servi
Petro

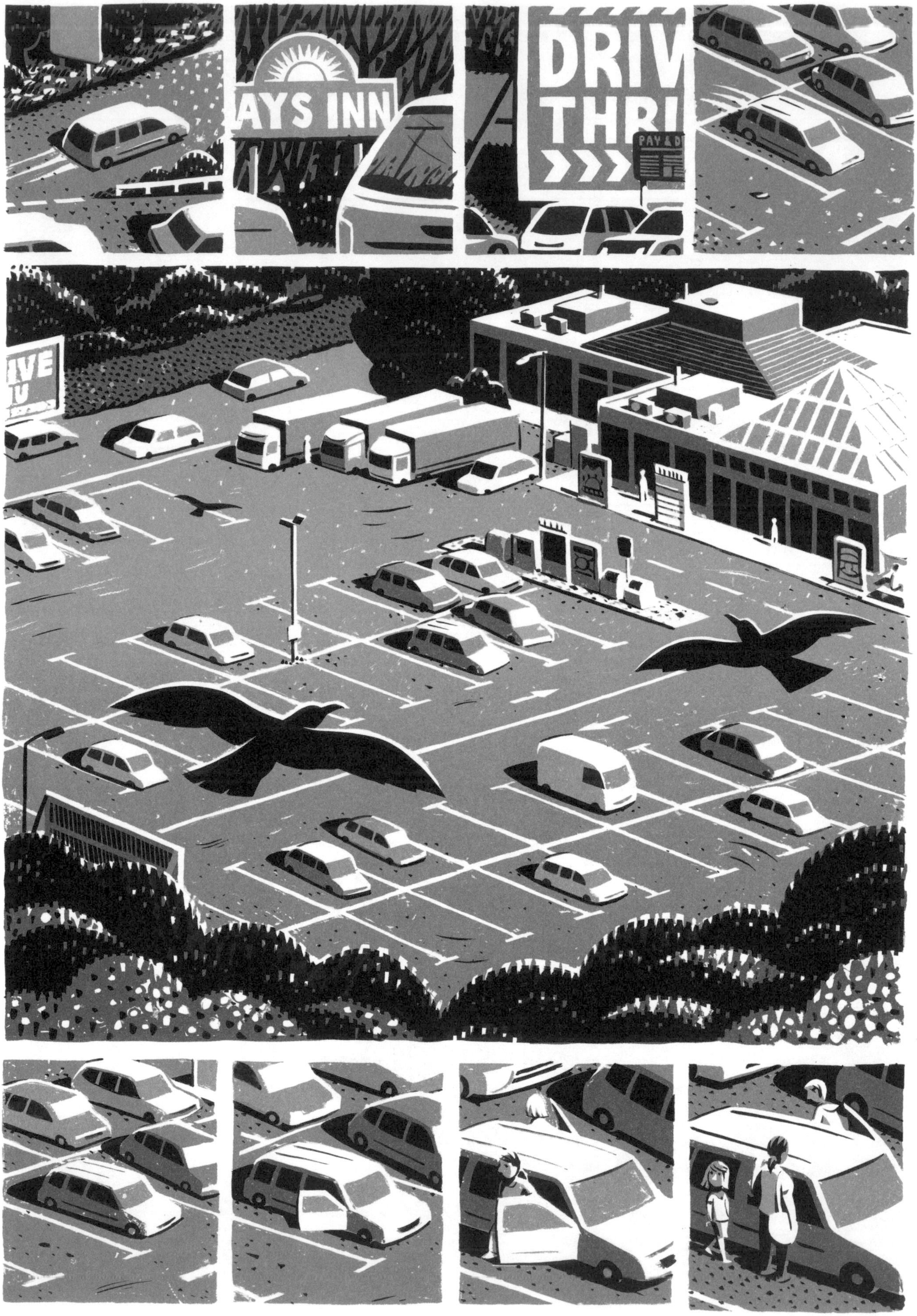
AYS INN
DRIV
THRI

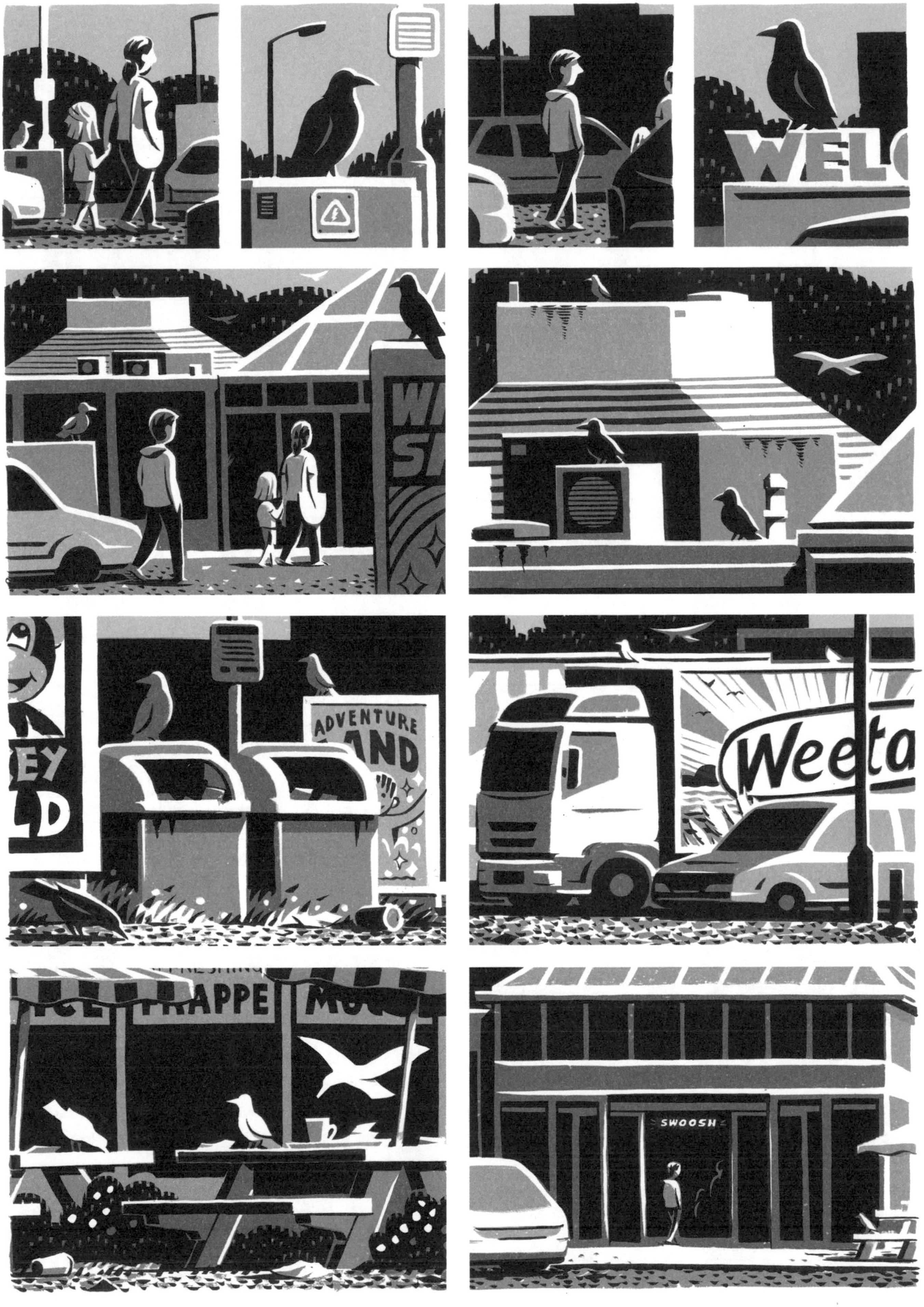
WEL
ADVENTURE
Weeta
FRAPPE
SWOOSH

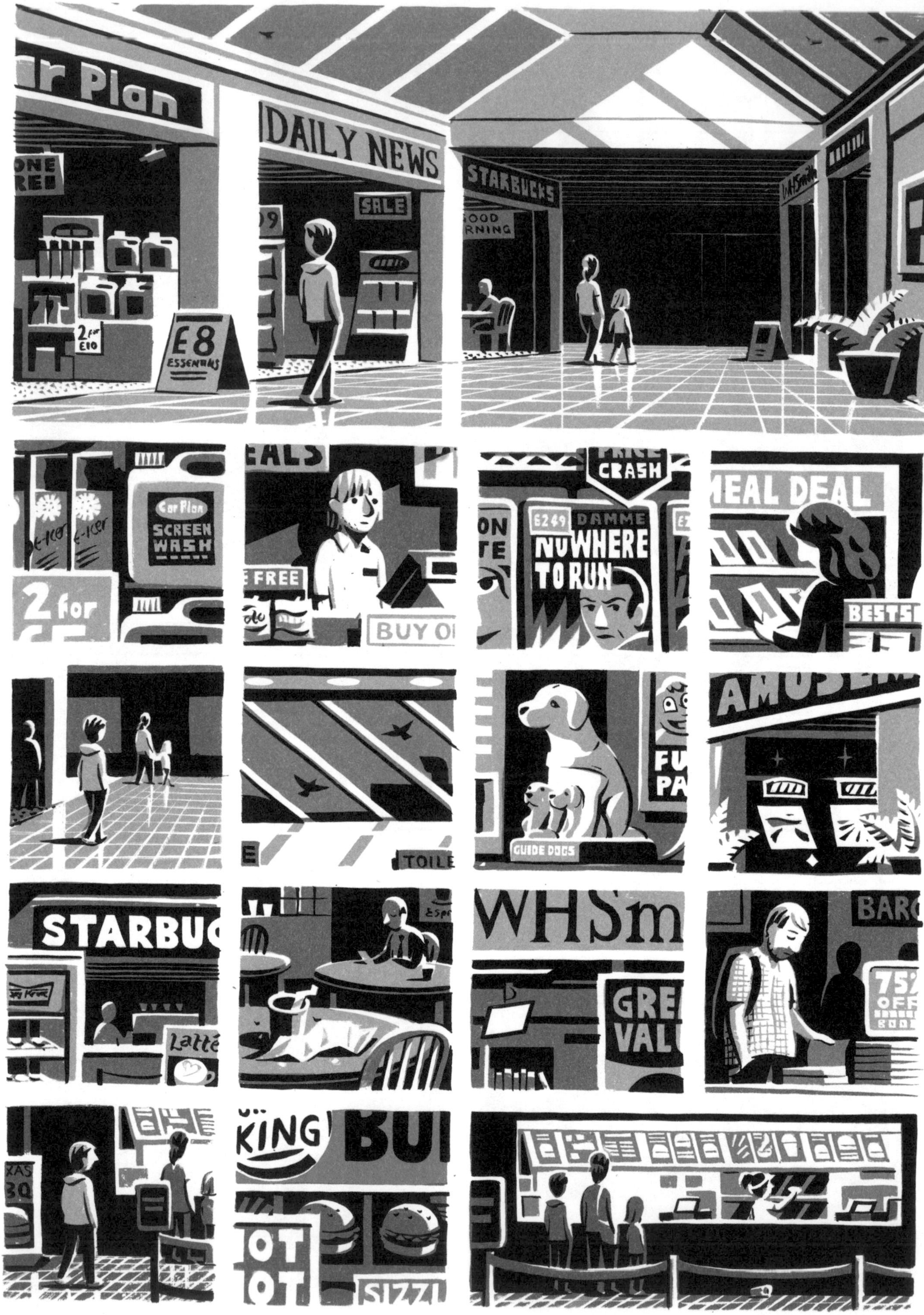

r Plan
DAILY NEWS
SALE
STARBUCKS
2 for £10
£8 ESSENTIALS
Car Plan
SCREEN WASH
2 for
E FREE
BUY O
CRASH
£249 DAMME
NOWHERE TO RUN
MEAL DEAL
BESTS
TOILE
GUIDE DOGS
AMUSE
STARBU
Latte
WHSm
GRE
VAL
BARG
75%
OFF
KING
BU
SIZZ

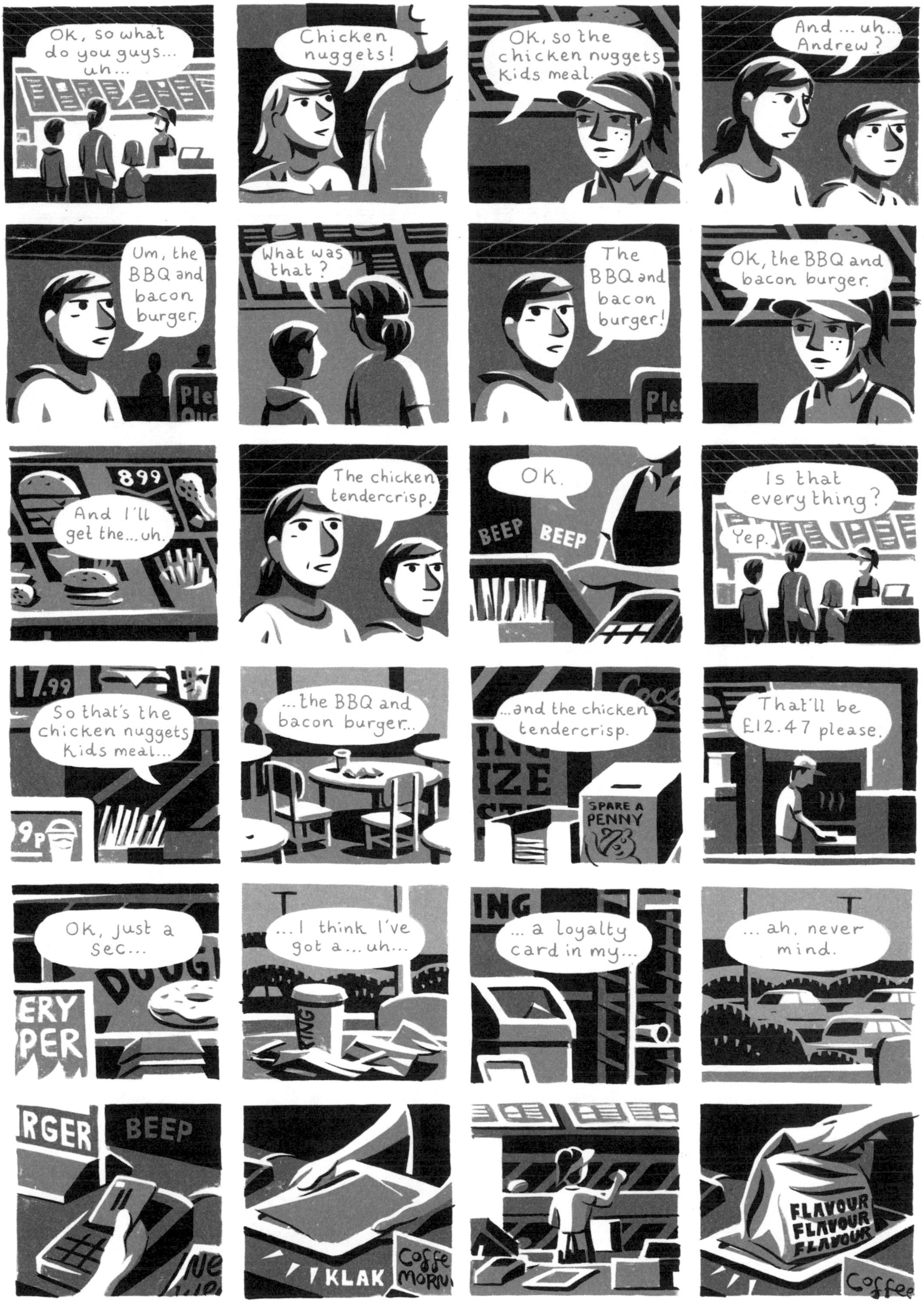
Ok, so what do you guys... uh...
Chicken nuggets!
Ok, so the chicken nuggets Kids meal.
And ... uh... Andrew?
Um, the BBQ and bacon burger.
What was that?
The BBQ and bacon burger!
OK, the BBQ and bacon burger.
899
And I'll get the... uh.
The chicken tendercrisp.
OK.
BEEP BEEP
Is that everything?
Yep.
17.99
So that's the chicken nuggets Kids meal...
...the BBQ and bacon burger...
...and the chicken tendercrisp.
SPARE A PENNY
That'll be £12.47 please.
Ok, just a sec...
...I think I've got a... uh...
... a loyalty card in my...
... ah, never mind.
BEEP
KLAK
FLAVOUR FLAVOUR FLAVOUR

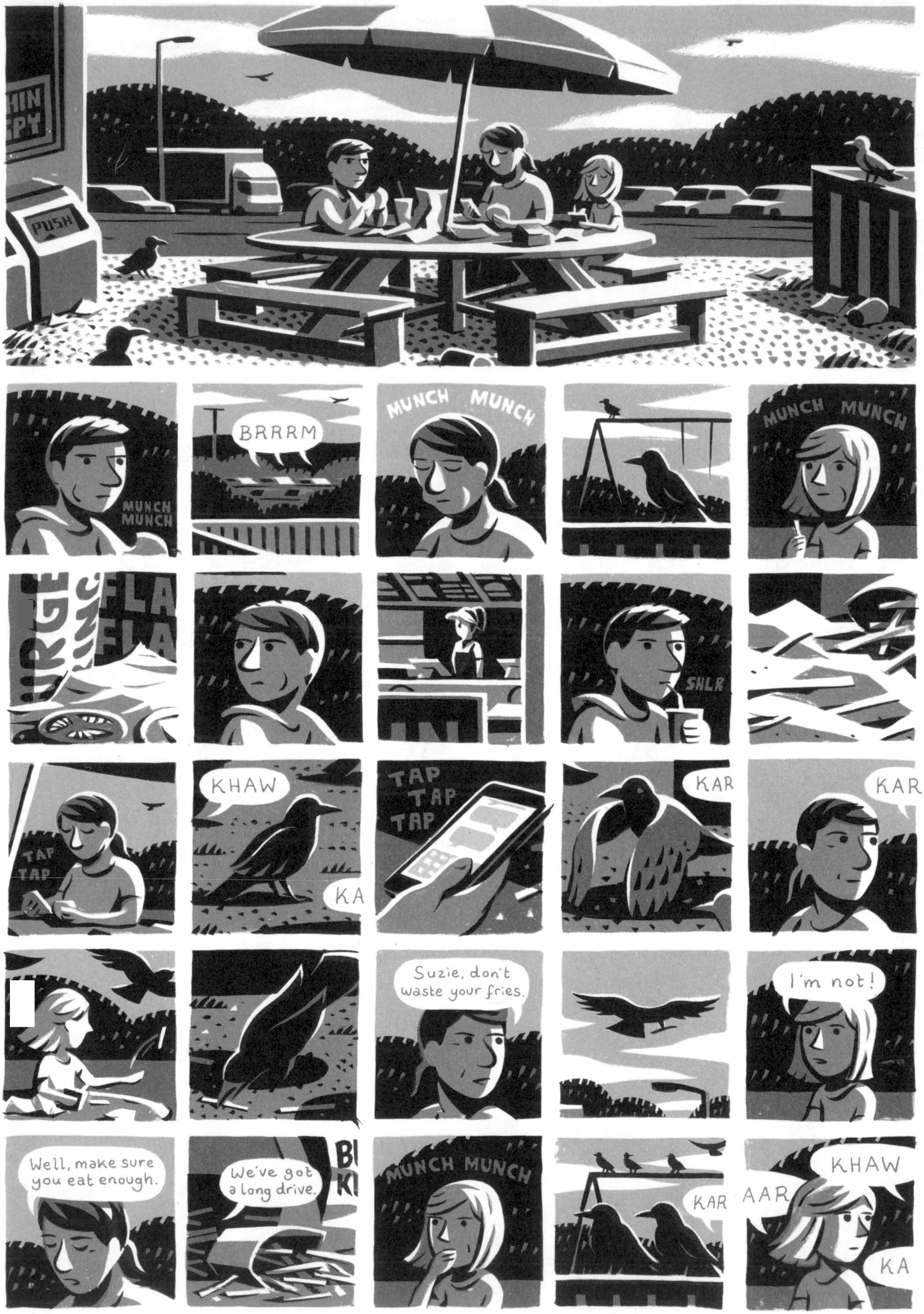
PUSH
MUNCH MUNCH
BRRRM
MUNCH MUNCH
MUNCH MUNCH
SHLR
TAP TAP
KHAW
KA
TAP TAP TAP
KAR
KAR
Suzie, don't waste your fries.
I'm not!
Well, make sure you eat enough.
We've got a long drive.
MUNCH MUNCH
KAR
AAR
KHAW
KA

How much further is it anyway?

Probably three hours or so...

...maybe four.

Four more hours!?

Why're we going somewhere so far away?

Well, cos it's a great place!

You guys will love it!

SHLRRRRRRR

It was my favourite place in the world when I was your age!

Me and your Uncle ... used to ...

...ring all of the caves and the dunes...
KLUNK

KLINK
CLUNK

...and even the end ... on th ... ly.
SHLR

Can I borrow some money for the arcade?

Sigh... not now, Andrew.

Just like a couple of quid.

No, sorry love.

I'm going to the bog.

Don't be too long!

WOOSH

Finished?

Yep.

KLIK

PUSH

PUSH

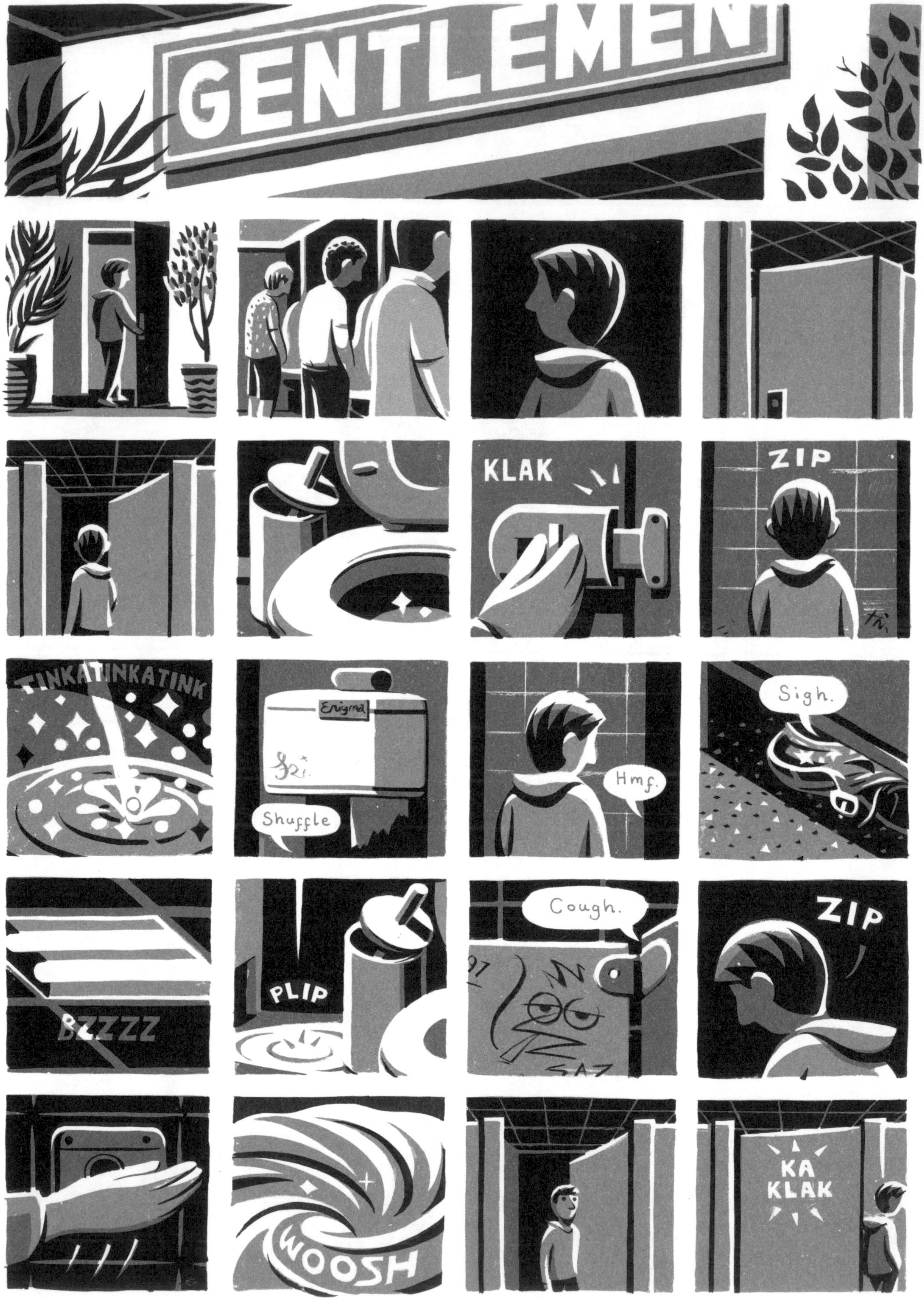
GENTLEMEN
KLAK
ZIP
TINKATINKATINK
Enigma
Shuffle
Hmf.
Sigh.
BZZZZ
PLIP
Cough.
ZIP
WOOSH
KA KLAK

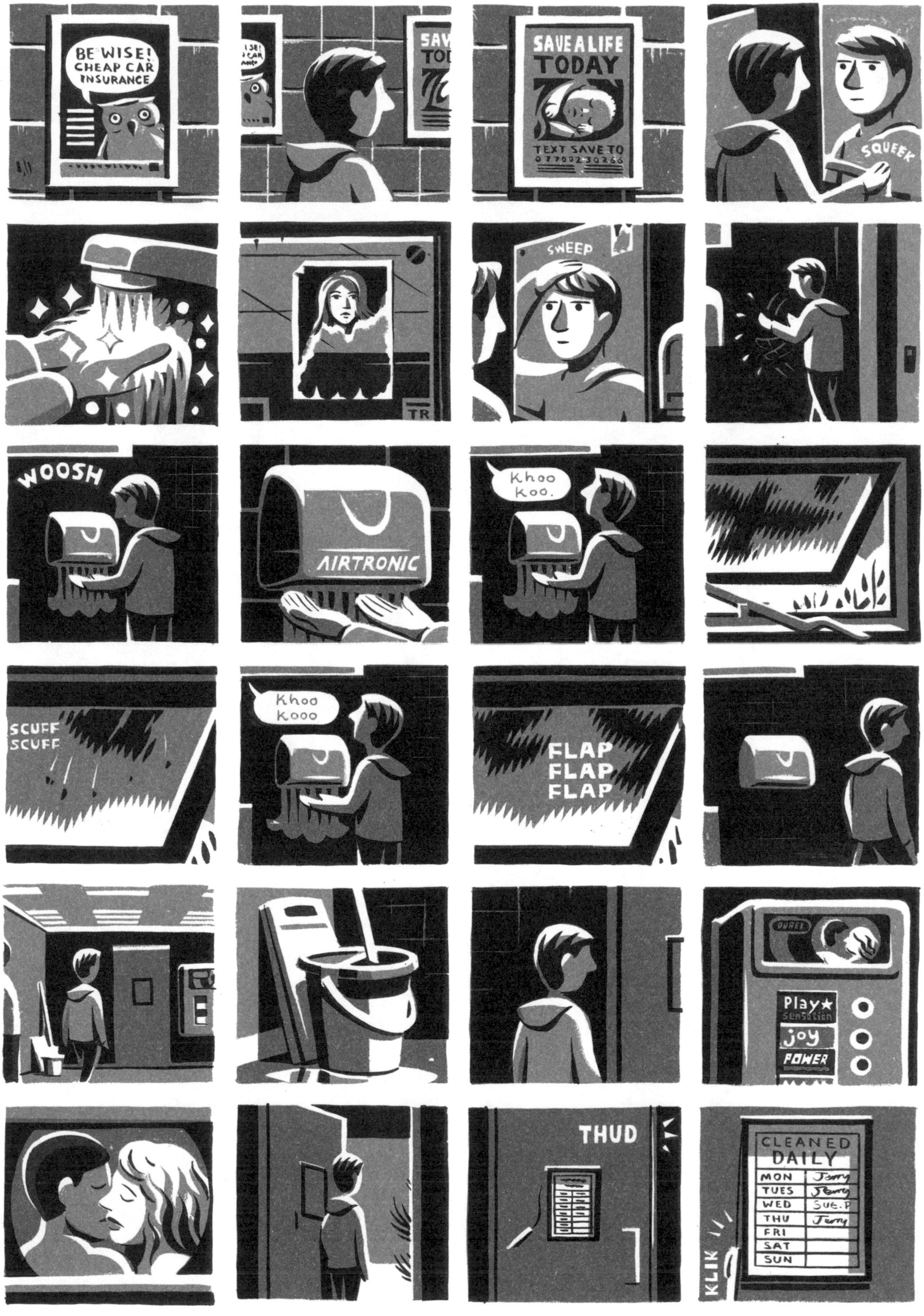
BE WISE! CHEAP CAR INSURANCE
SAVE A LIFE TODAY
TEXT SAVE TO 07700230266
SQUEEK
SWEEP
TR
WOOSH
AIRTRONIC
Khoo koo.
SCUFF SCUFF
Khoo kooo
FLAP FLAP FLAP
Play★ sensation
joy
POWER
THUD
CLEANED DAILY
MON Jerry
TUES Jerry
WED Sue.P
THU Jerry
FRI
SAT
SUN
KLIK

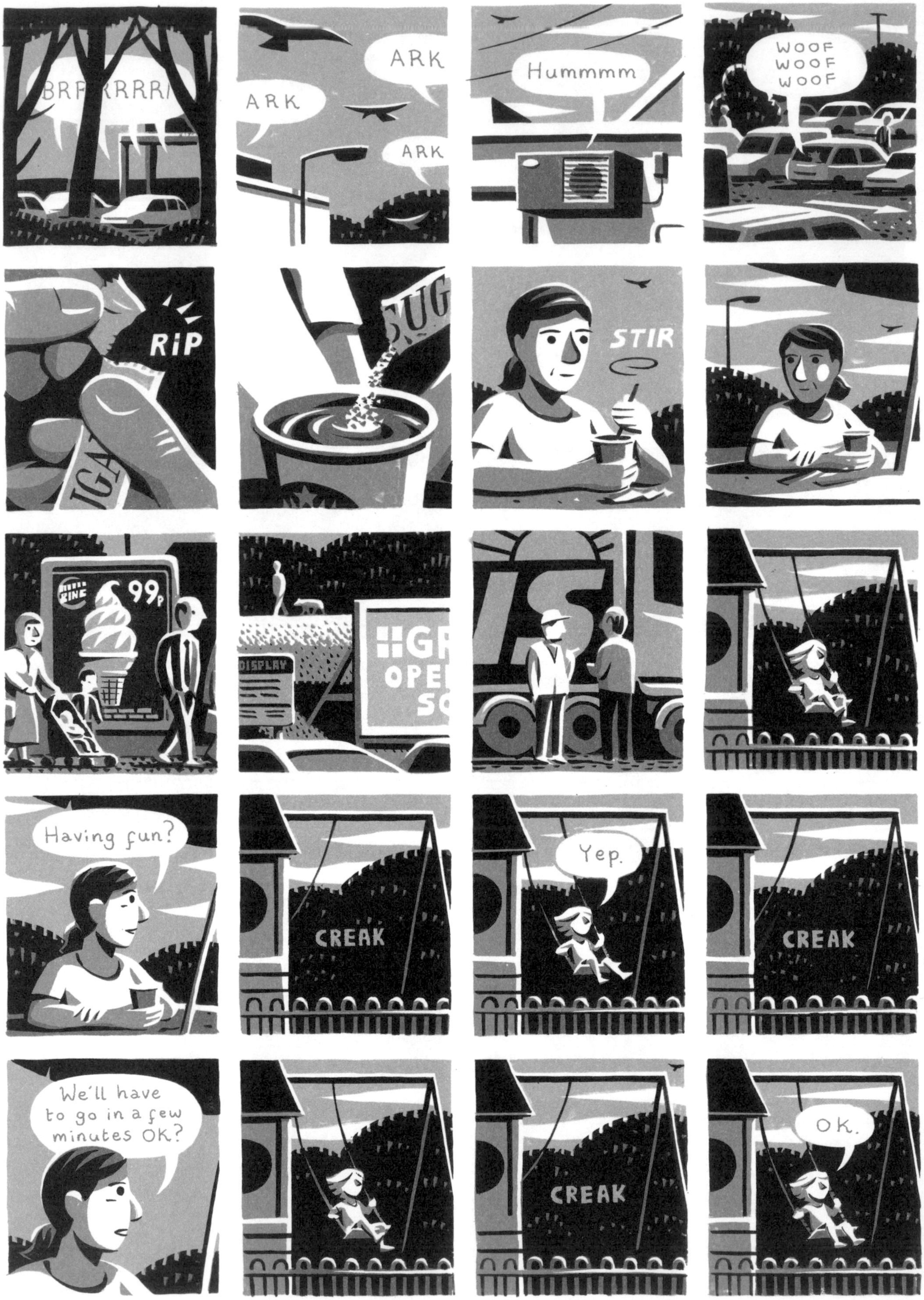
ARK
ARK
ARK
Hummmm
WOOF WOOF WOOF
RIP
STIR
99p
DISPLAY
Having fun?
CREAK
Yep.
CREAK
We'll have to go in a few minutes OK?
CREAK
OK.

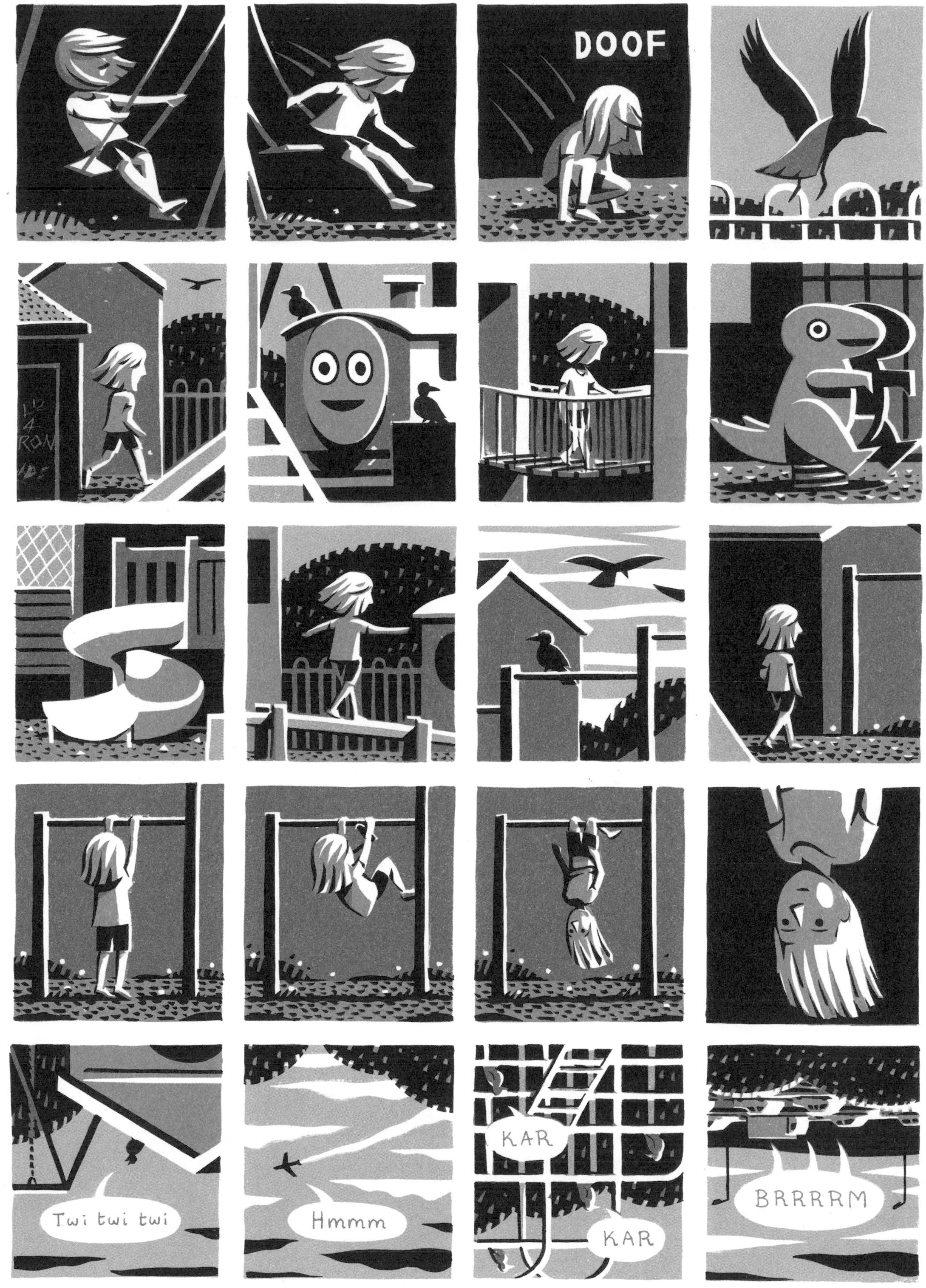
DOOF
Twi twi twi
Hmmm
KAR
KAR
BRRRRM

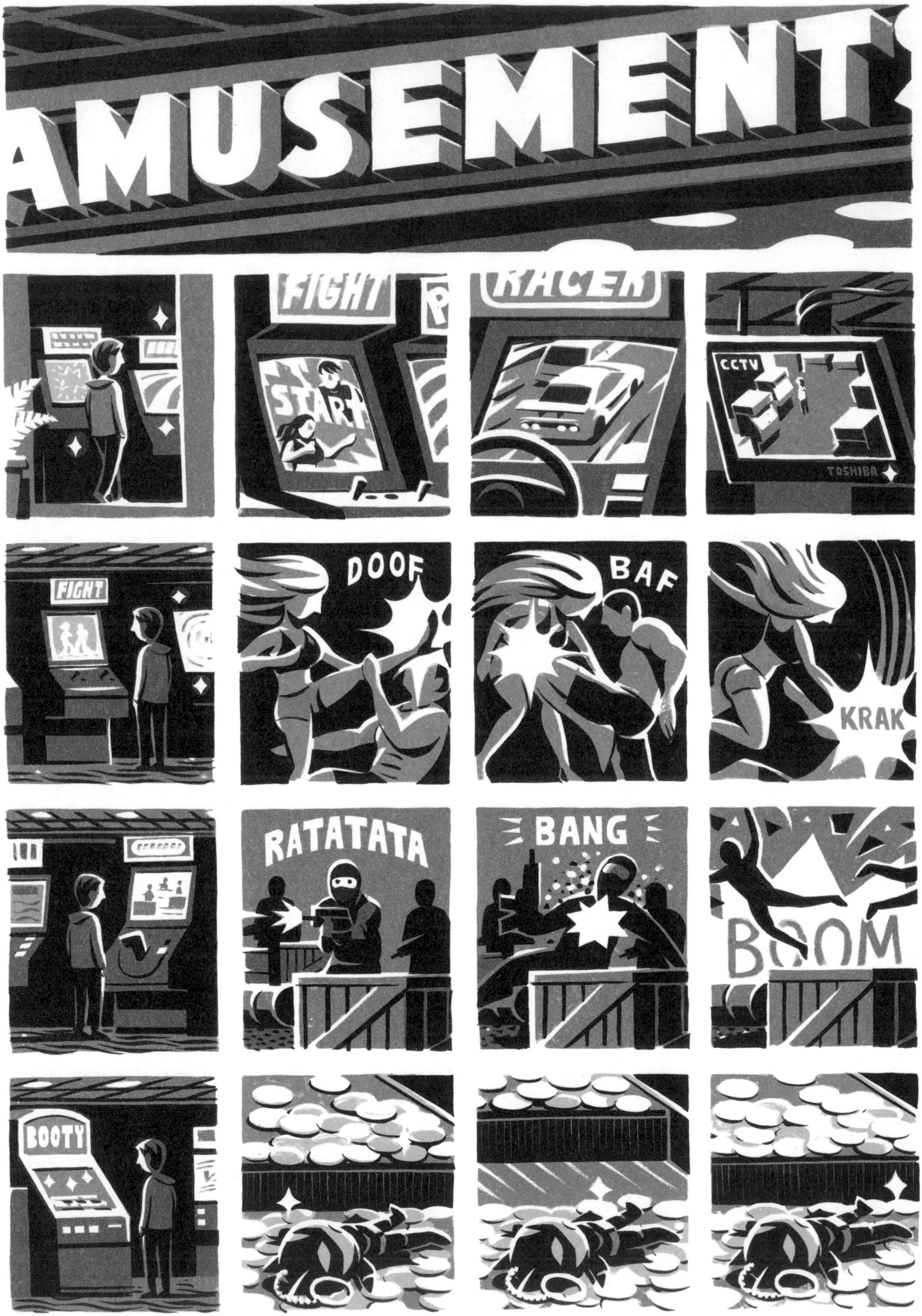
AMUSEMENT
FIGHT
START
RACER
CCTV
TOSHIBA
FIGHT
DOOF
BAF
KRAK
RATATATA
BANG
BOOM
BOOTY

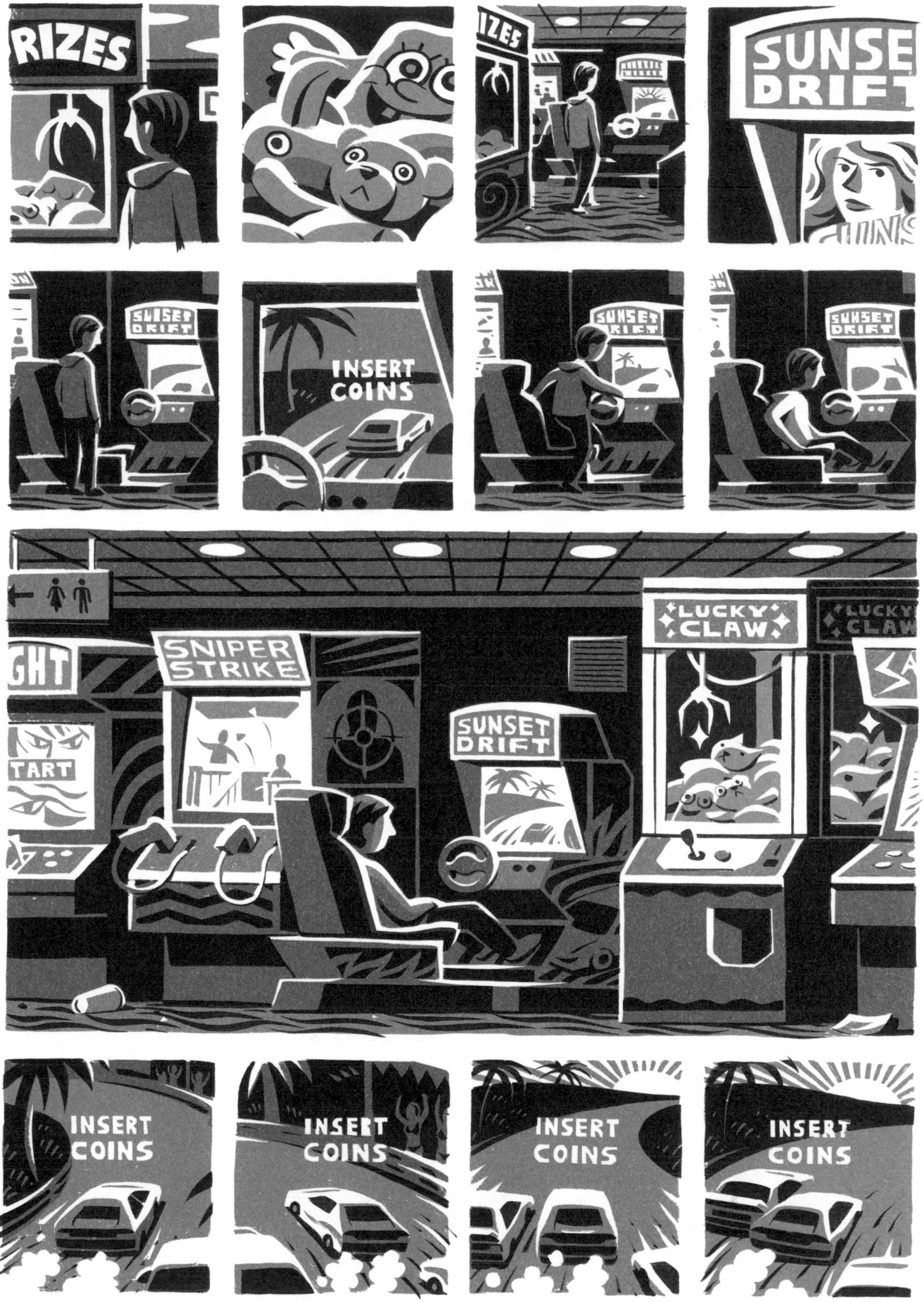

RIZES
IZES
SUNSE
DRIF
SUNSET DRIFT
INSERT
COINS
SUNSET DRIFT
SUNSET DRIFT
GHT
SNIPER
STRIKE
TART
SUNSET
DRIFT
LUCKY
CLAW
LUCKY
CLAW
INSERT
COINS
INSERT
COINS
INSERT
COINS
INSERT
COINS

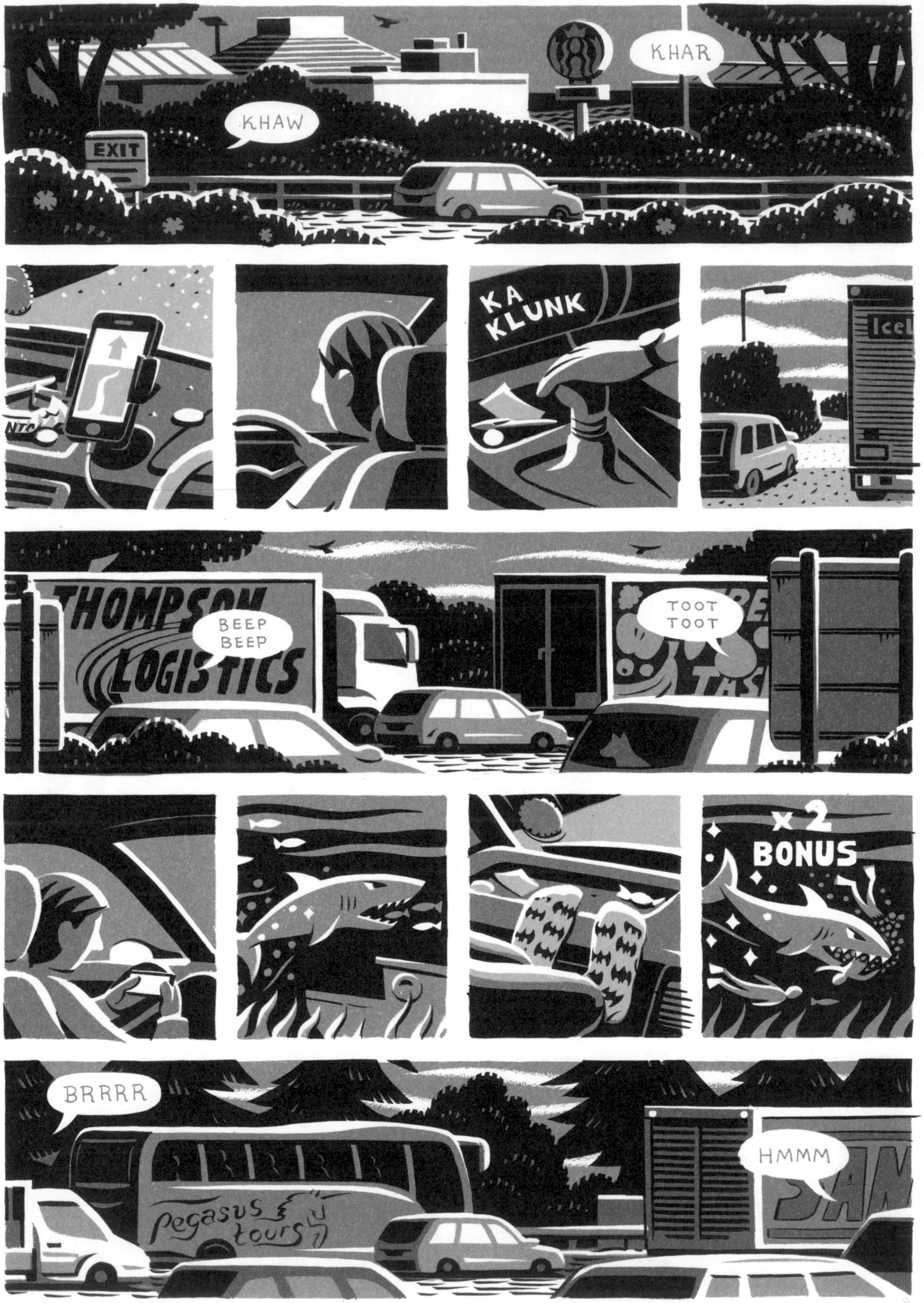
EXIT
KHAW
KHAR
KA KLUNK
THOMPSON LOGISTICS
BEEP BEEP
TOOT TOOT
x 2
BONUS
BRRRR
pegasus tours
HMMM

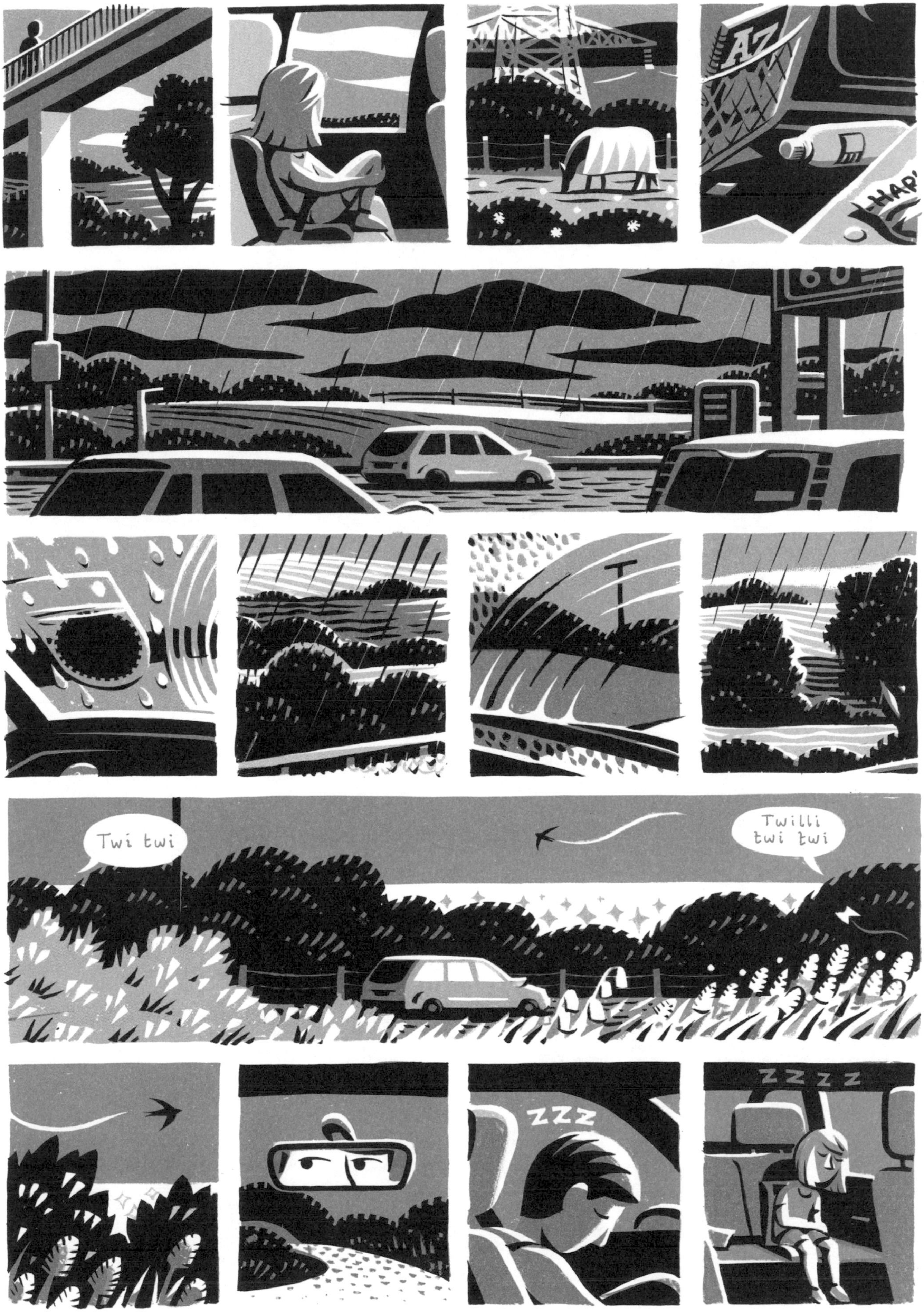
A-Z
-HAP
Twi twi
Twilli
twi twi
ZZZ
ZZZZ

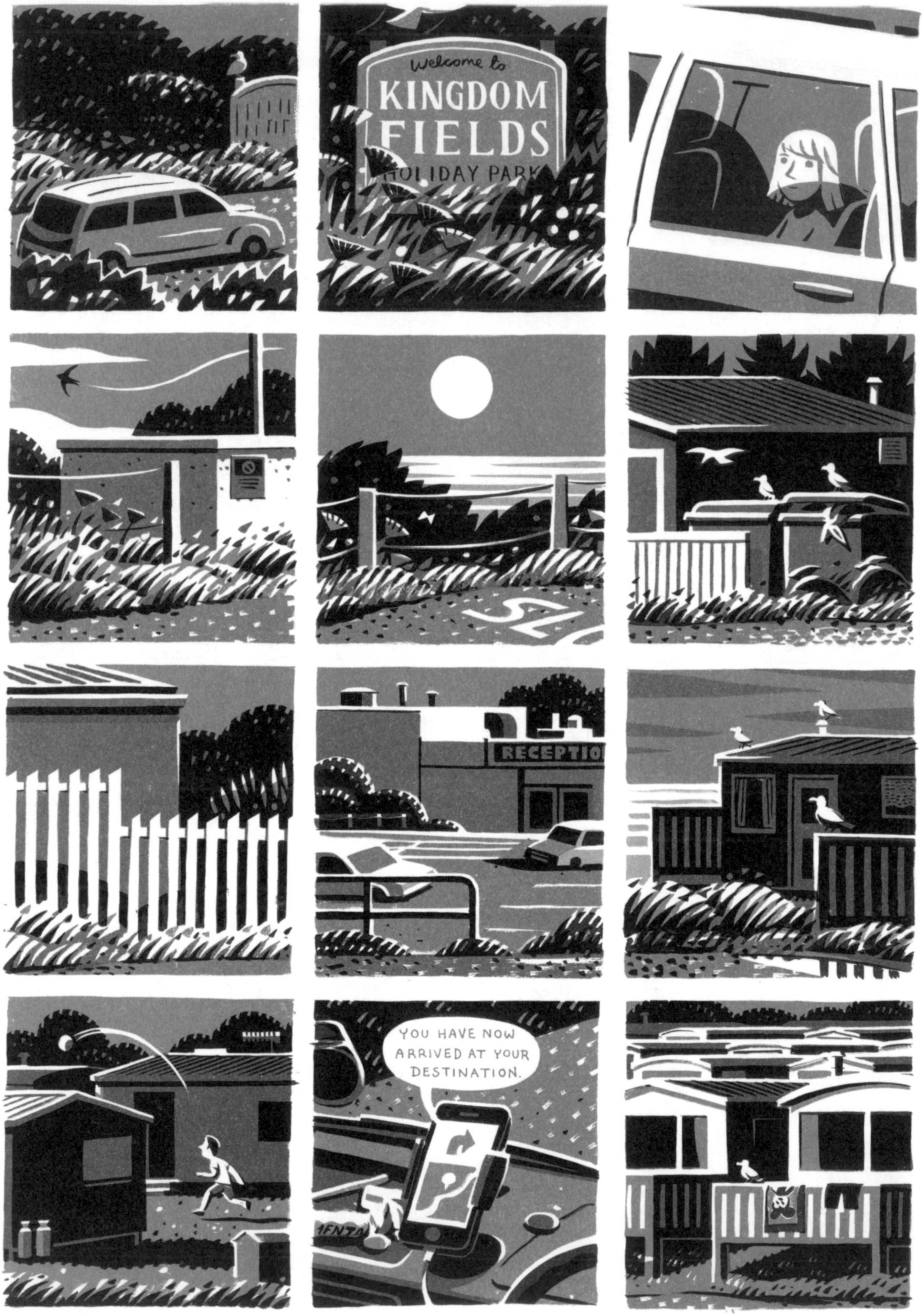
Welcome to
KINGDOM FIELDS
HOLIDAY PARK
RECEPTION
YOU HAVE NOW ARRIVED AT YOUR DESTINATION.

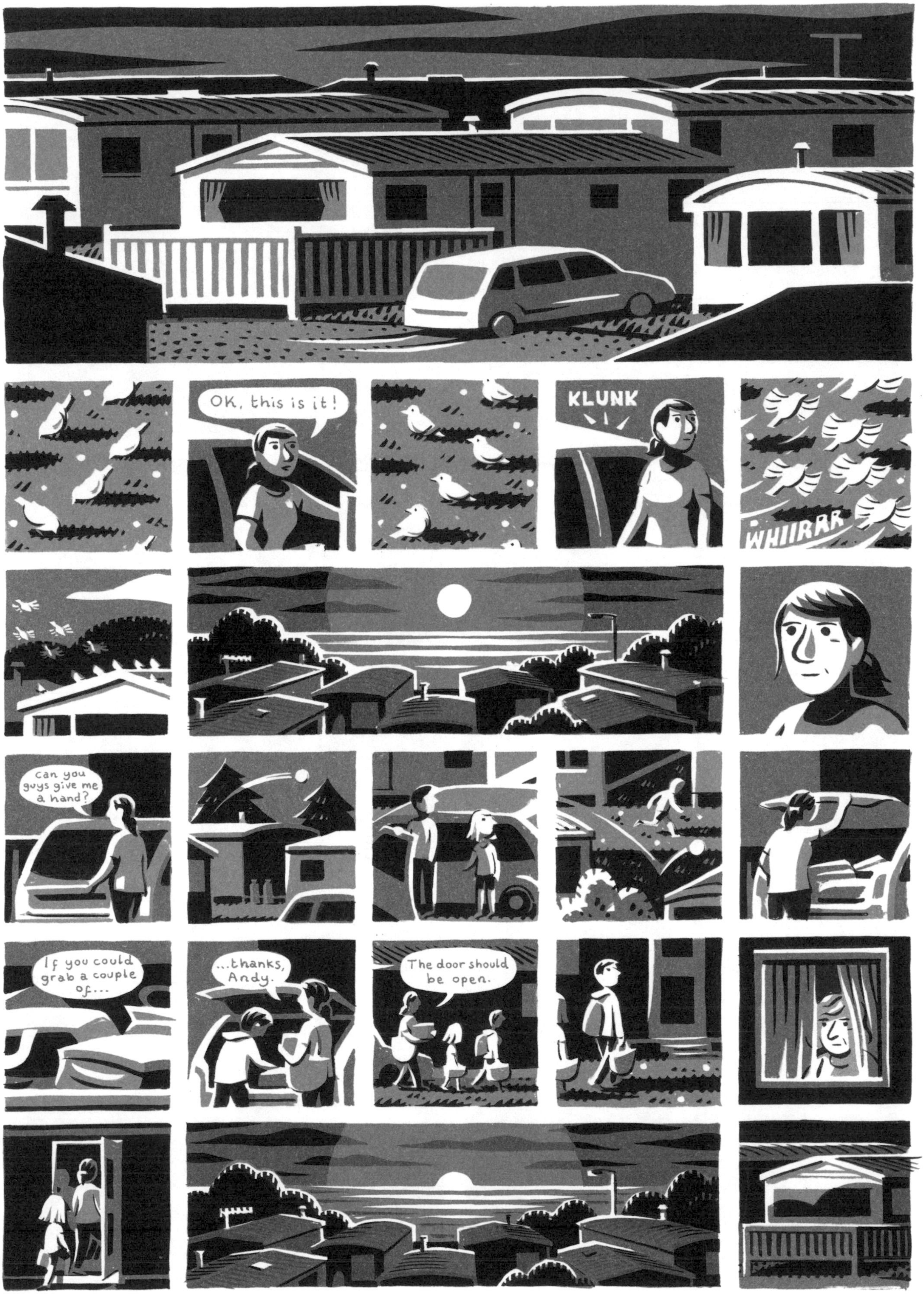
OK, this is it!
KLUNK
WHIIRRR
Can you guys give me a hand?
If you could grab a couple of...
...thanks, Andy.
The door should be open.

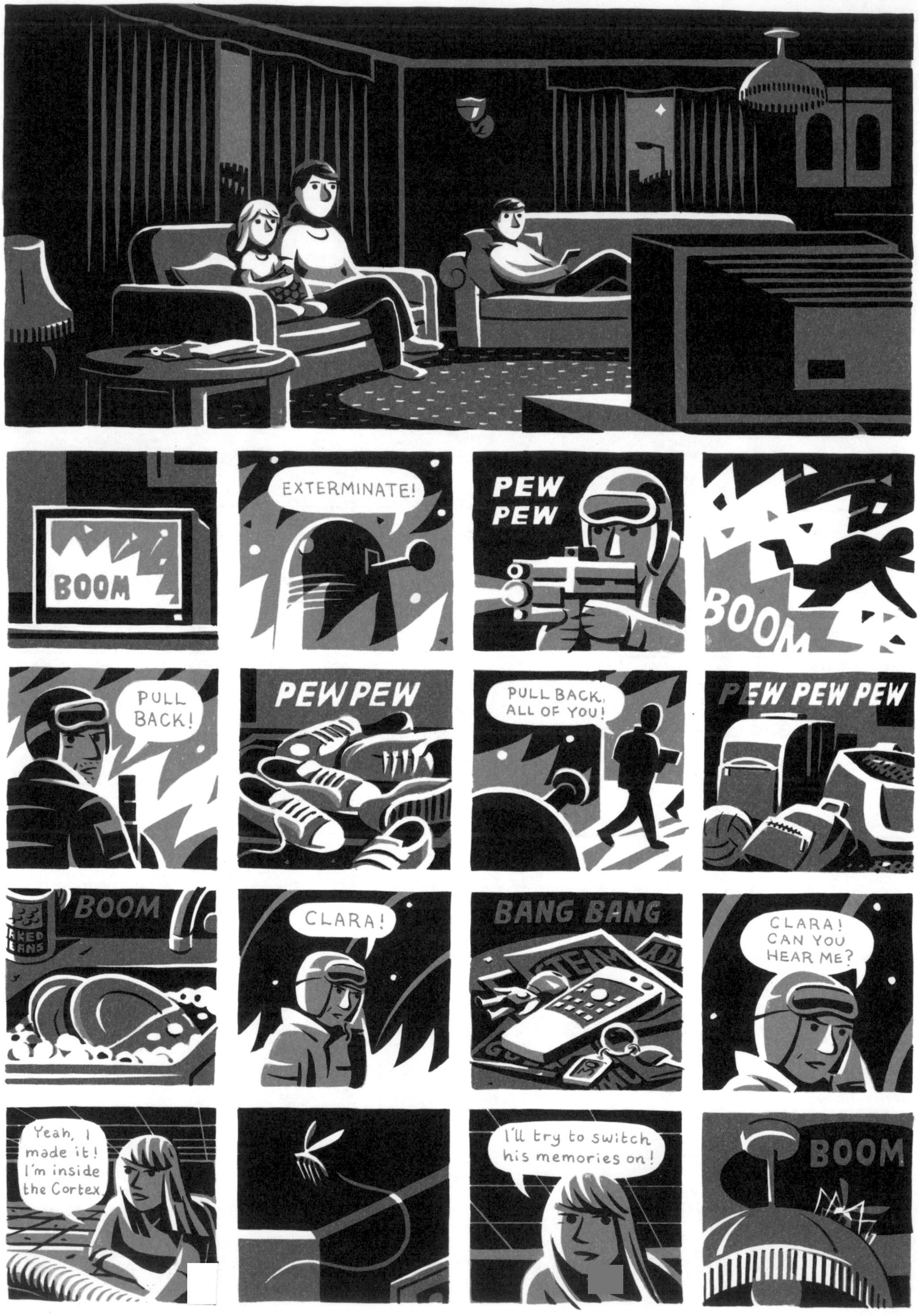
BOOM
EXTERMINATE!
PEW PEW
BOOM
PULL BACK!
PEW PEW
PULL BACK, ALL OF YOU!
PEW PEW PEW
BOOM
CLARA!
BANG BANG
CLARA! CAN YOU HEAR ME?
Yeah, I made it! I'm inside the Cortex.
I'll try to switch his memories on!
BOOM

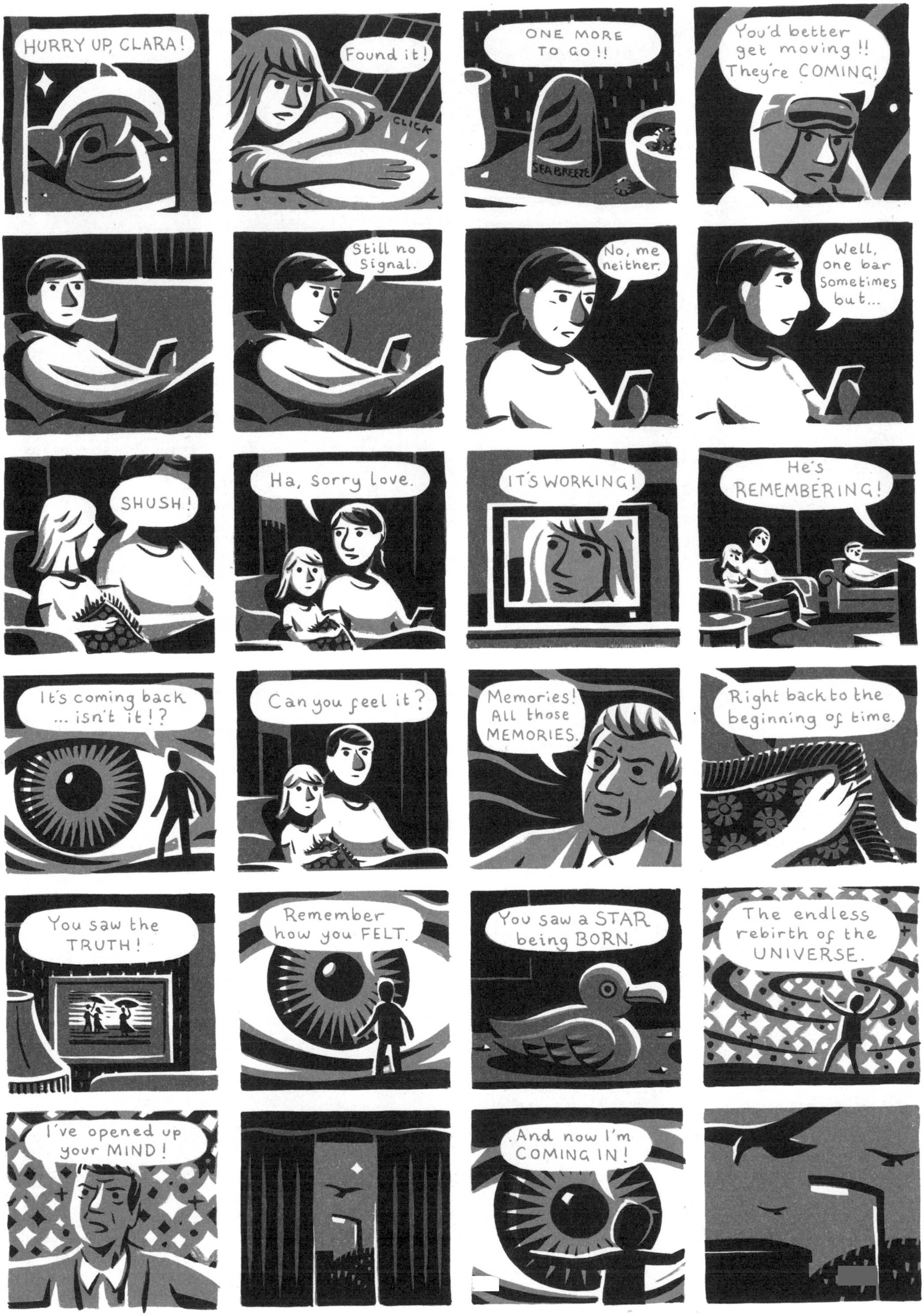
HURRY UP, CLARA!
Found it!
CLICK
ONE MORE TO GO!!
SEA BREEZE
You'd better get moving!! They're COMING!
Still no signal.
No, me neither.
Well, one bar sometimes but...
SHUSH!
Ha, sorry love.
IT'S WORKING!
He's REMEMBERING!
It's coming back ... isn't it!?
Can you feel it?
Memories! All those MEMORIES.
Right back to the beginning of time.
You saw the TRUTH!
Remember how you FELT.
You saw a STAR being BORN.
The endless rebirth of the UNIVERSE.
I've opened up your MIND!
And now I'm COMING IN!

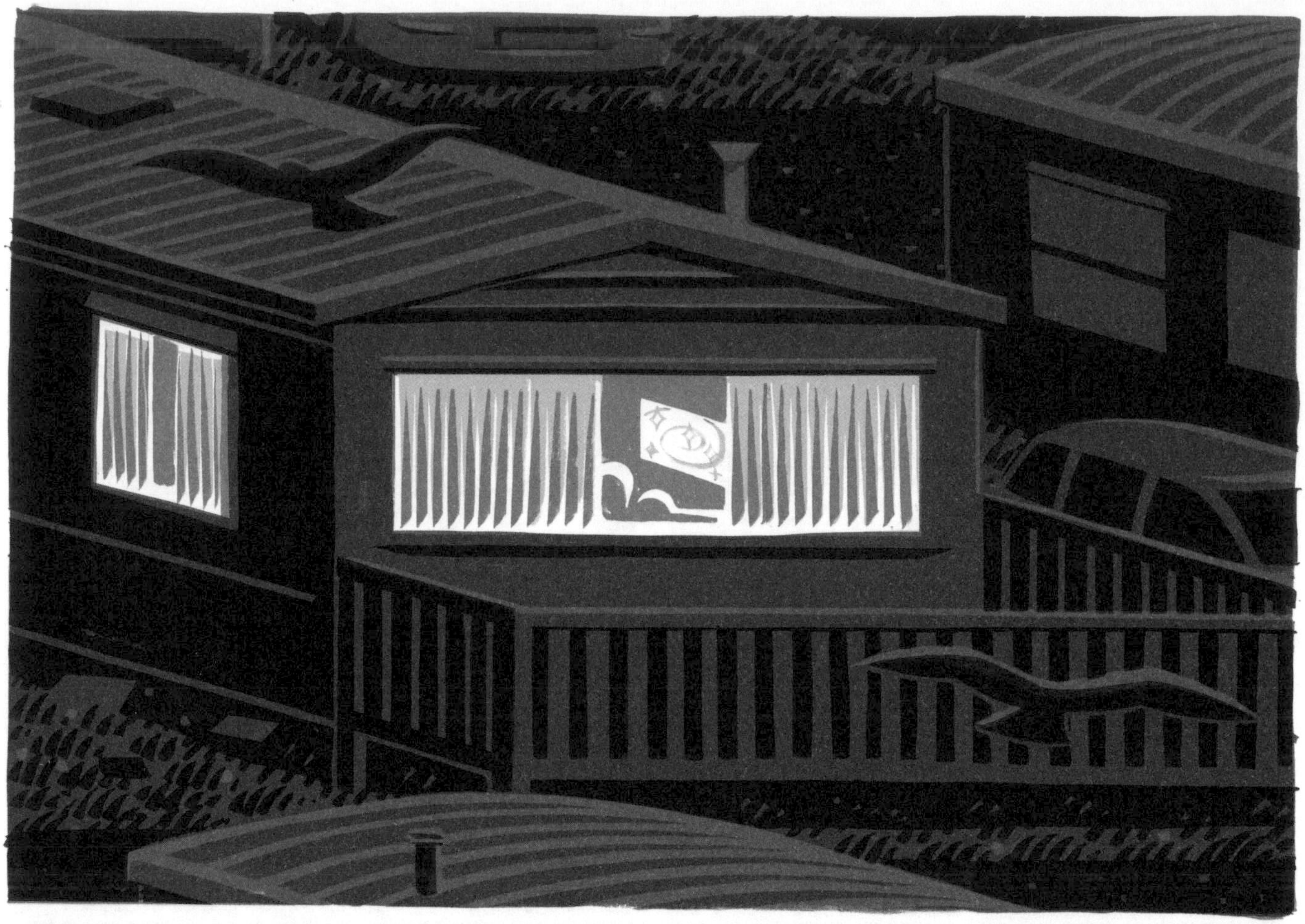
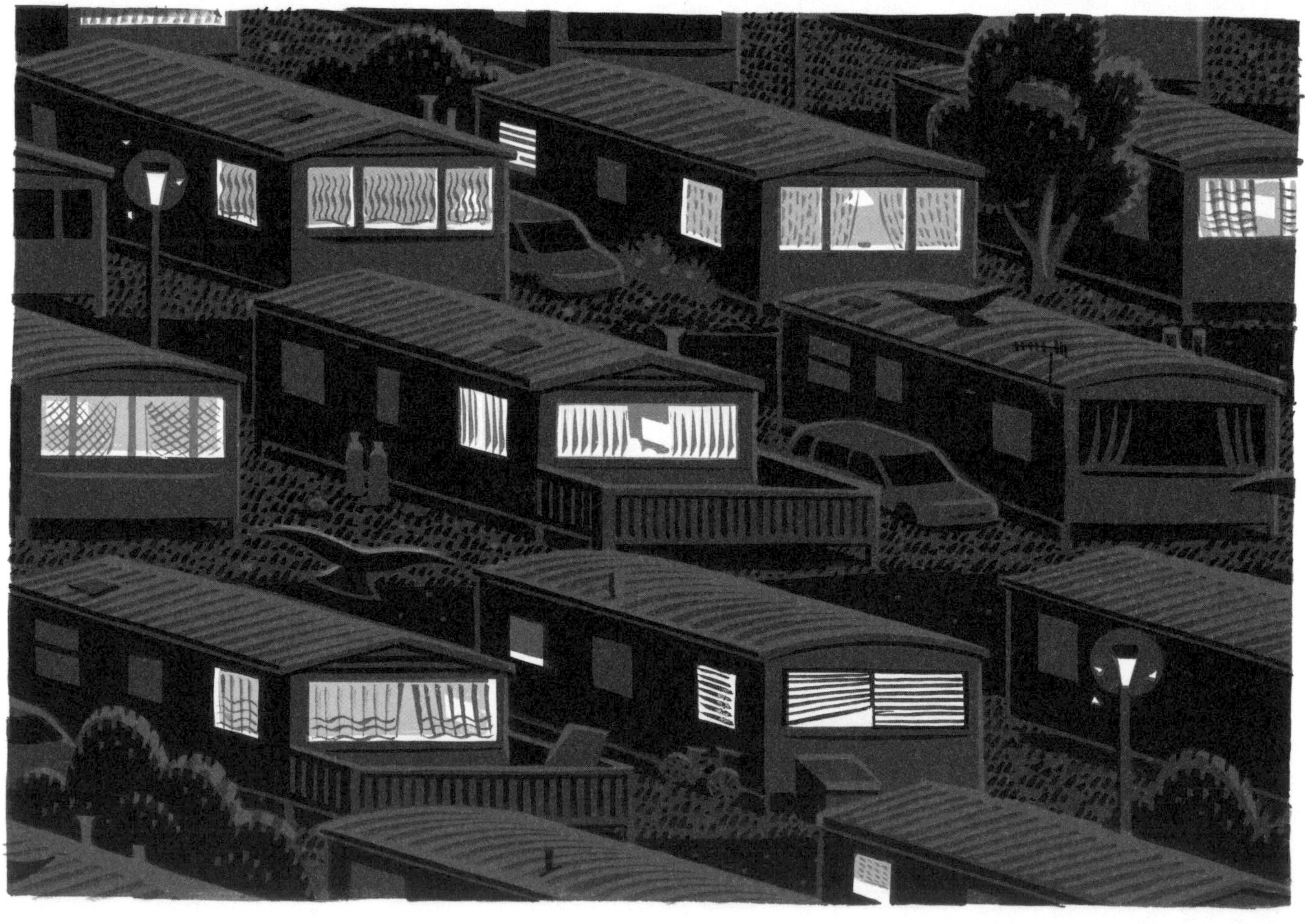

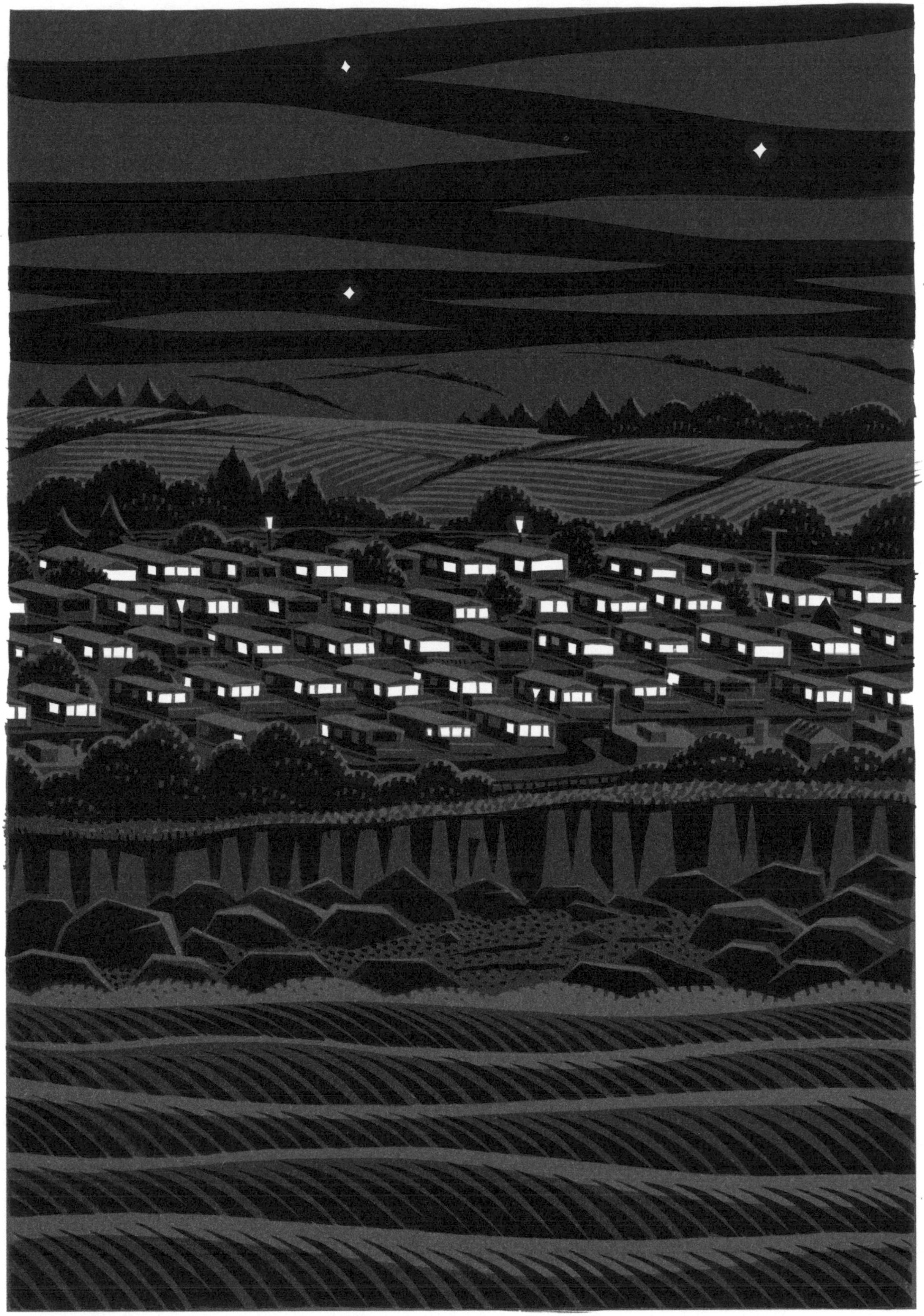

Landmarks

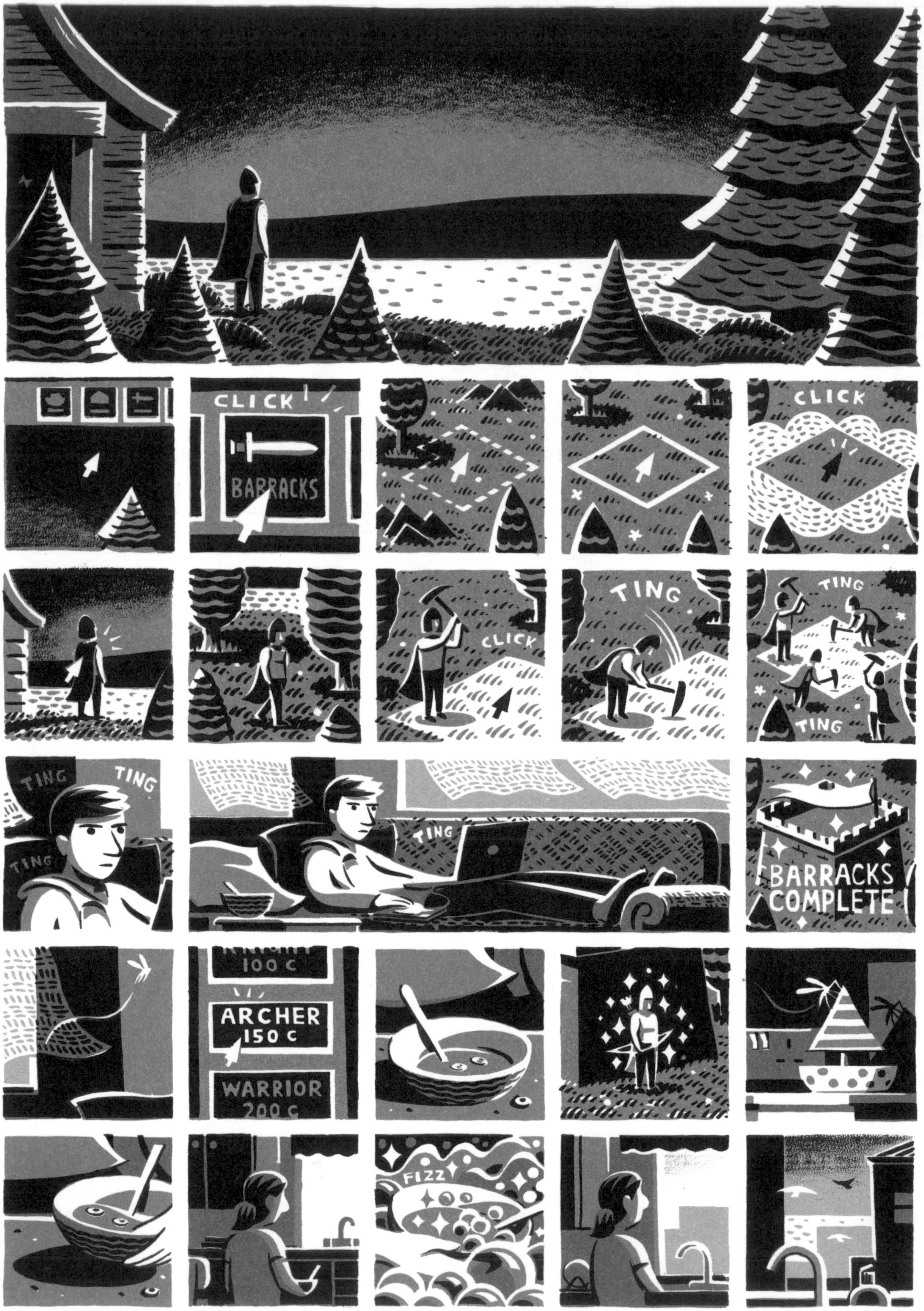
CLICK
BARRACKS
CLICK
CLICK
TING
TING
TING
TING
TING
TING
TING
BARRACKS COMPLETE
100 C
ARCHER
150 C
WARRIOR
200 C
FIZZ

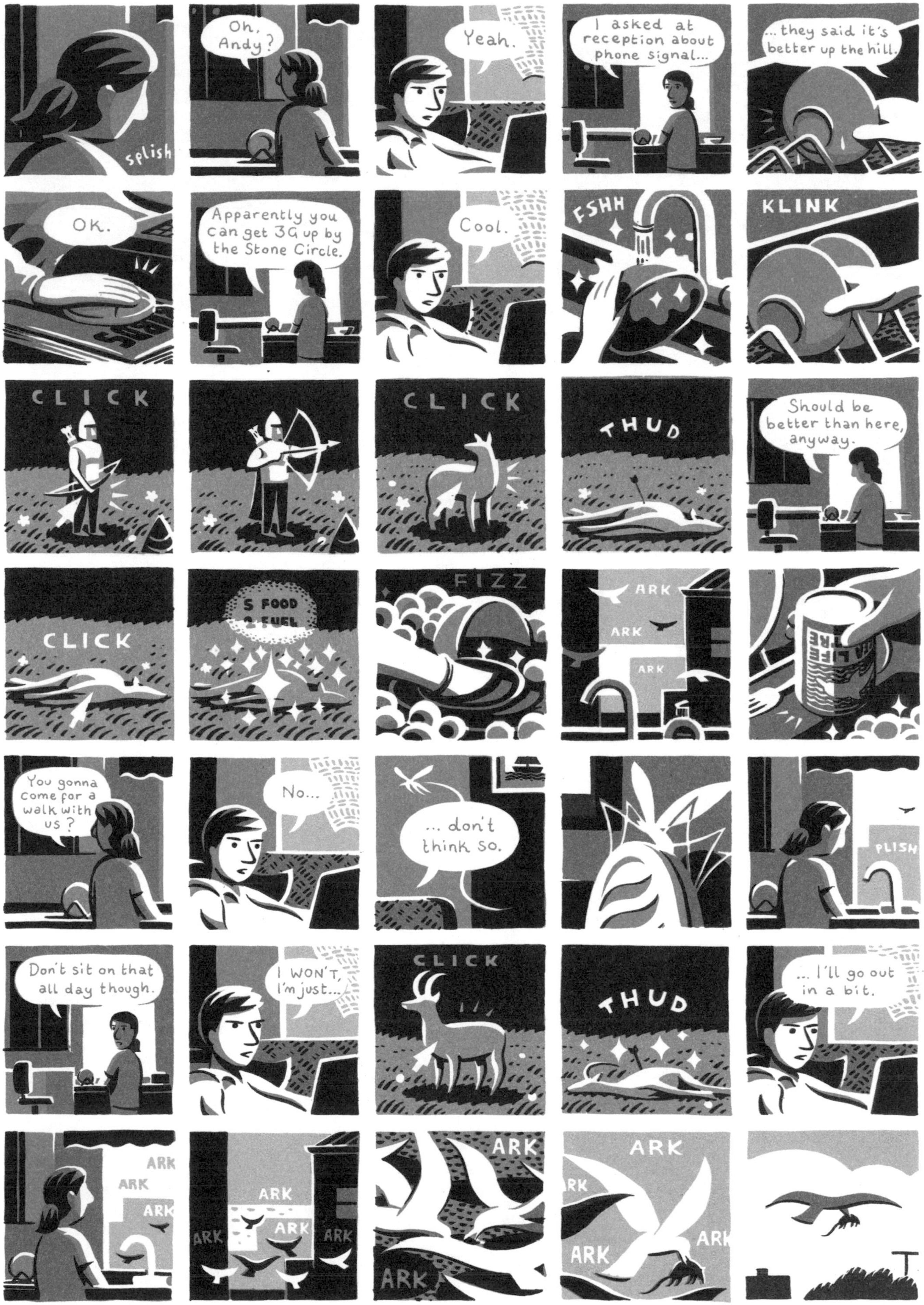
splish
Oh, Andy?
Yeah.
I asked at reception about phone signal...
... they said it's better up the hill.
OK.
Apparently you can get 3G up by the Stone Circle.
Cool.
FSHH
KLINK
CLICK
CLICK
THUD
Should be better than here, anyway.
CLICK
5 FOOD
FIZZ
ARK
ARK
ARK
You gonna come for a walk with us?
No...
... don't think so.
PLISH
Don't sit on that all day though.
I WON'T, I'm just...
CLICK
THUD
... I'll go out in a bit.
ARK
ARK
ARK
ARK
ARK
ARK
ARK
ARK
ARK
ARK
ARK
ARK

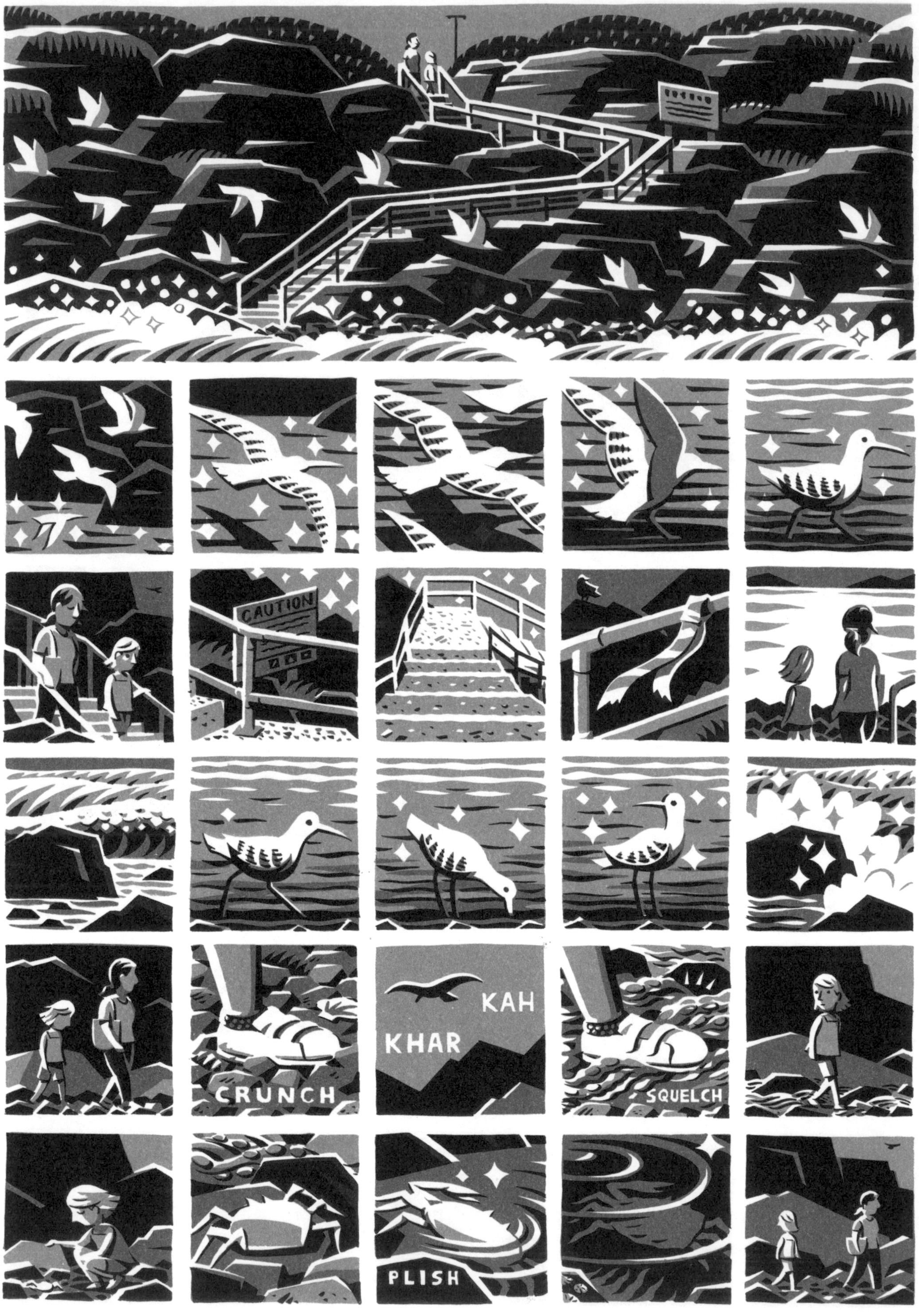
CAUTION
CRUNCH
KAH
KHAR
SQUELCH
PLISH

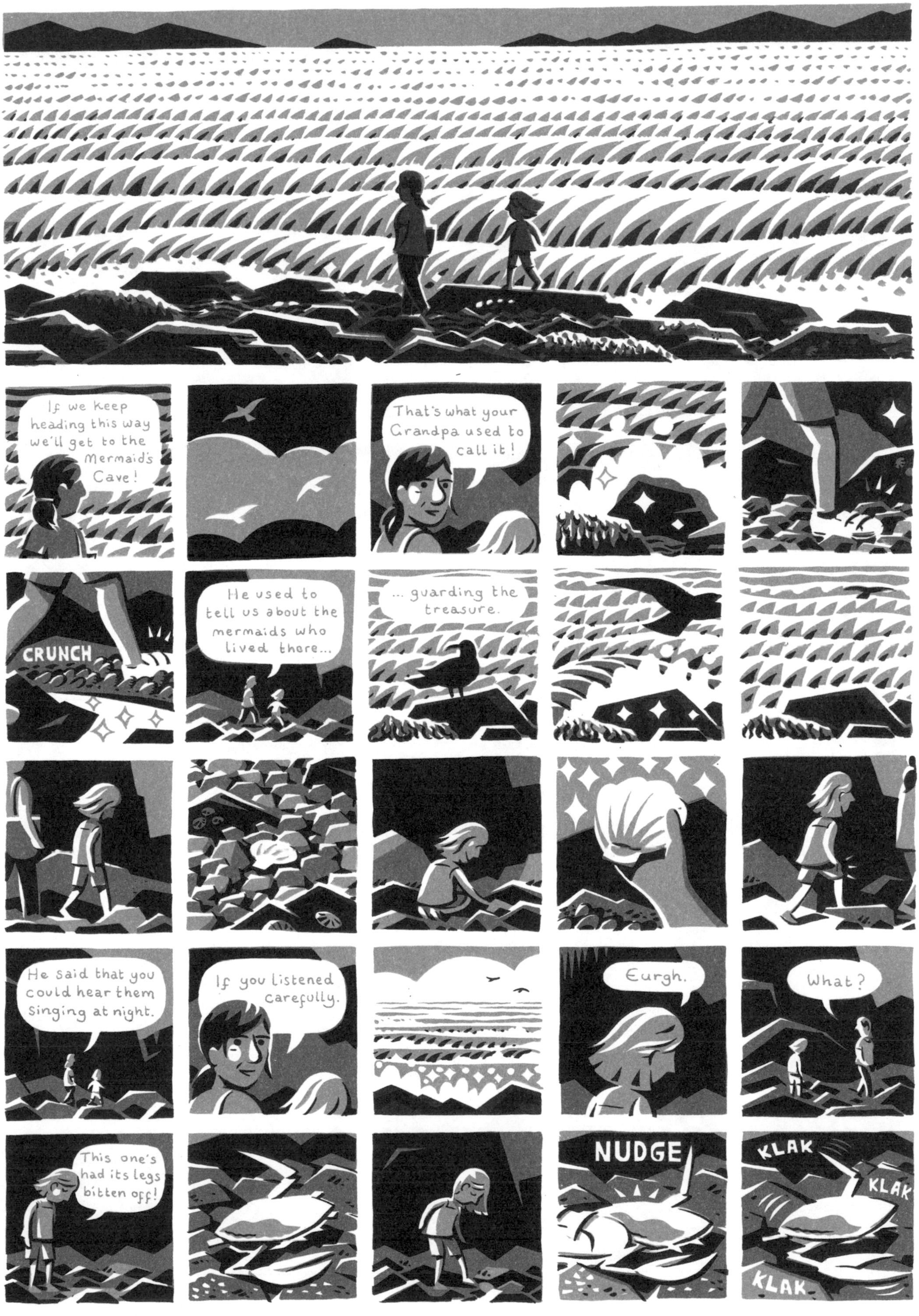
If we keep heading this way we'll get to the Mermaid's Cave!
That's what your Grandpa used to call it!
CRUNCH
He used to tell us about the mermaids who lived there...
... guarding the treasure.
He said that you could hear them singing at night.
If you listened carefully.
Eurgh.
What?
This one's had its legs bitten off!
NUDGE
KLAK
KLAK
KLAK

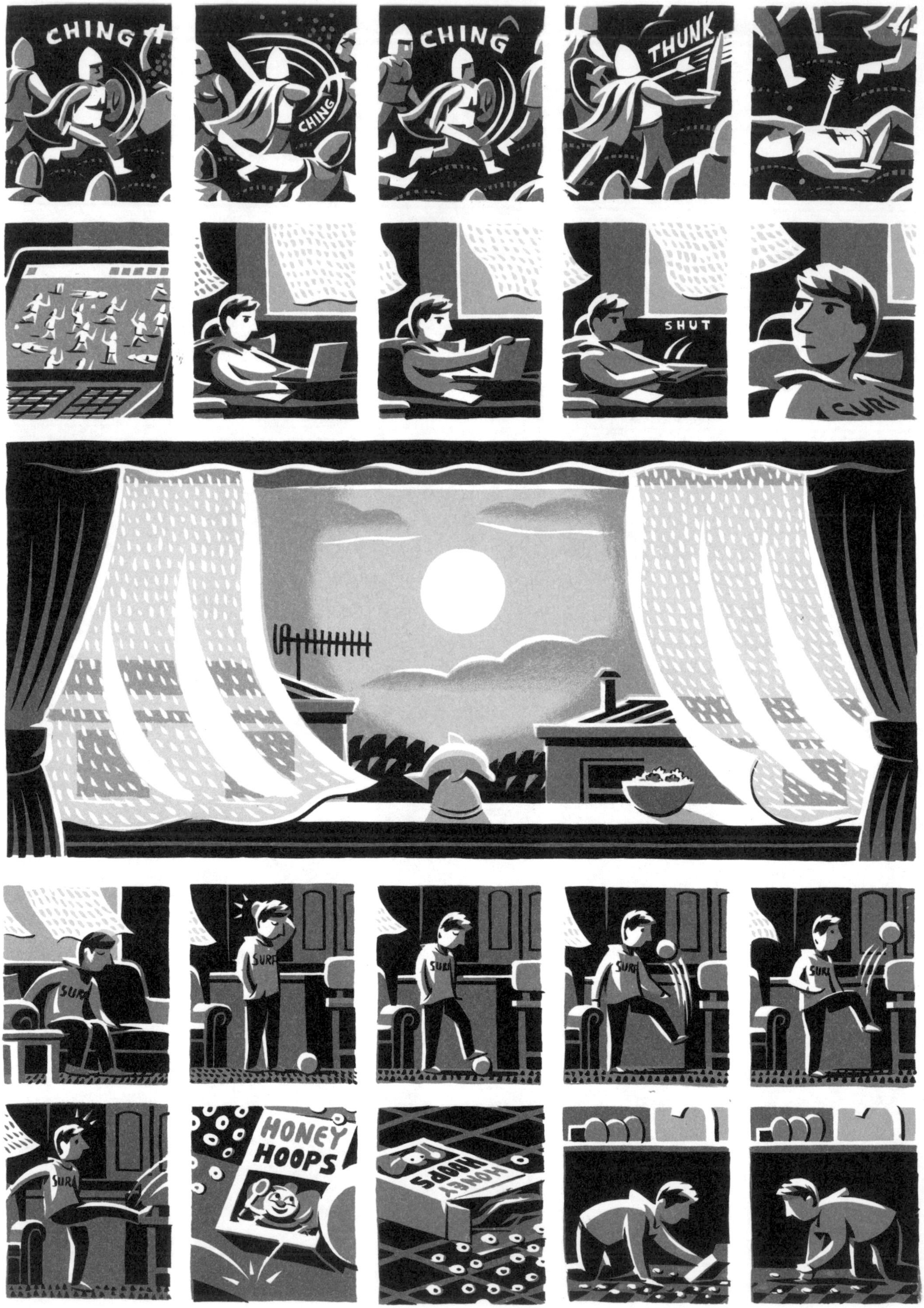
CHING
CHING
CHING
THUNK
SHUT
SURF
HONEY
HOOPS

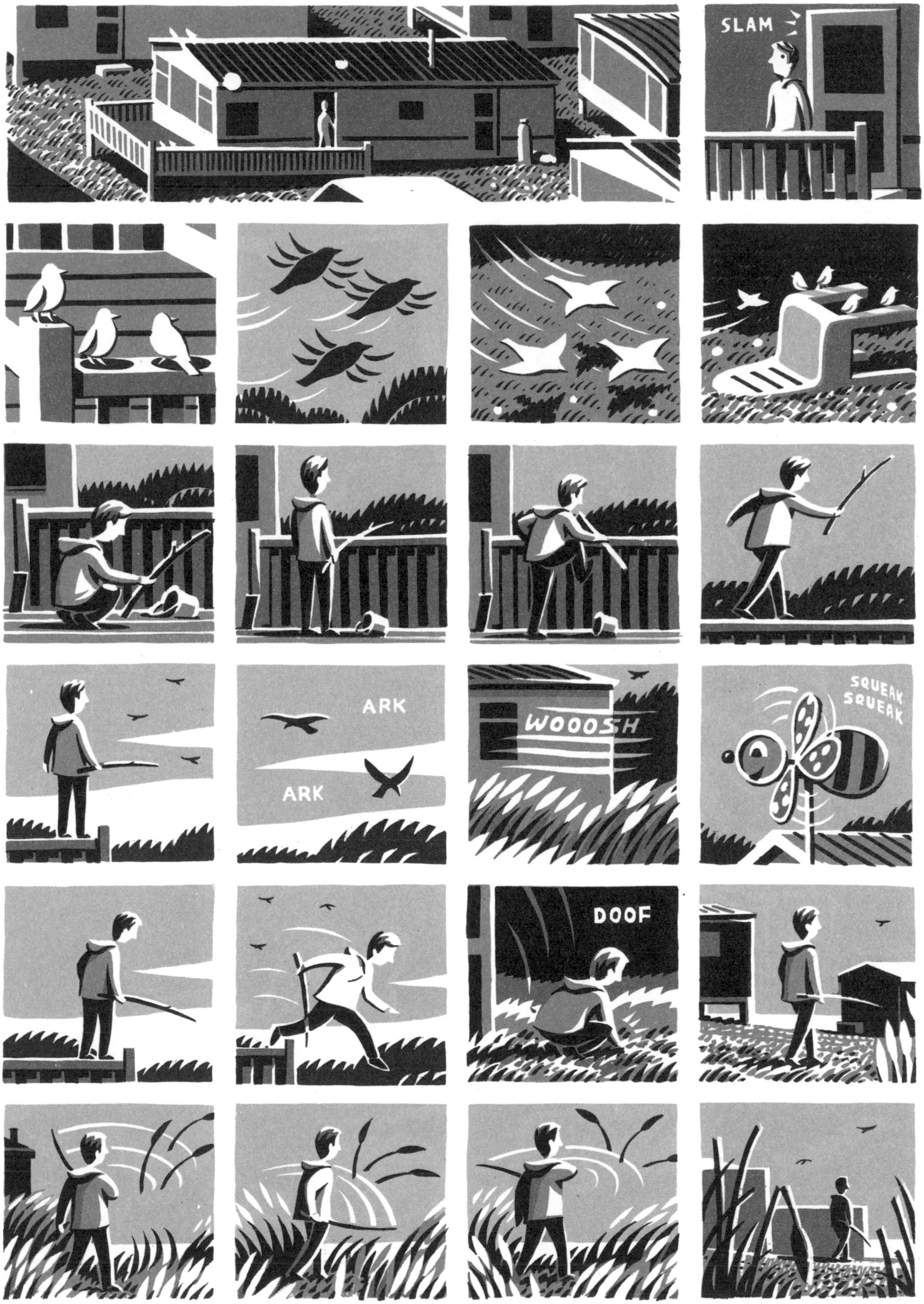
SLAM
ARK
ARK
WOOOSH
SQUEAK
SQUEAK
DOOF

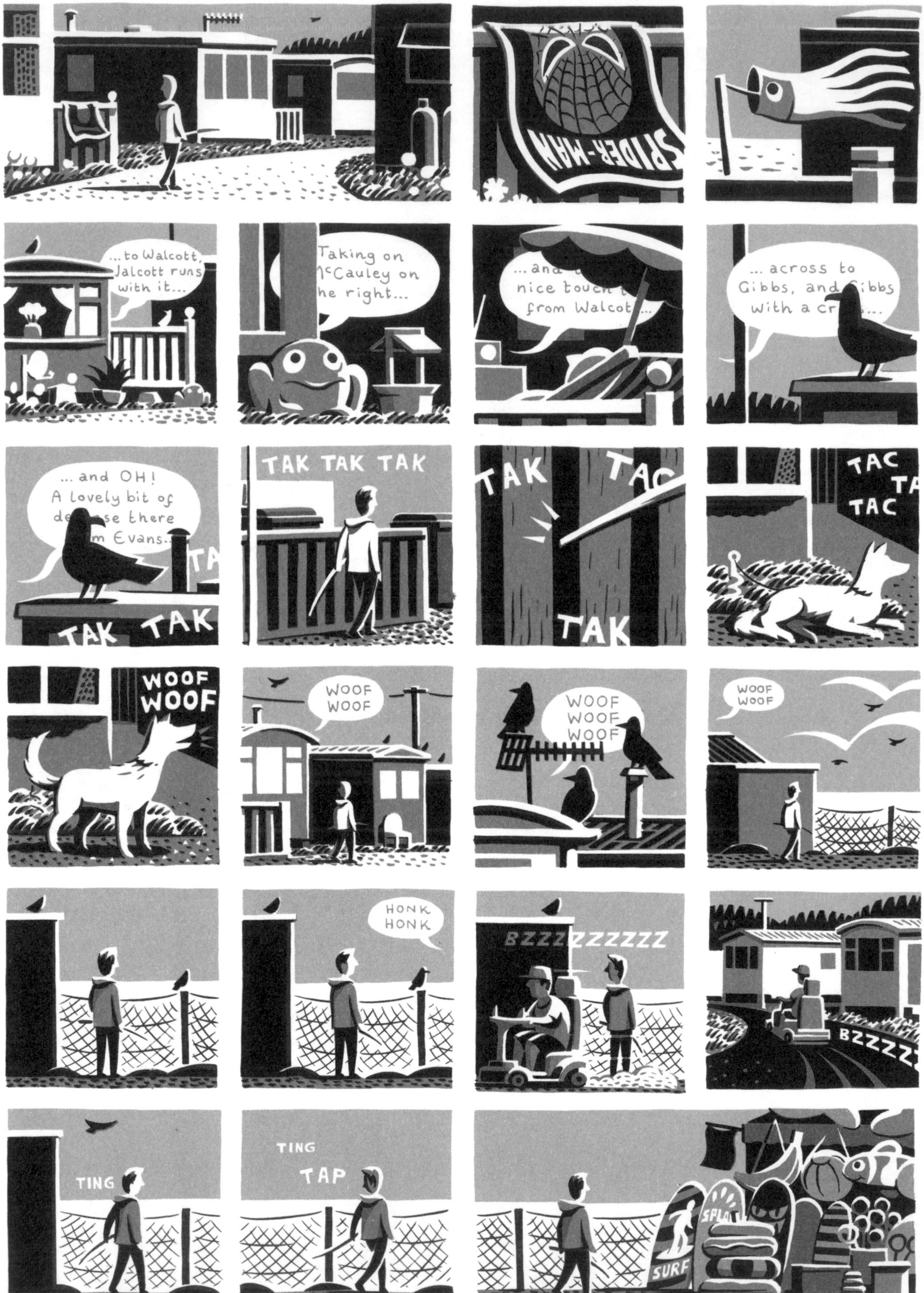
SPIDER-MAN
... to Walcott, Walcott runs with it...
Taking on McCauley on the right...
... and a nice touch from Walcott...
... across to Gibbs, and Gibbs with a cr...
... and OH! A lovely bit of de...se there ...m Evans...
TA
TAK TAK
TAK TAK TAK
TAK
TAC
TAK
TAC
TA
TAC
WOOF
WOOF
WOOF
WOOF
WOOF
WOOF
WOOF
WOOF
WOOF
HONK
HONK
BZZZZZZZZZ
BZZZZ
TING
TING
TAP
SURF
SPLA

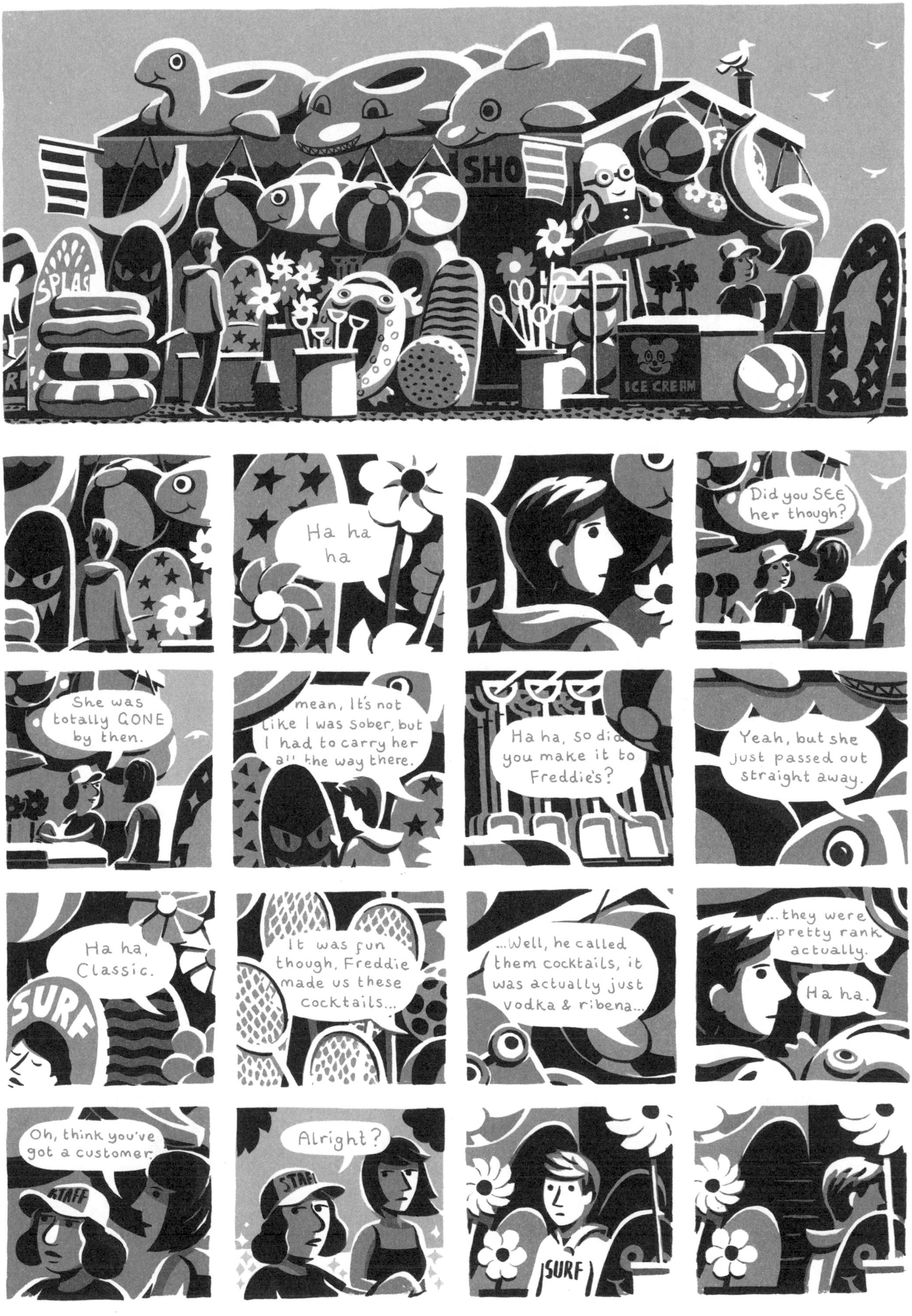
SPLAS
SHO
ICE CREAM
Ha ha ha
Did you SEE her though?
She was totally GONE by then.
mean, It's not like I was sober, but I had to carry her all the way there.
Ha ha, so did you make it to Freddie's?
Yeah, but she just passed out straight away.
Ha ha, Classic.
SURF
It was fun though, Freddie made us these cocktails...
...Well, he called them cocktails, it was actually just vodka & ribena...
...they were pretty rank actually.
Ha ha.
Oh, think you've got a customer.
STAFF
Alright?
STAFF
SURF

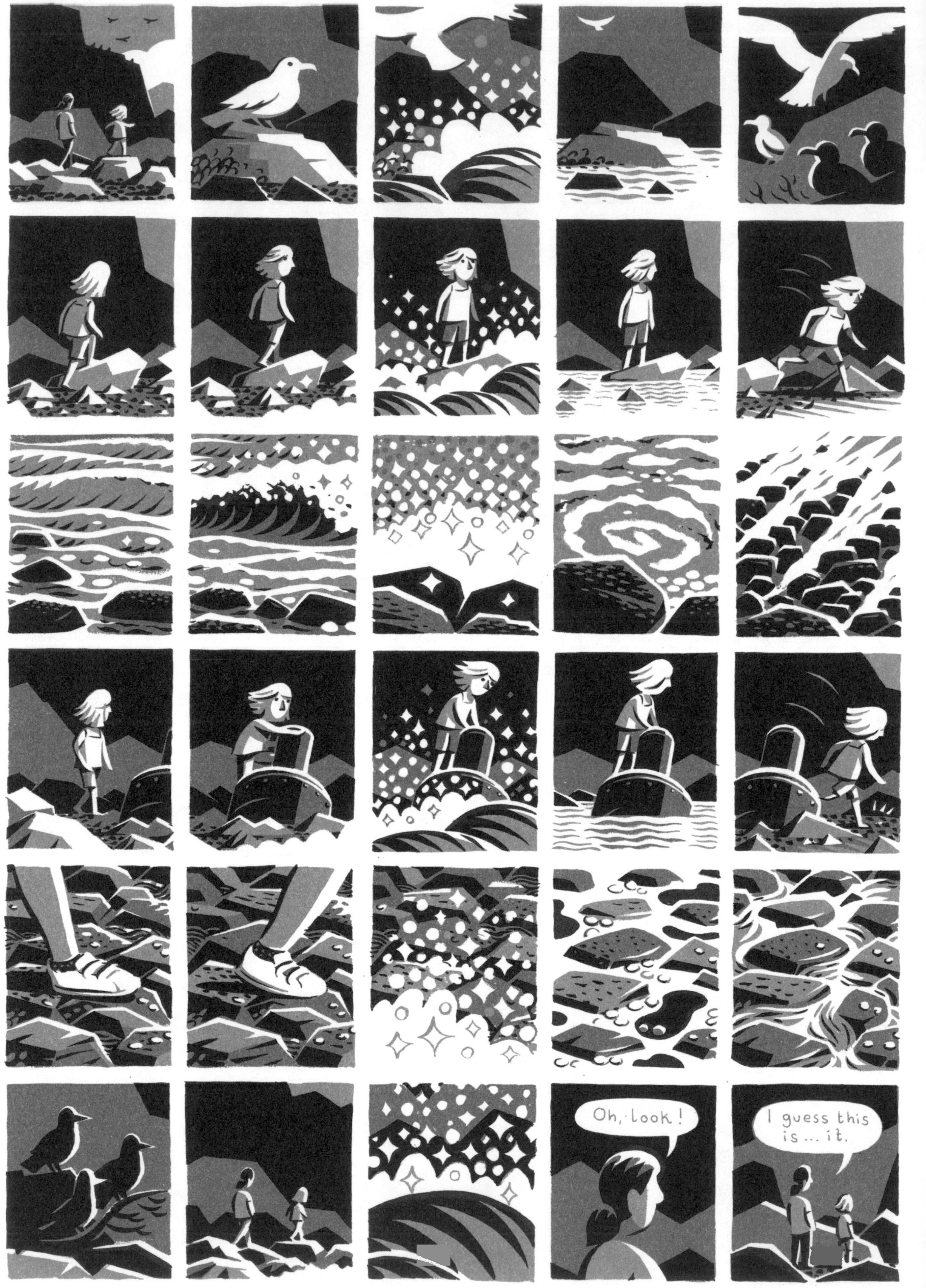
Oh, look!
I guess this is ... it.

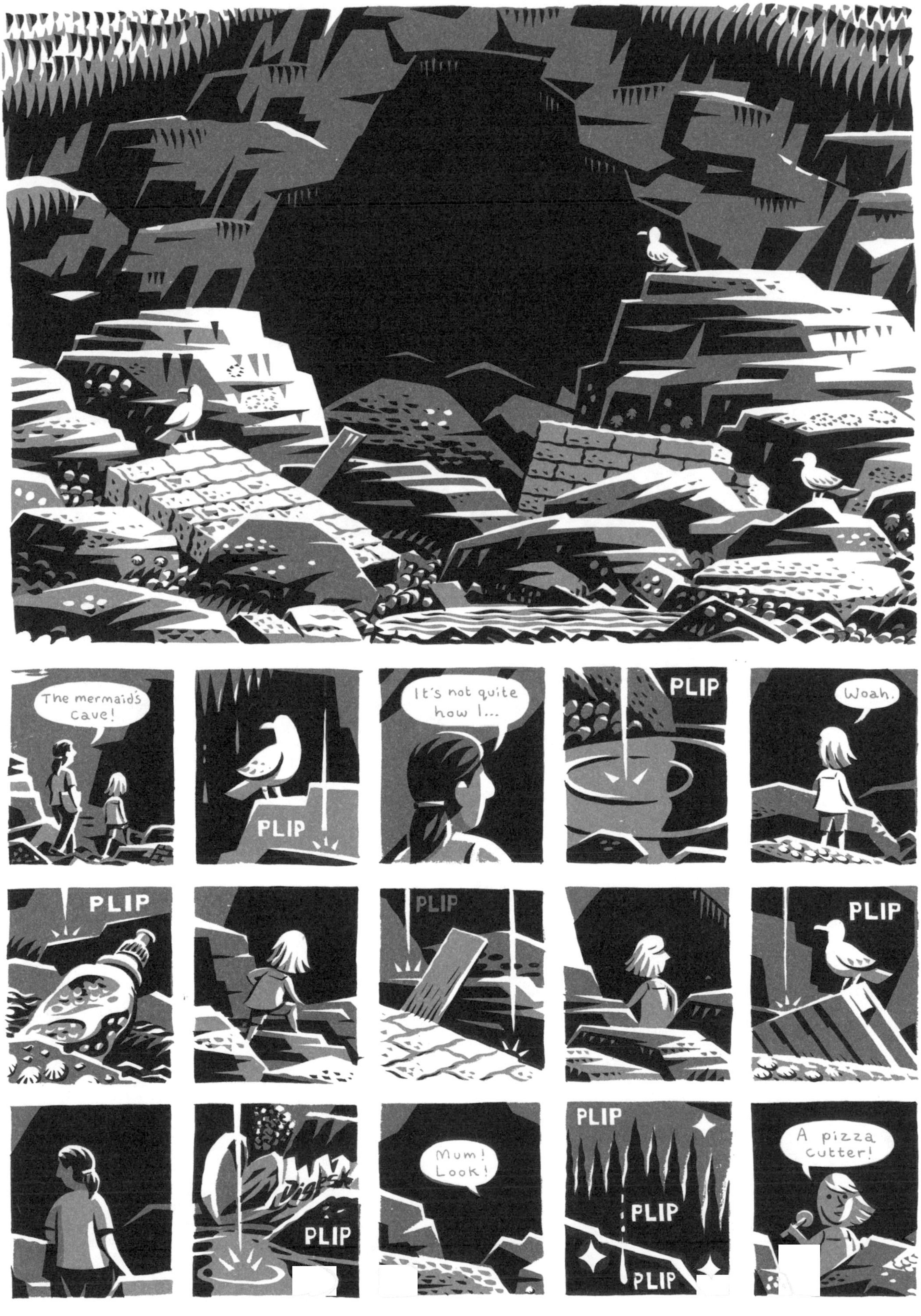

The mermaid's cave!
PLIP
It's not quite how I...
PLIP
Woah.
PLIP
PLIP
PLIP
PLIP
PLIP
Mum! Look!
PLIP
PLIP
PLIP
A pizza cutter!

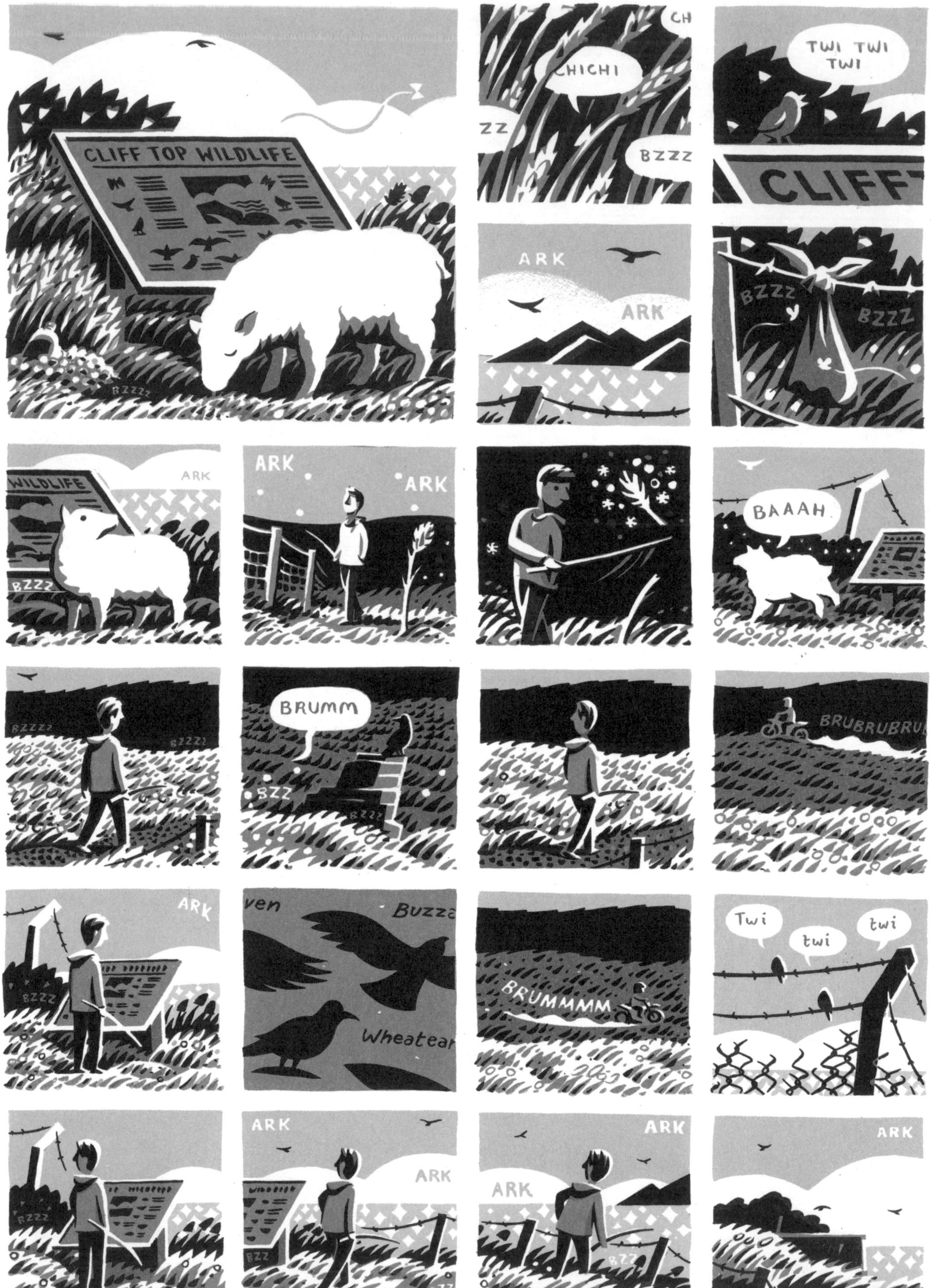
CLIFF TOP WILDLIFE
BZZZZ
CH
CHICHI
ZZ
BZZZ
TWI TWI TWI
CLIFF
ARK
ARK
BZZZ
BZZZ
WILDLIFE
ARK
BZZZ
ARK
ARK
BAAAH
BZZZZ
BZZZZ
BRUMM
BZZ
BZZZ
BRUBRUBRU
ARK
BZZZ
ven
Buzza
Wheatear
BRUMMMM
Twi
twi
twi
BZZZ
ARK
ARK
BZZ
BZZ
ARK
ARK
BZZ
ARK

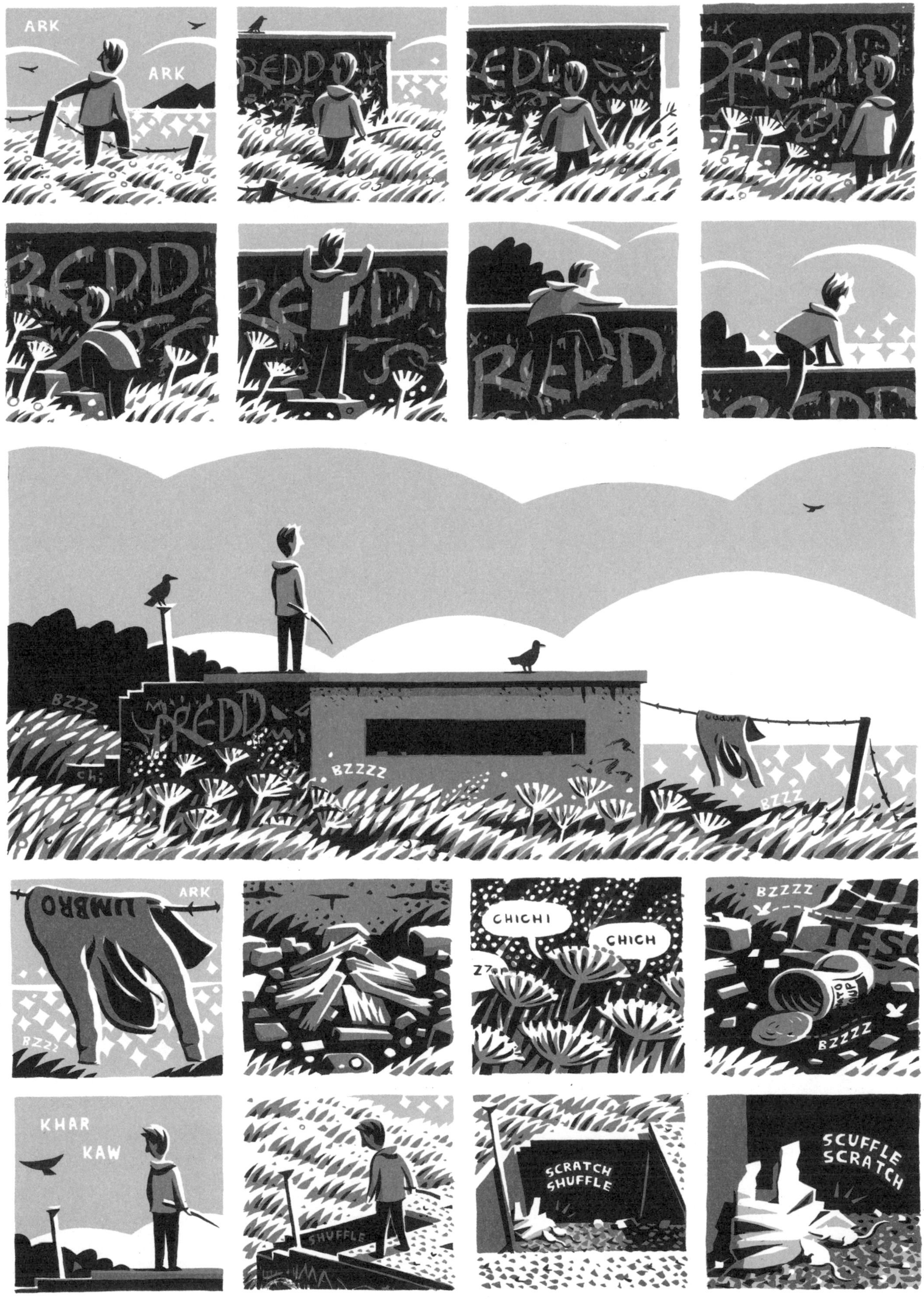
ARK
ARK
REDD
REDD
REDD
REDD
REDD
BZZZ
REDD
BZZZZ
BZZZ
UMBRO
ARK
BZZZ
CHICHI
CHICH
BZZZZ
BZZZZ
KHAR
KAW
SHUFFLE
SCRATCH
SHUFFLE
SCUFFLE
SCRATCH

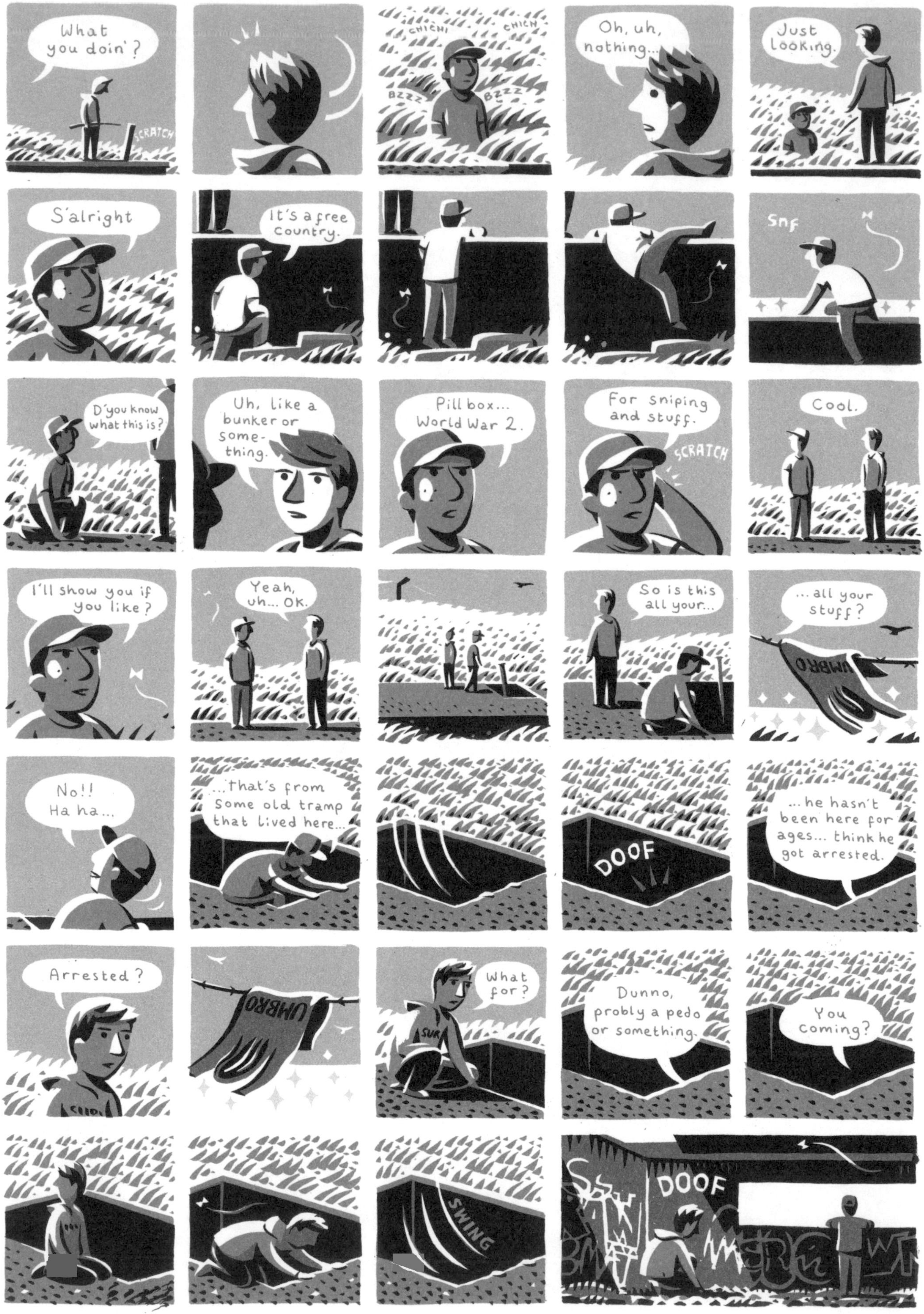
What you doin'?
SCRATCH
CHICHI
CHICH
BZZZ
BZZZ
Oh, uh, nothing...
Just looking.
S'alright
It's a free country.
Snf
D'you know what this is?
Uh, like a bunker or some-thing.
Pill box... World War 2.
For sniping and stuff.
SCRATCH
Cool.
I'll show you if you like?
Yeah, uh... OK.
So is this all your...
...all your stuff?
UMBRO
No!! Ha ha...
...that's from some old tramp that lived here...
DOOF
...he hasn't been here for ages... think he got arrested.
Arrested?
UMBRO
What for?
Dunno, probly a pedo or something.
You coming?
SWING
DOOF

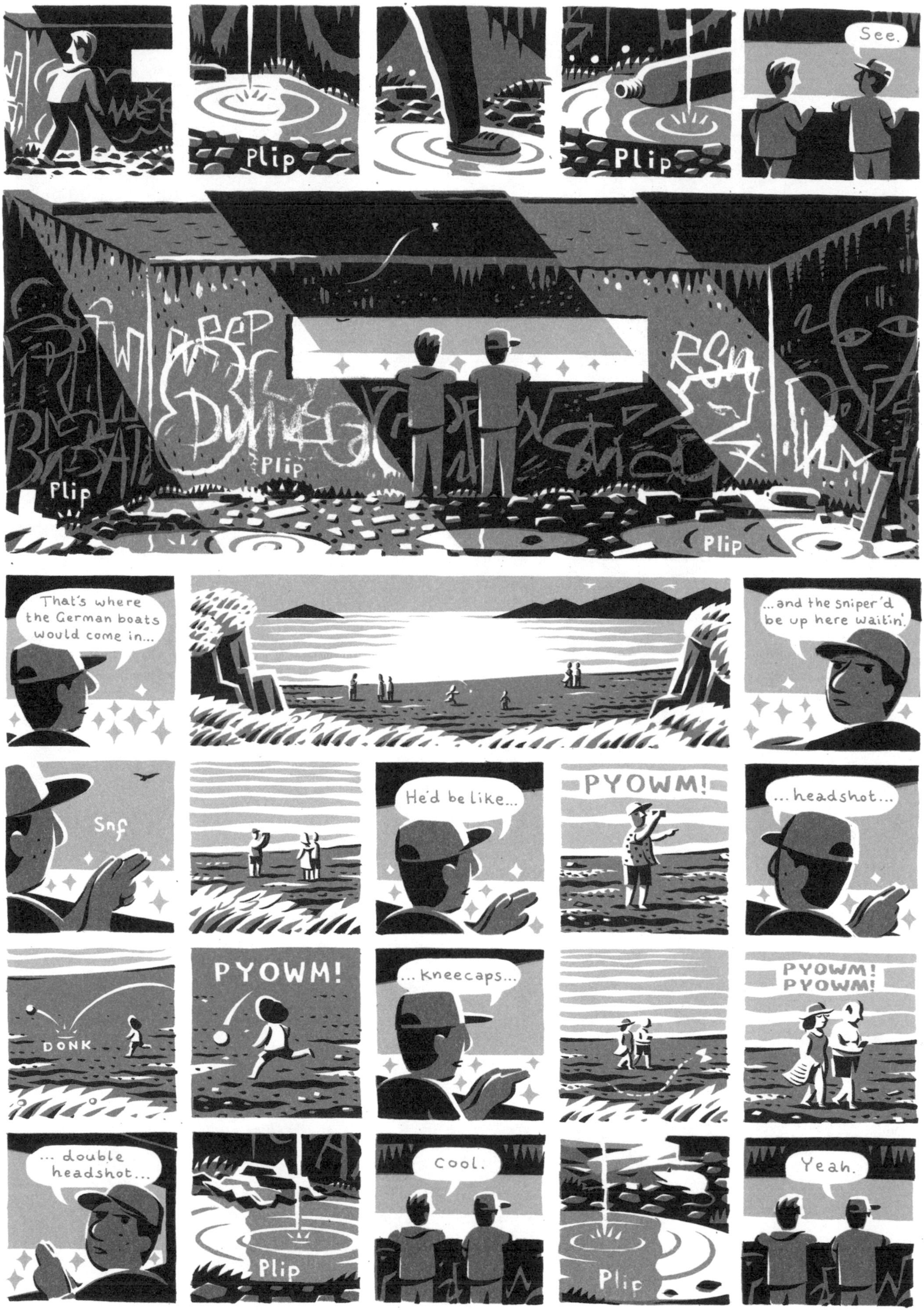
Plip
Plip
See.
Plip
Plip
Plip
Plip
That's where the German boats would come in...
...and the sniper'd be up here waitin'.
Snf
He'd be like...
PYOWM!
...headshot...
DONK
PYOWM!
...kneecaps...
PYOWM! PYOWM!
... double headshot...
Plip
Cool.
Plip
Yeah.

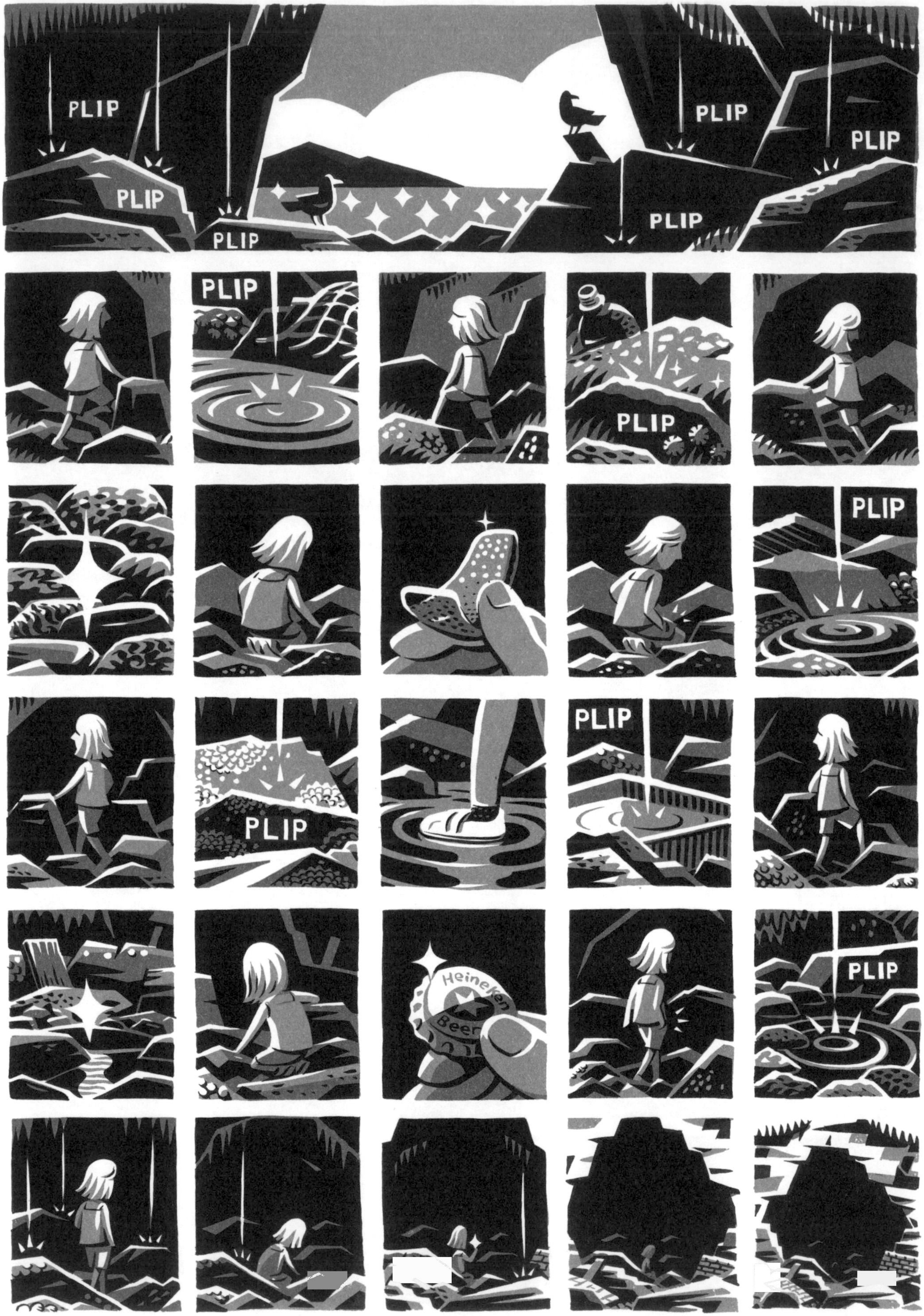
PLIP
PLIP
PLIP
PLIP
PLIP
PLIP
PLIP
PLIP
PLIP
PLIP
PLIP
Heineken
Beer
PLIP

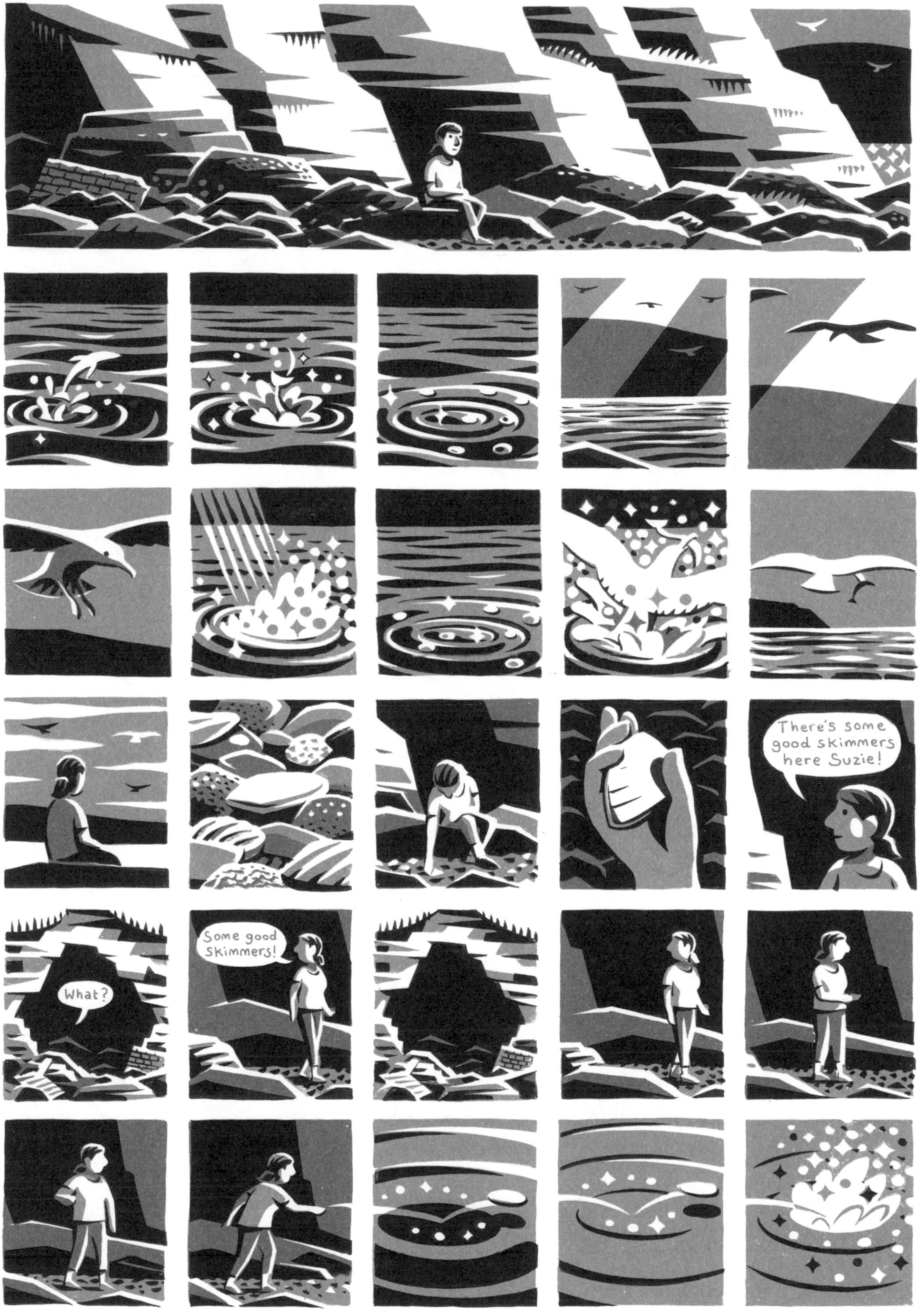
There's some good skimmers here Suzie!
What?
Some good skimmers!

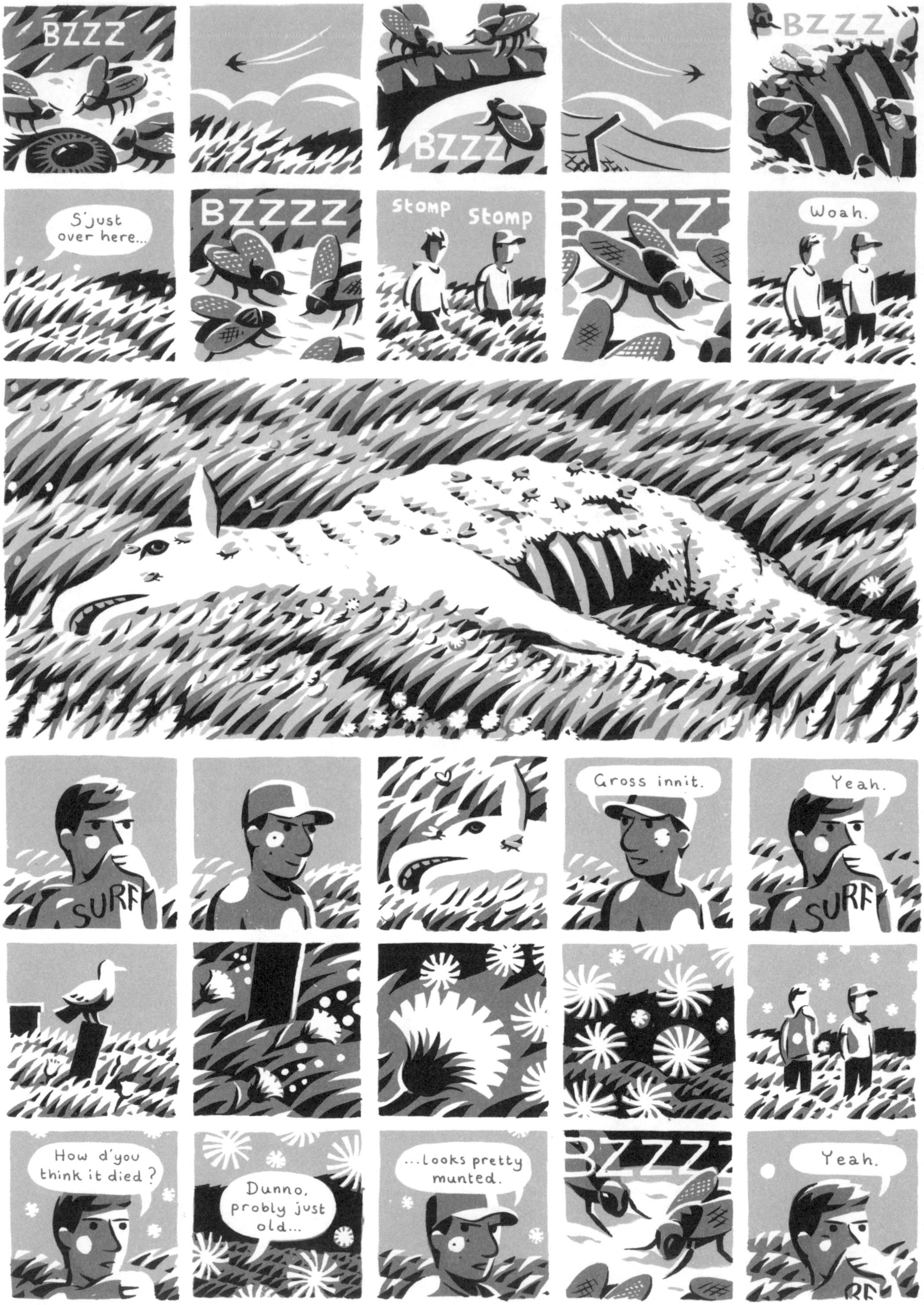
BZZZ
BZZZ
BZZZ
S'just over here...
BZZZZ
stomp
stomp
BZZZZ
Woah.
SURF
Gross innit.
Yeah.
SURF
How d'you think it died?
Dunno, probly just old...
...Looks pretty munted.
BZZZZ
Yeah.

You ever seen a dead PERSON?

No..?

Nah... me neither.

MUNCH MUNCH

Actually, there was my Grandad...

I saw him in the hospital when he was...uh...

...I mean, he wasn't actually DEAD when I saw him, but...

Doesn't count then.

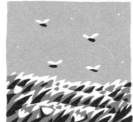

NUDGE NUDGE

Would you rather eat ALL of those maggots...

...or suck out its eyeball?

BZZZ

BZZ

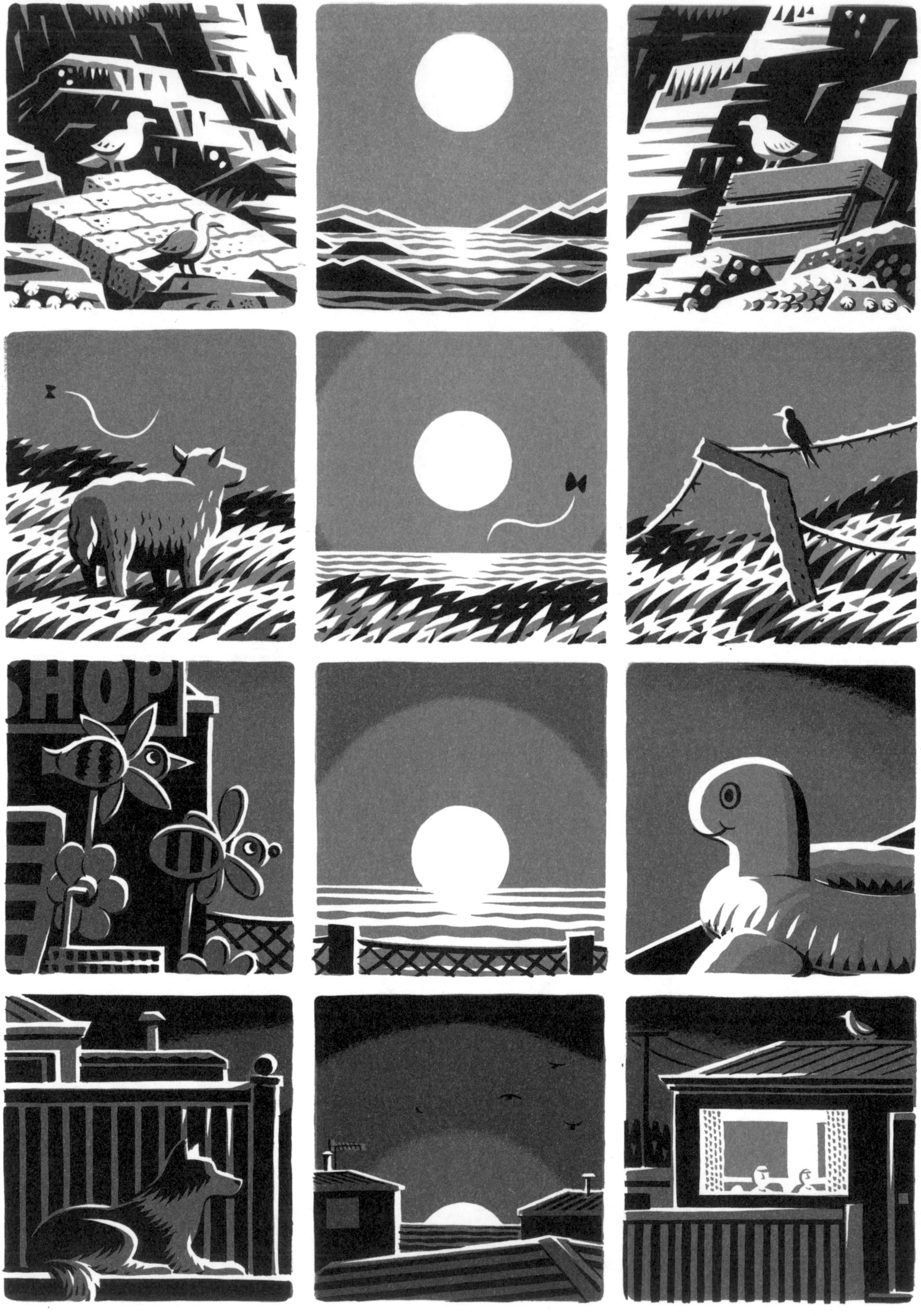
SHOP

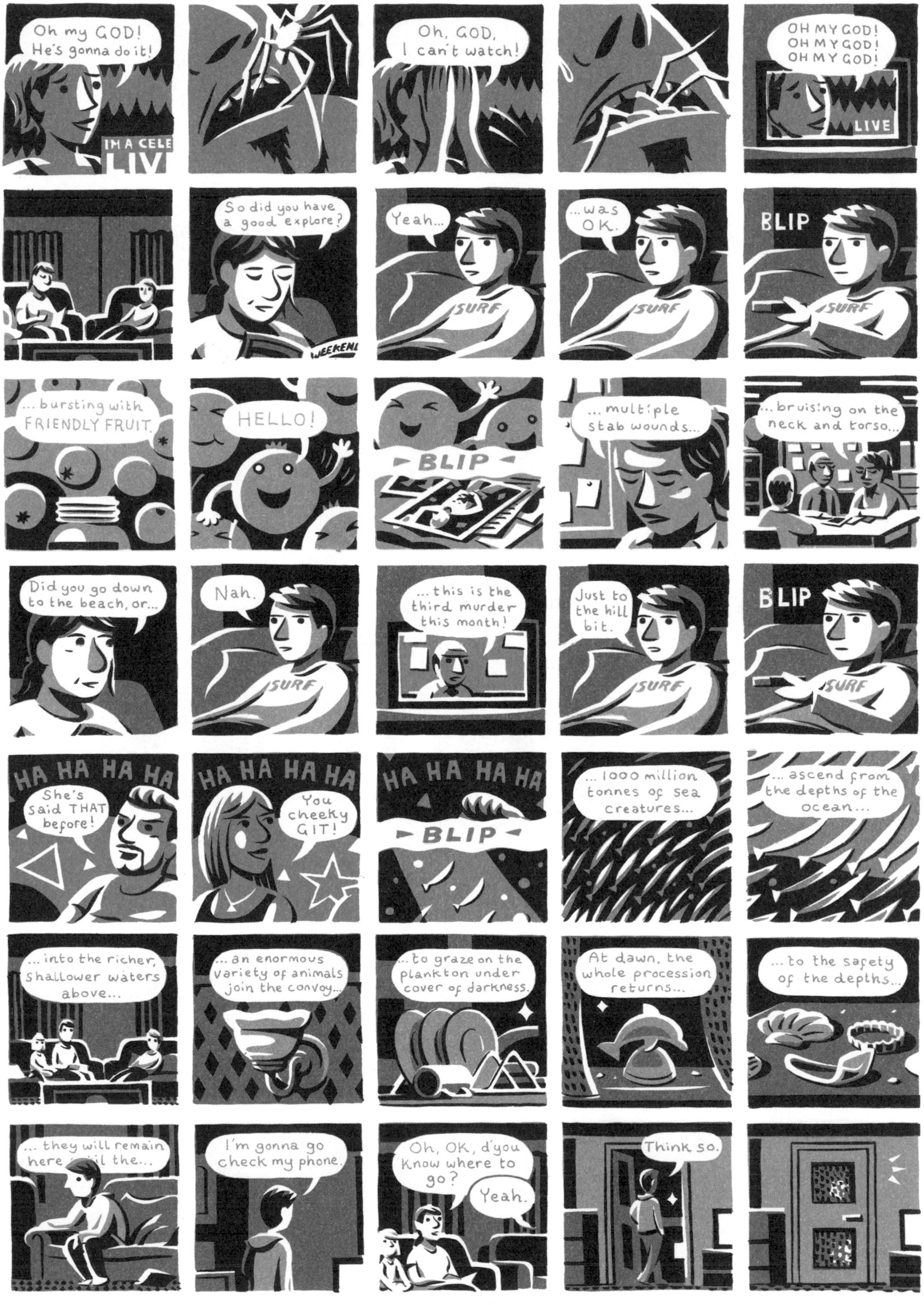
Oh my GOD! He's gonna do it!
IM A CELE
LIV
Oh, GOD, I can't watch!
OH MY GOD! OH MY GOD! OH MY GOD!
LIVE
So did you have a good explore?
WEEKEN
Yeah...
...was OK.
BLIP
...bursting with FRIENDLY FRUIT.
HELLO!
BLIP
...multiple stab wounds...
...bruising on the neck and torso...
Did you go down to the beach, or...
Nah.
...this is the third murder this month!
Just to the hill bit.
BLIP
HA HA HA HA
She's said THAT before!
HA HA HA HA
You cheeky GIT!
HA HA HA HA
BLIP
...1000 million tonnes of sea creatures...
...ascend from the depths of the ocean...
...into the richer, shallower waters above...
...an enormous variety of animals join the convoy...
...to graze on the plankton under cover of darkness.
At dawn, the whole procession returns...
...to the safety of the depths...
... they will remain here il the...
I'm gonna go check my phone.
Oh, OK, d'you know where to go?
Yeah.
Think so.

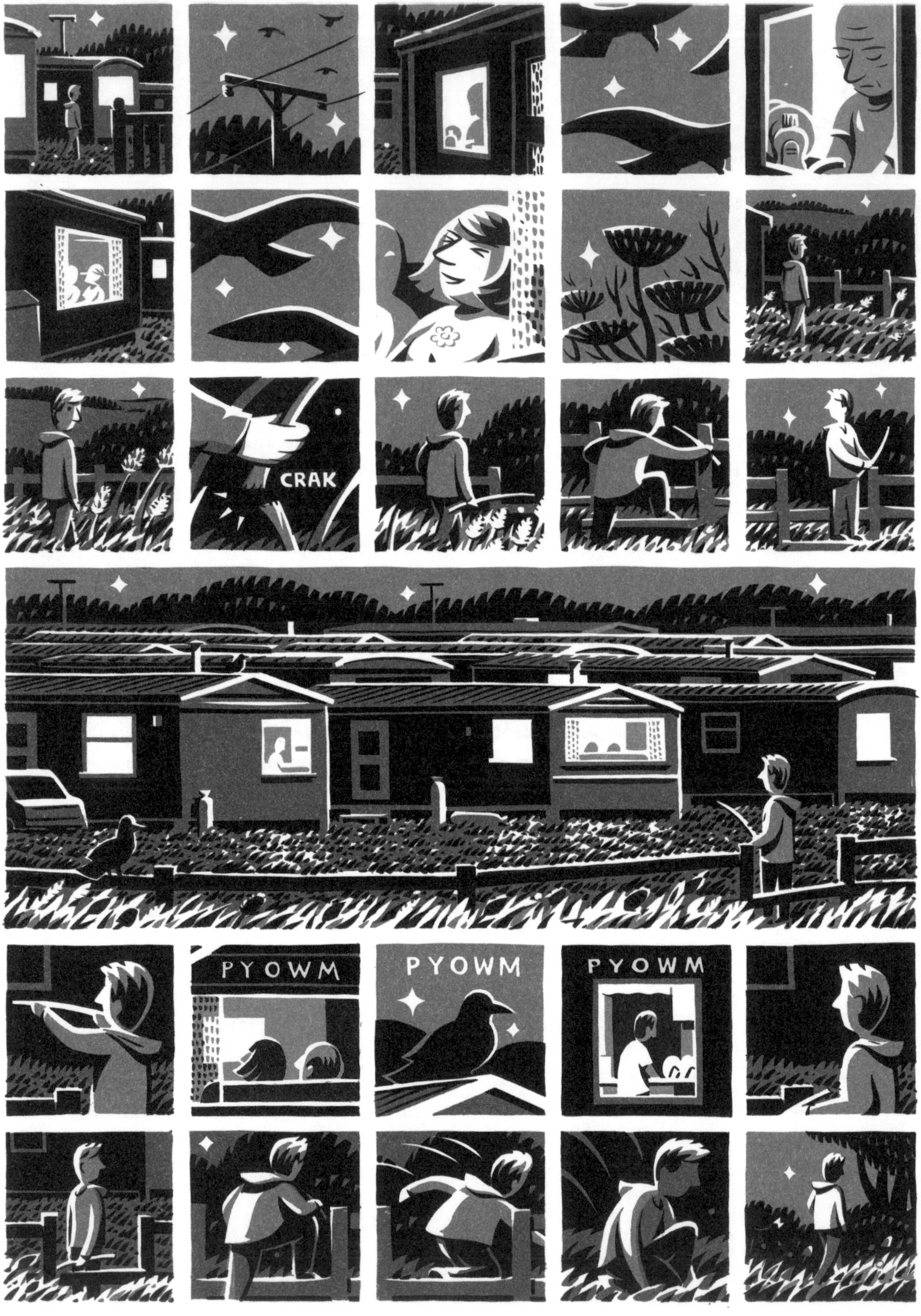
CRAK
PYOWM
PYOWM
PYOWM

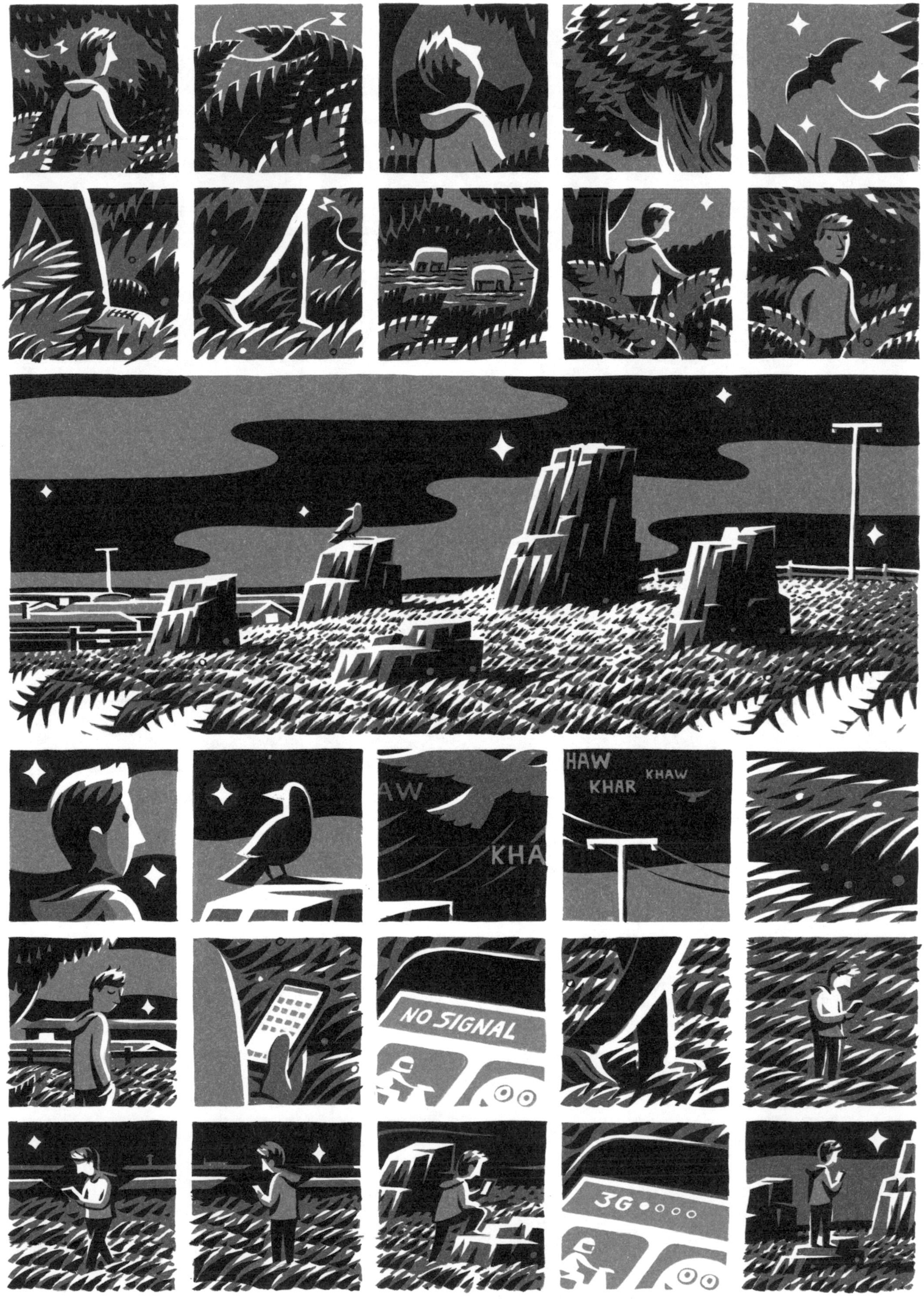
AW
KHA
HAW
KHAR
KHAW
NO SIGNAL
3G

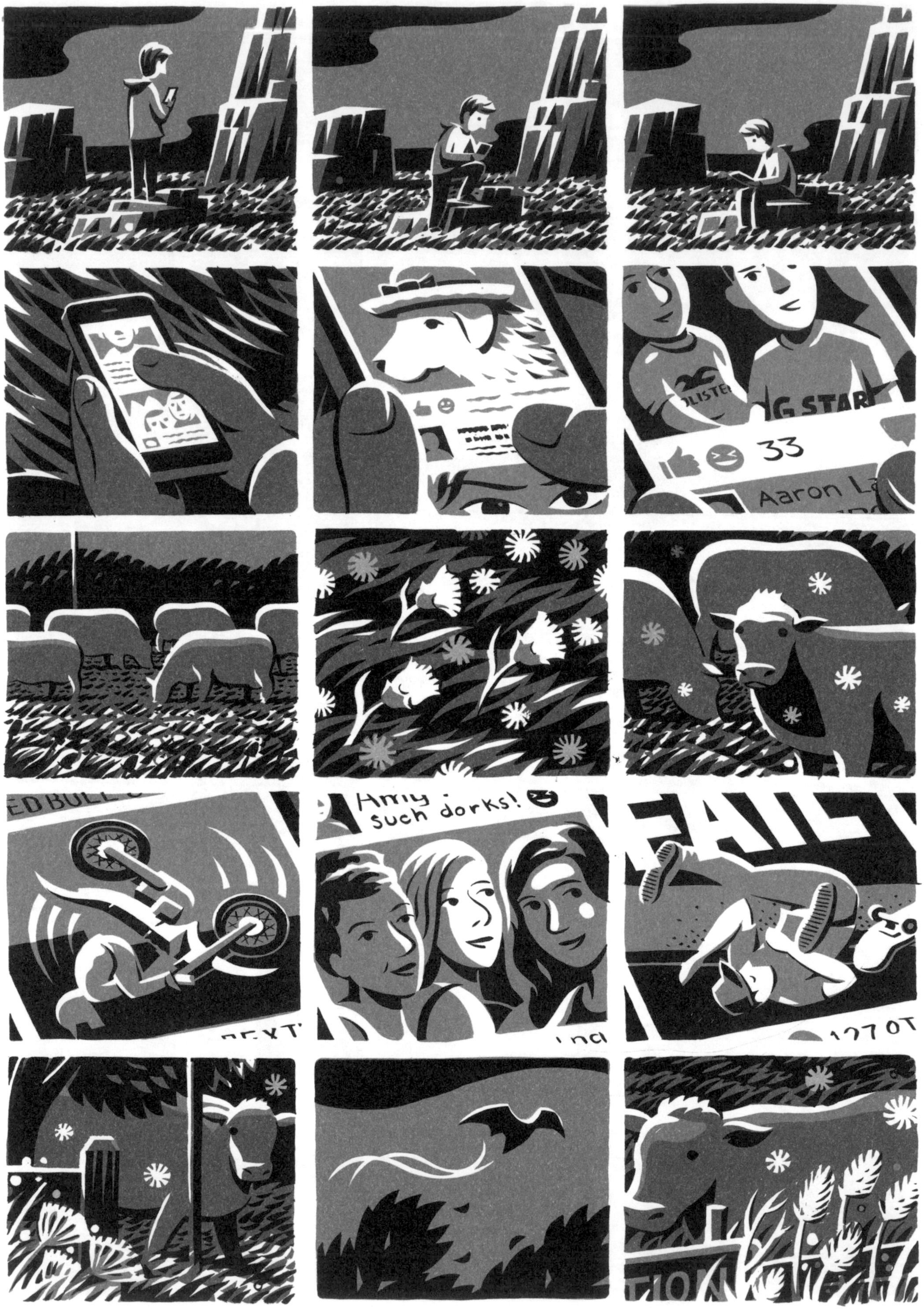
G STAR
33
Aaron La
ED BULL
Amy ·
such dorks!
FAIL

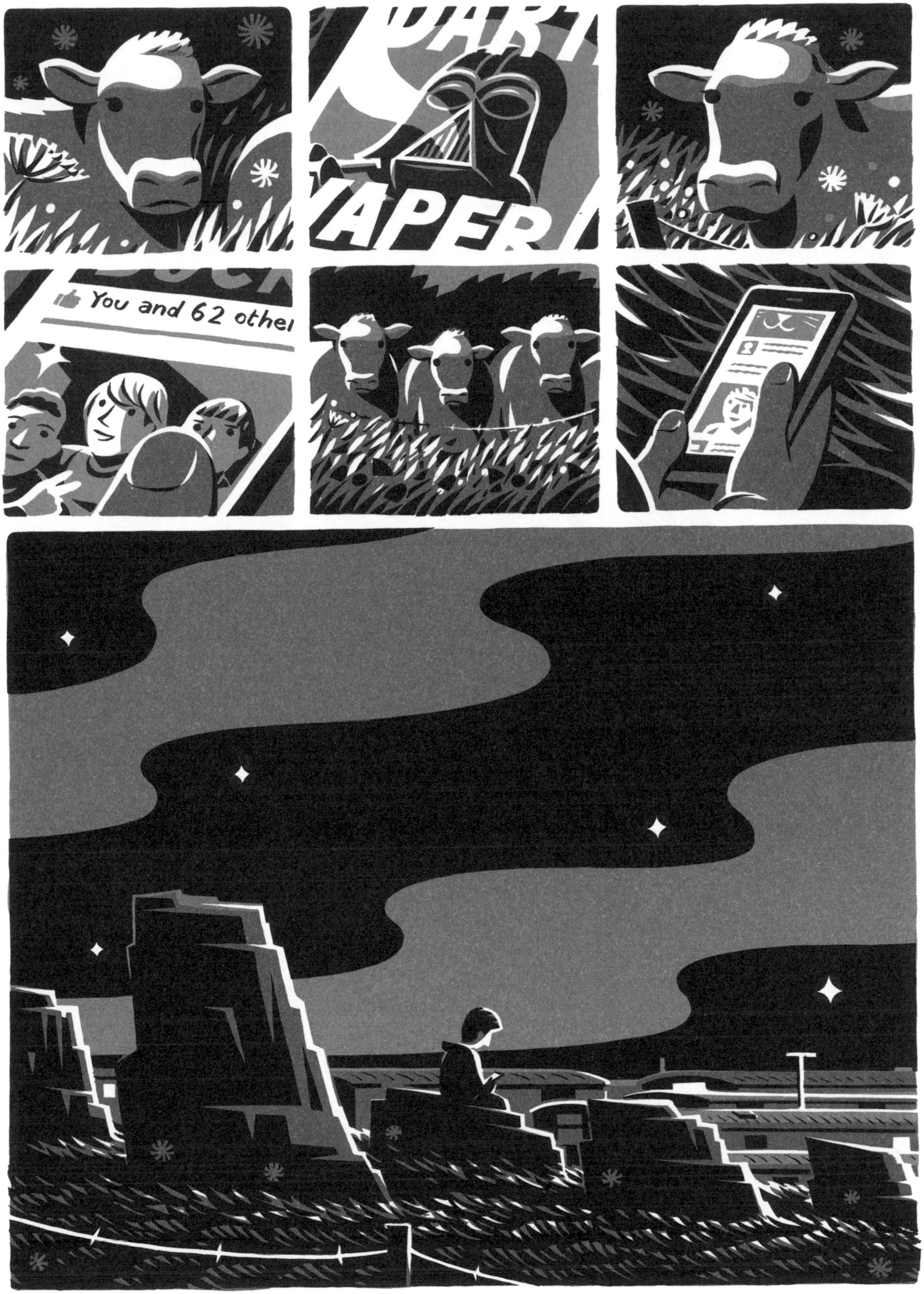
You and 62 othe

Passing Time

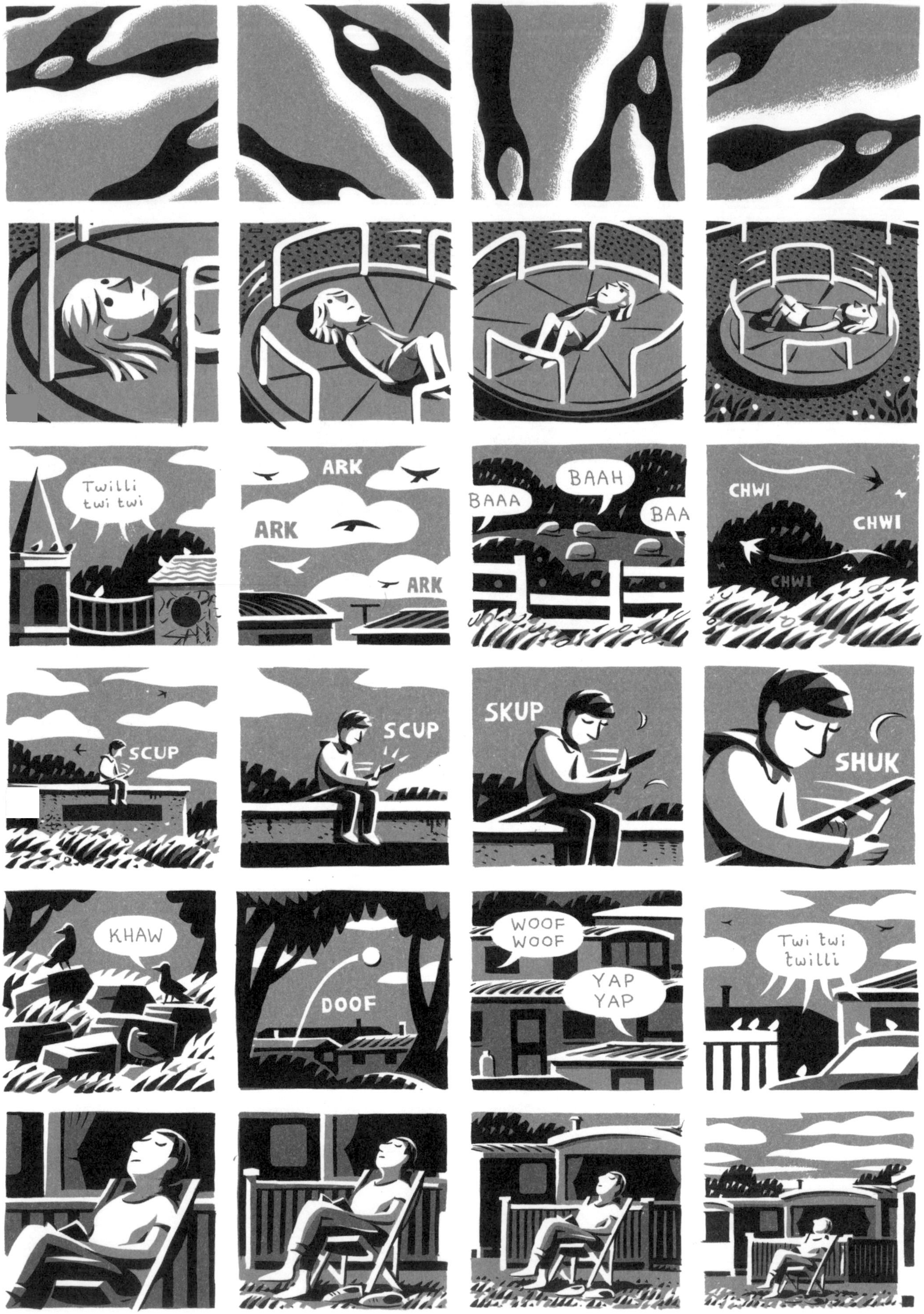
Twilli twi twi
ARK
ARK
ARK
BAAA
BAAH
BAA
CHWI
CHWI
CHWI
SCUP
SCUP
SKUP
SHUK
KHAW
DOOF
WOOF WOOF
YAP YAP
Twi twi twilli

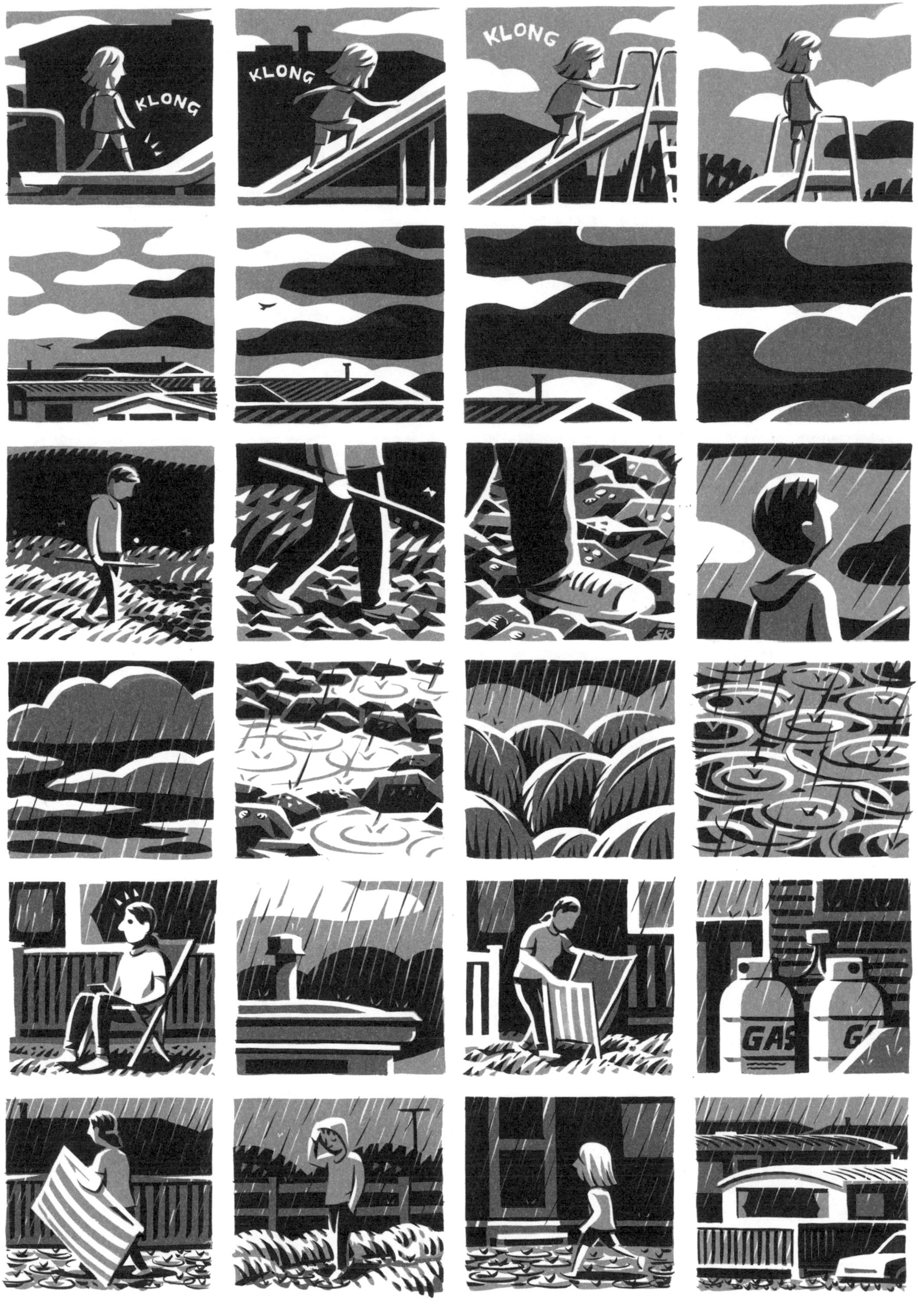
KLONG
KLONG
KLONG
GAS

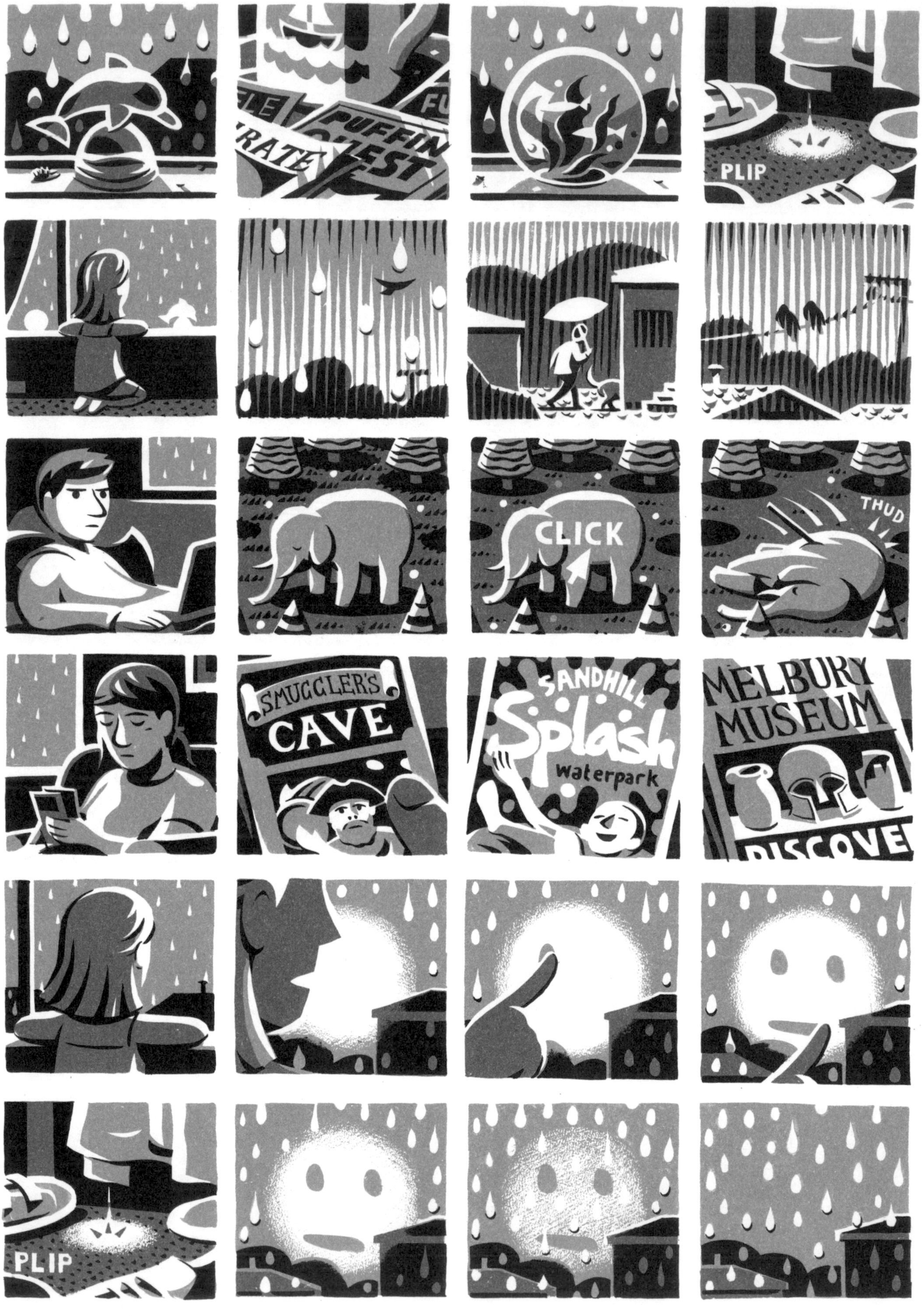
PUFFIN
PLIP
CLICK
THUD
SMUGGLER'S
CAVE
SANDHILL
Splash
waterpark
MELBURY
MUSEUM
PLIP

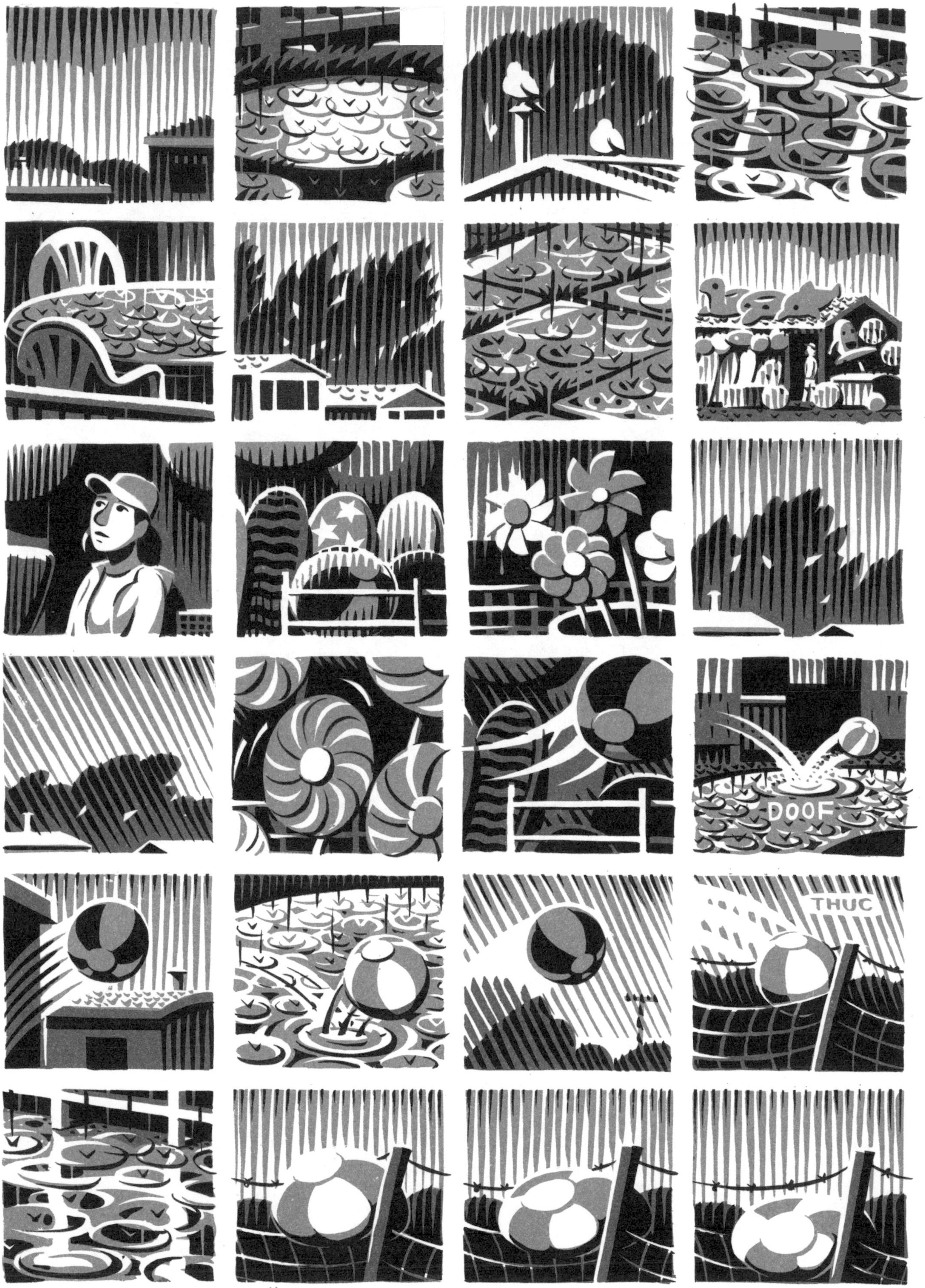
DOOF
THUC

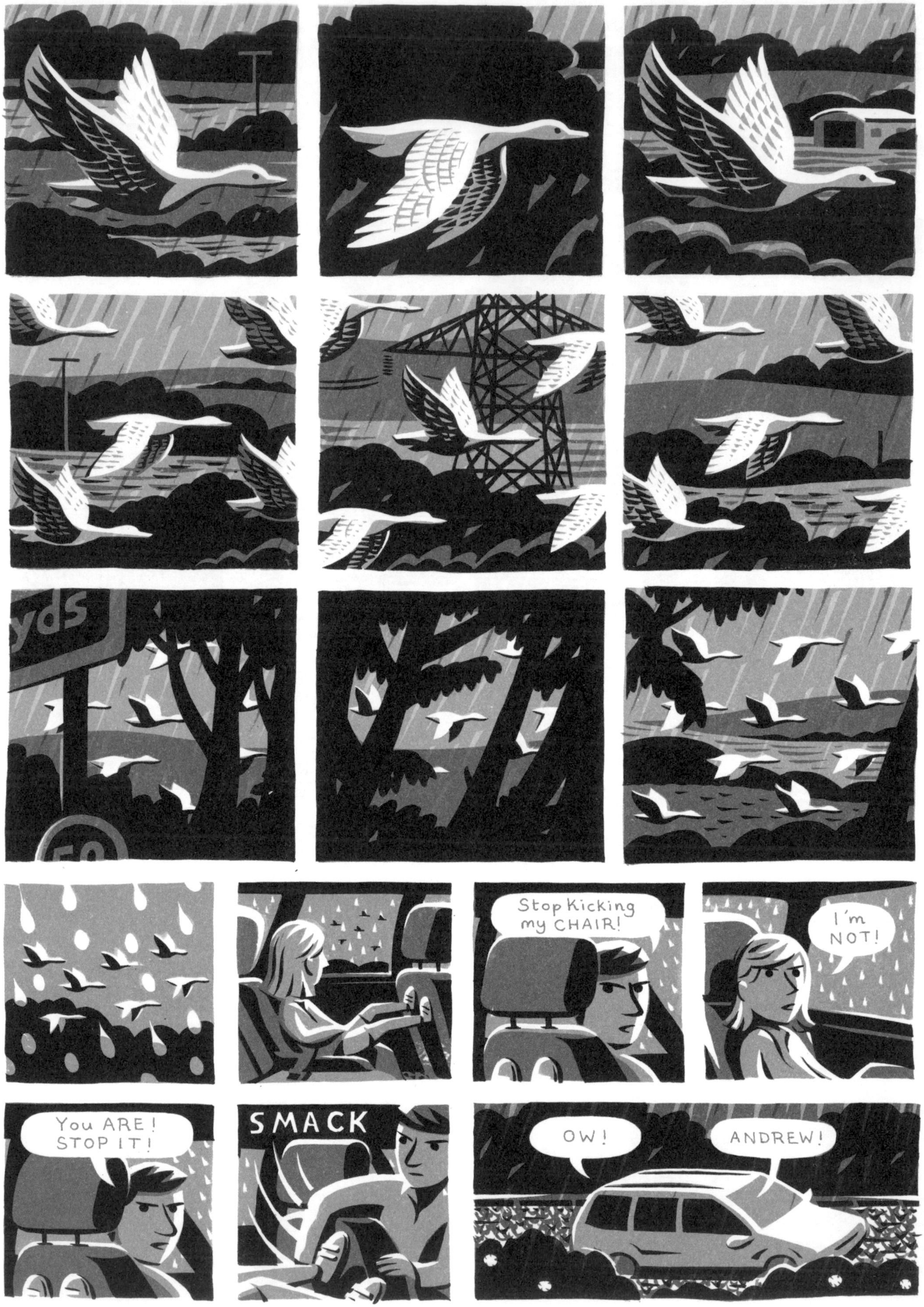
Stop Kicking my CHAIR!
I'm NOT!
You ARE! STOP IT!
SMACK
OW!
ANDREW!

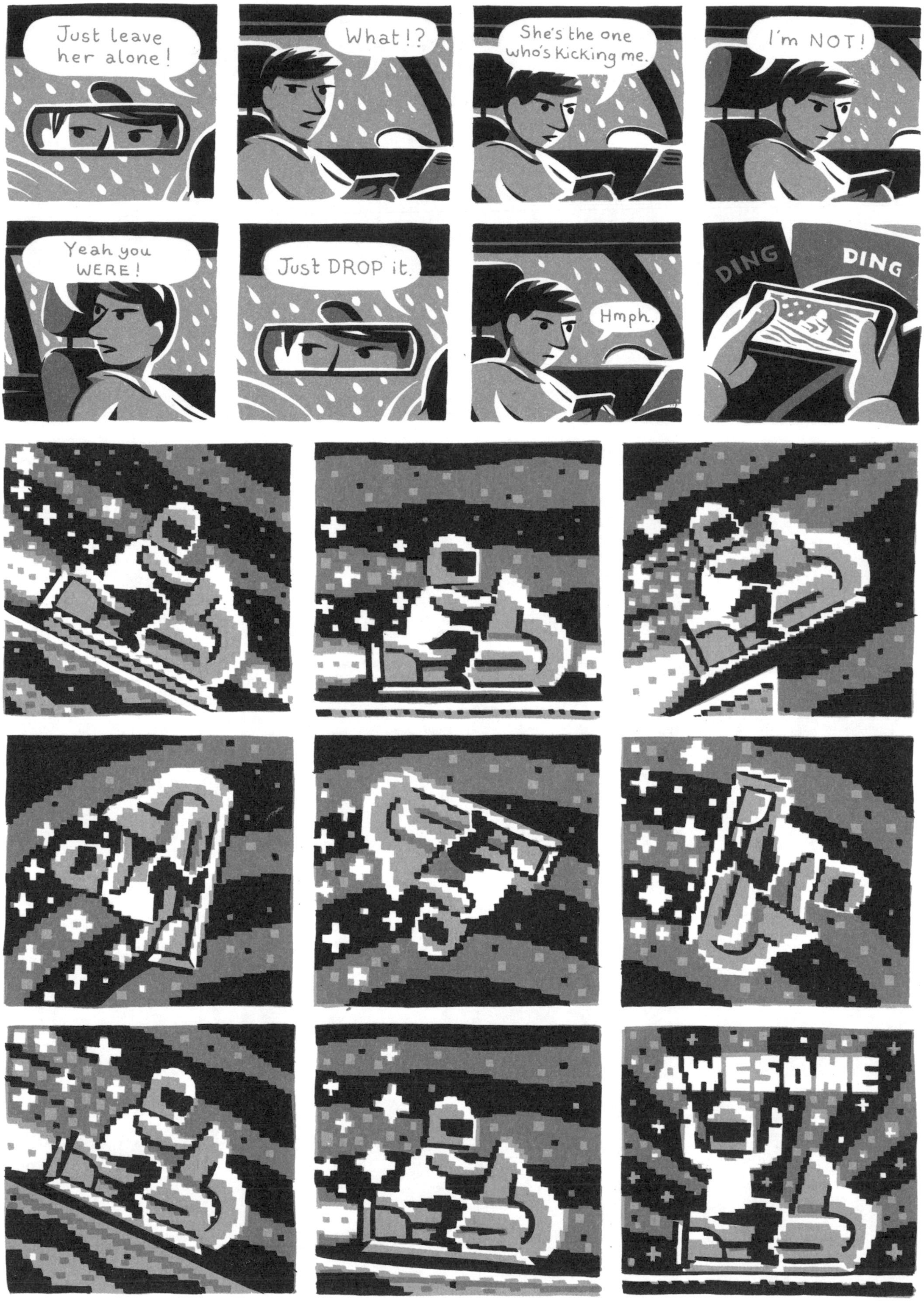
Just leave her alone!
What!?
She's the one who's kicking me.
I'm NOT!
Yeah you WERE!
Just DROP it.
Hmph.
DING
DING
AWESOME

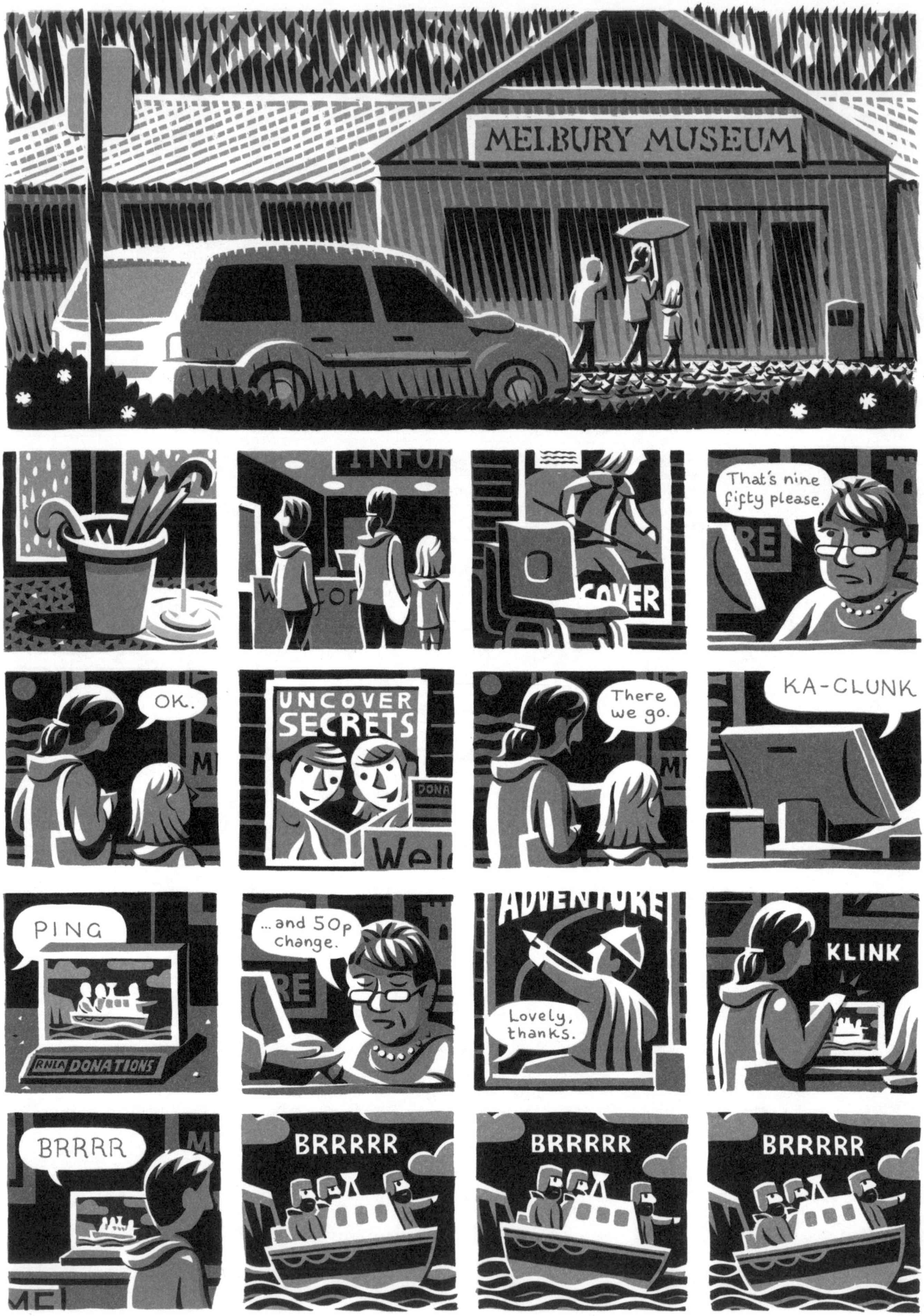
MELBURY MUSEUM
That's nine fifty please.
OK.
UNCOVER SECRETS
There we go.
KA-CLUNK
PING
RNLI DONATIONS
...and 50p change.
ADVENTURE
Lovely, thanks.
KLINK
BRRRR
BRRRRR
BRRRRR
BRRRRR

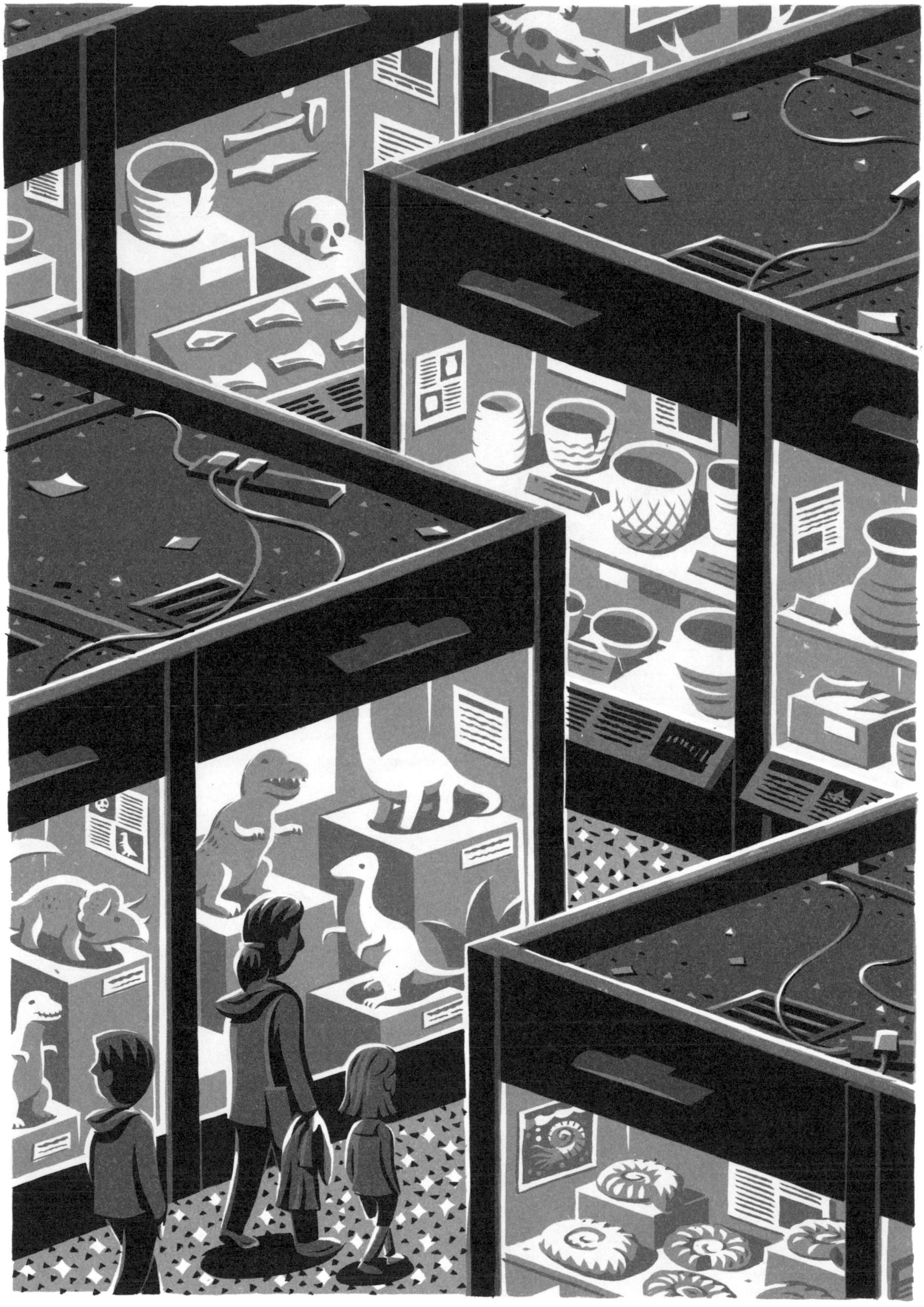

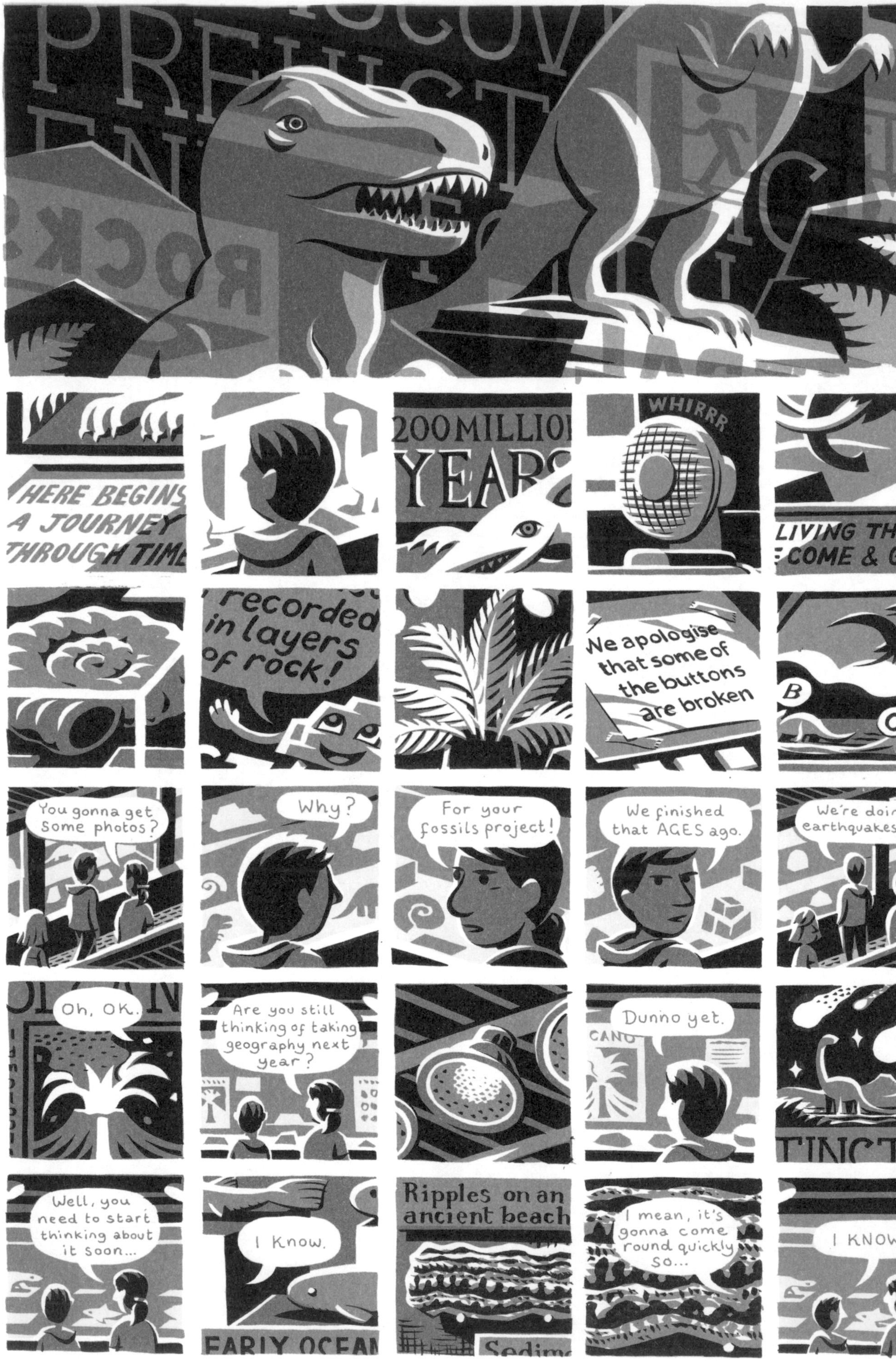
HERE BEGINS A JOURNEY THROUGH TIME
WHIRRR
LIVING THINGS COME & GONE
recorded in layers of rock!
We apologise that some of the buttons are broken
B
C
E
You gonna get some photos?
Why?
For your fossils project!
We finished that AGES ago.
We're doing earthquakes now.
Oh, OK.
Are you still thinking of taking geography next year?
Dunno yet.
Well, you need to start thinking about it soon...
I know.
Ripples on an ancient beach
I mean, it's gonna come round quickly so...
I KNOW!

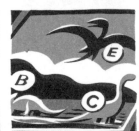

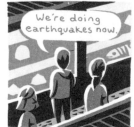

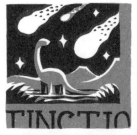

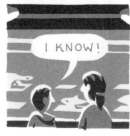

VAST SHEETS OF ICE

VENT AXIA

Ⓐ Ⓑ Ⓒ
COLD PLANES OF BRITAIN

A mammoth's tusk found c

③

THIS DOOR IS ALARMED

a deliberate blow to the head (c)

What?

Nothing.

Stop following me around!

CLICK

GREETINGS FRIEND!

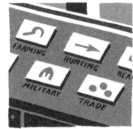
WELCOME TO THE IRON AGE VILLAGE.

MY NAME IS BRIOK REN, AND I WILL BE YOUR GUIDE...

...TO THE SECRETS OF THESE ANCIENT HILLS.

SELECT A SUBJECT FROM THE BUTTONS BELOW...

...AND I WILL BEGIN.

FARMING HUNTING
MILITARY TRADE

BRONZE AGE

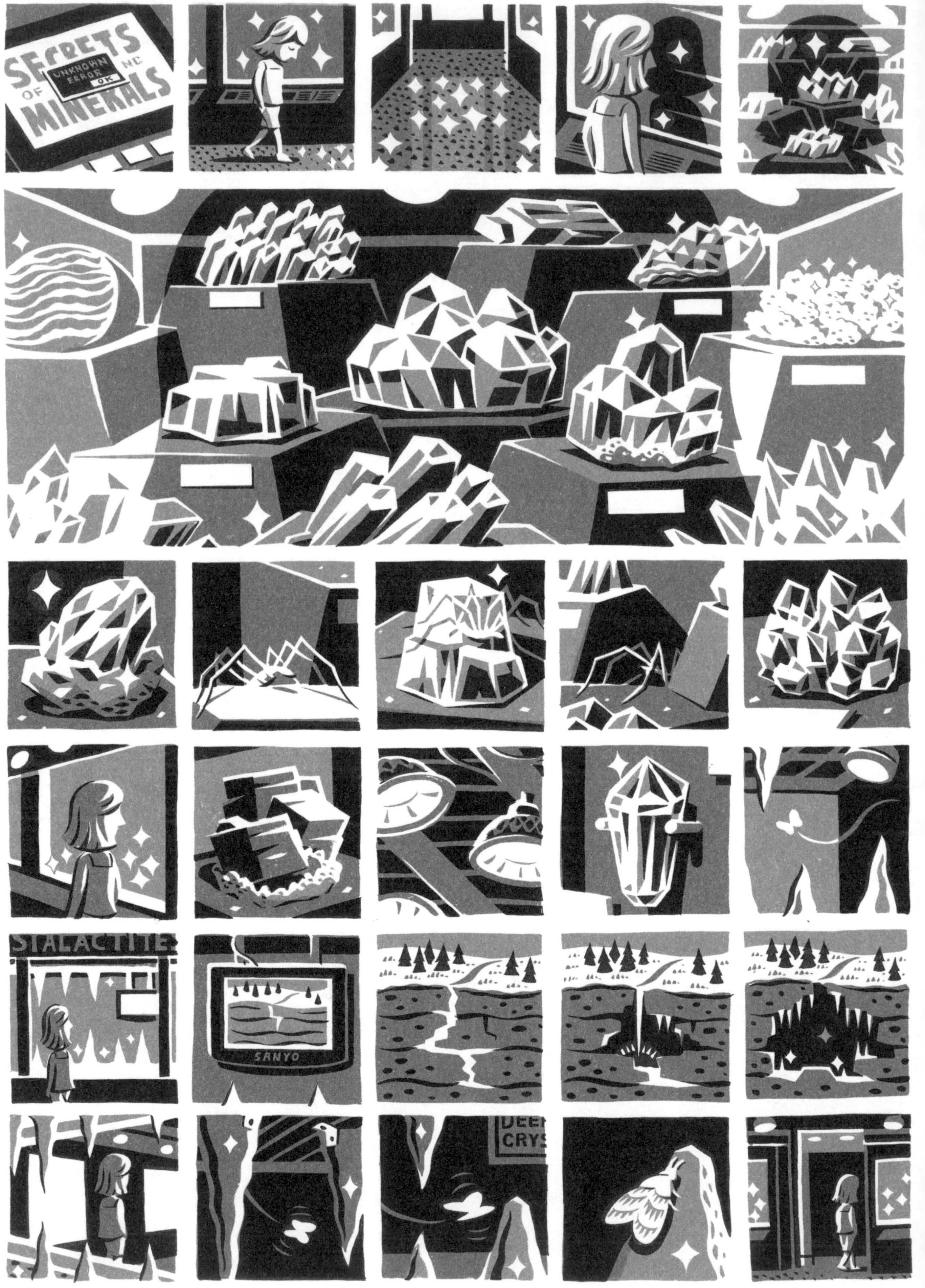
SECRETS OF MINERALS
UNKNOWN ERROR
OK
STALACTITES
SANYO

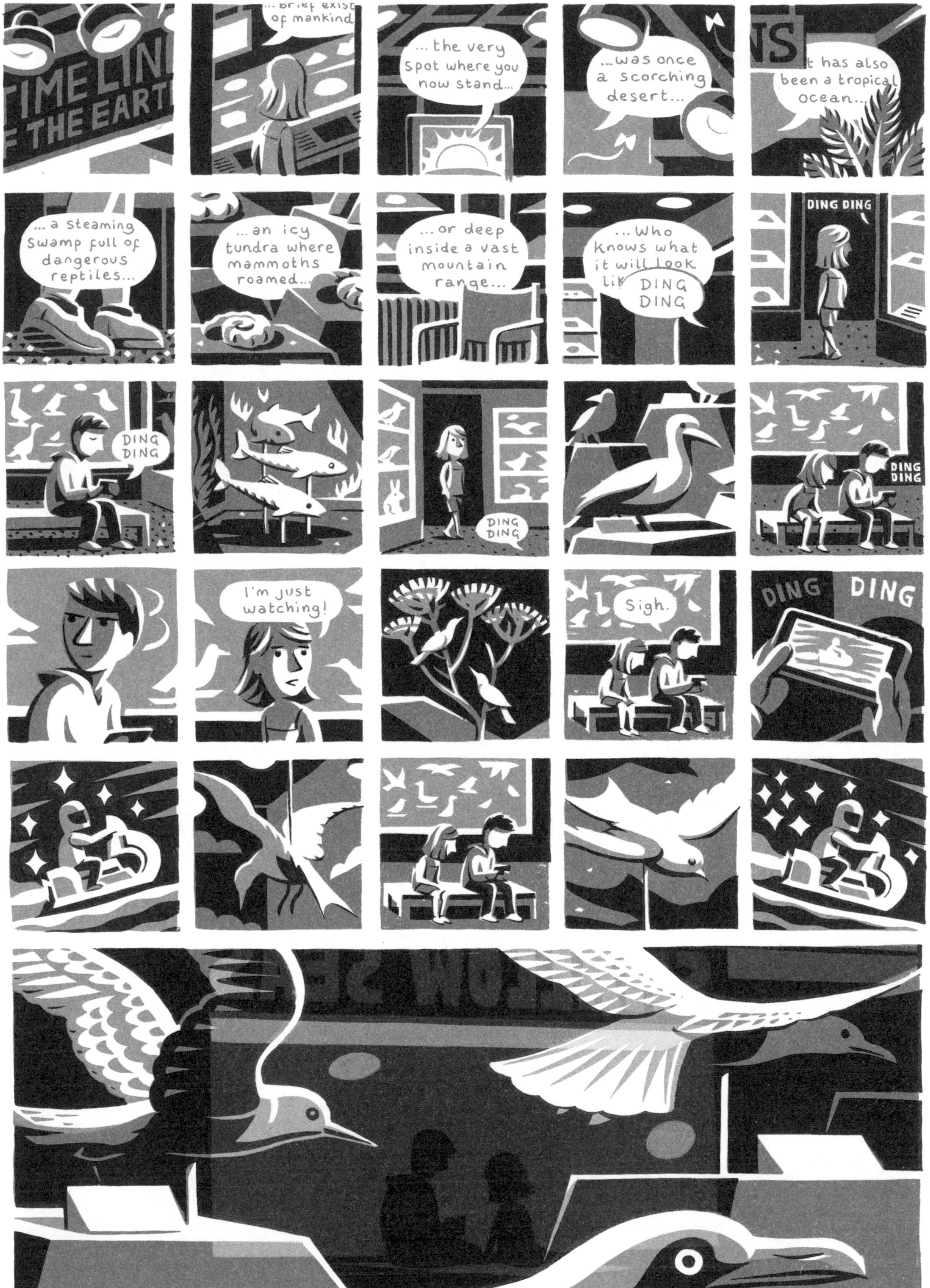
TIMELIN
F THE EART
... brief exist
of mankind
... the very spot where you now stand...
...was once a scorching desert...
NS
t has also been a tropical ocean...
... a steaming swamp full of dangerous reptiles...
... an icy tundra where mammoths roamed...
... or deep inside a vast mountain range...
... Who knows what it will look lik
DING DING
DING DING
DING DING
DING DING
DING DING
I'm just watching!
Sigh.
DING
DING

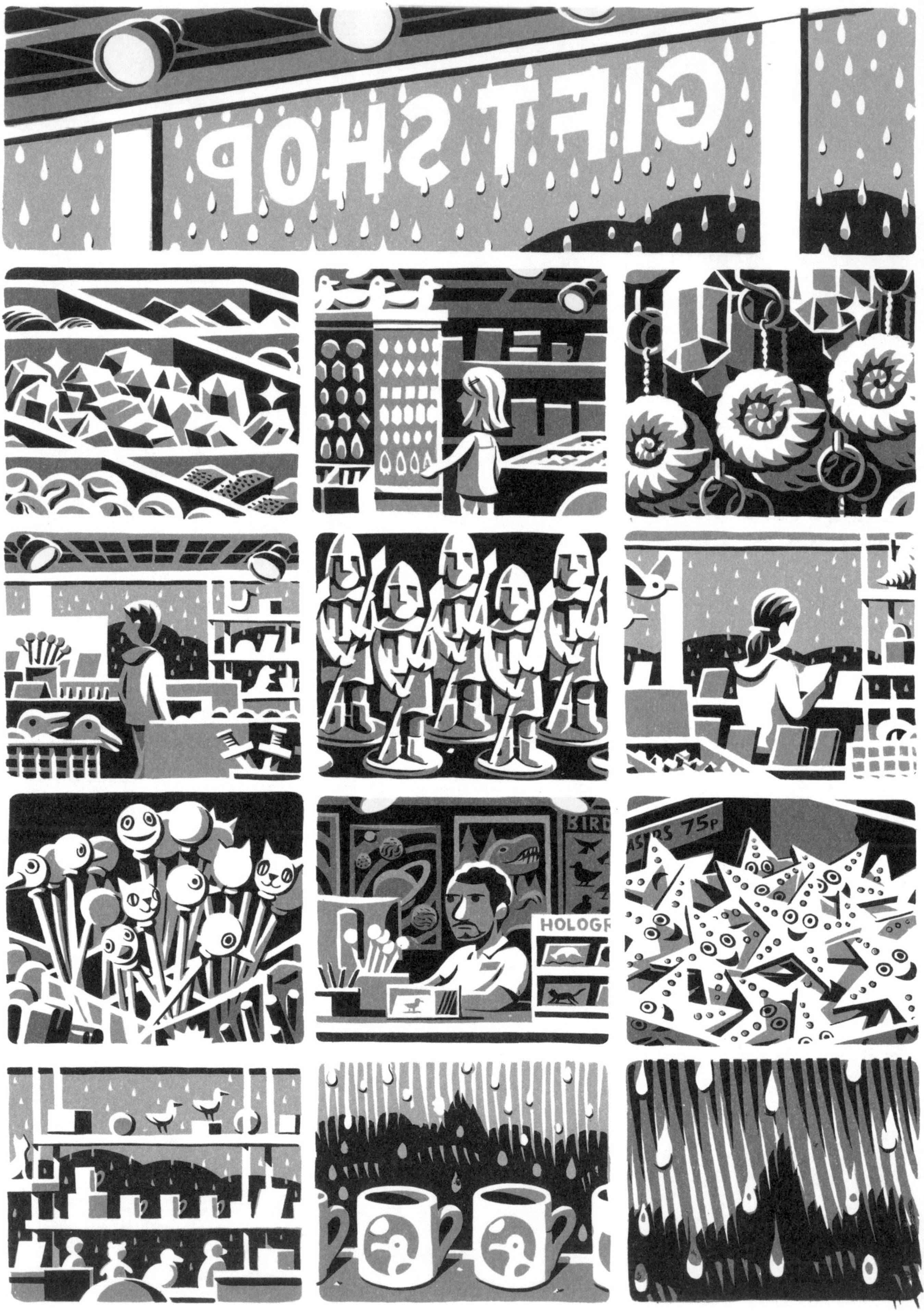
GIFT SHOP
BIRD
HOLOGR
75p

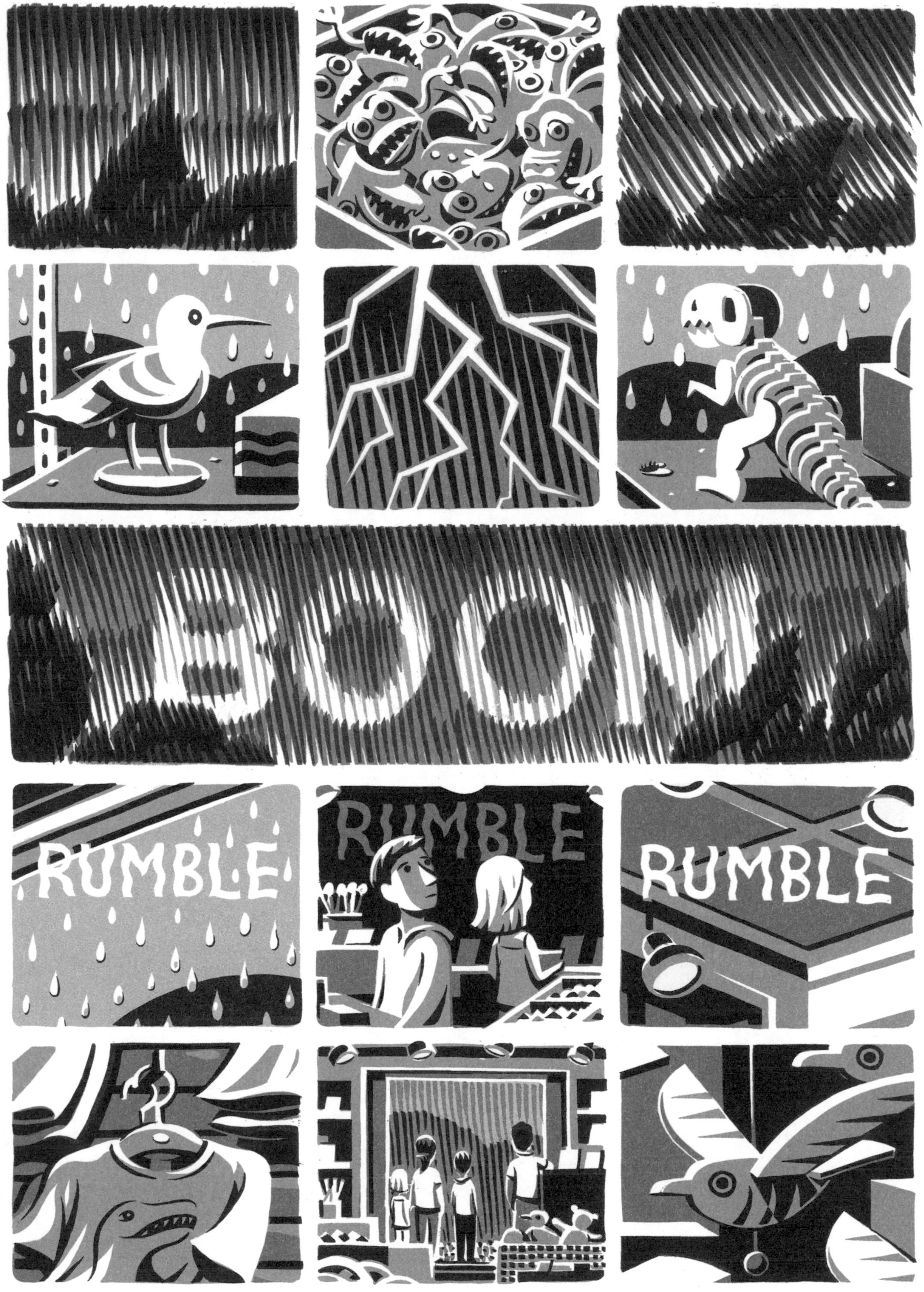
BOOM
RUMBLE
RUMBLE
RUMBLE

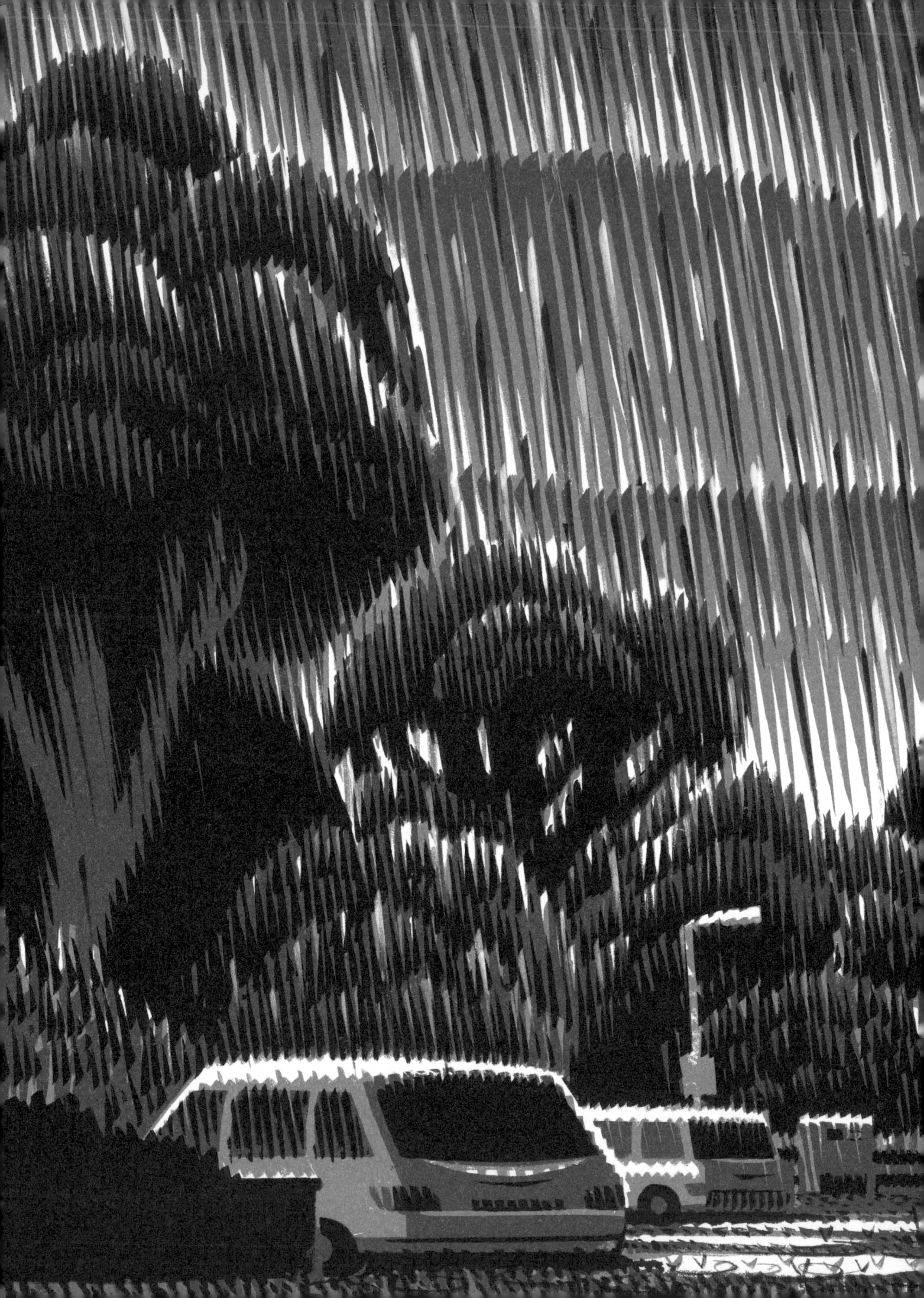

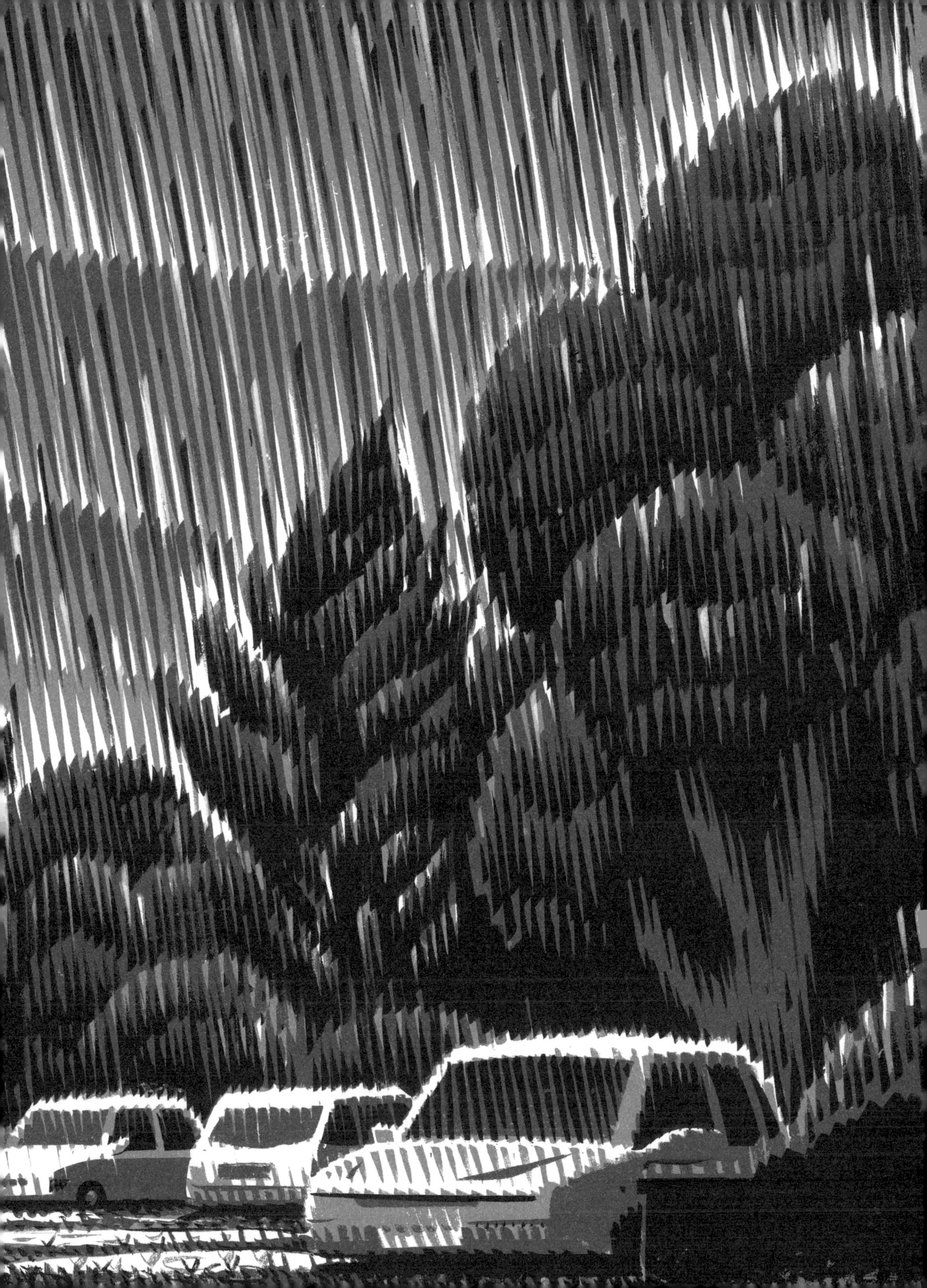

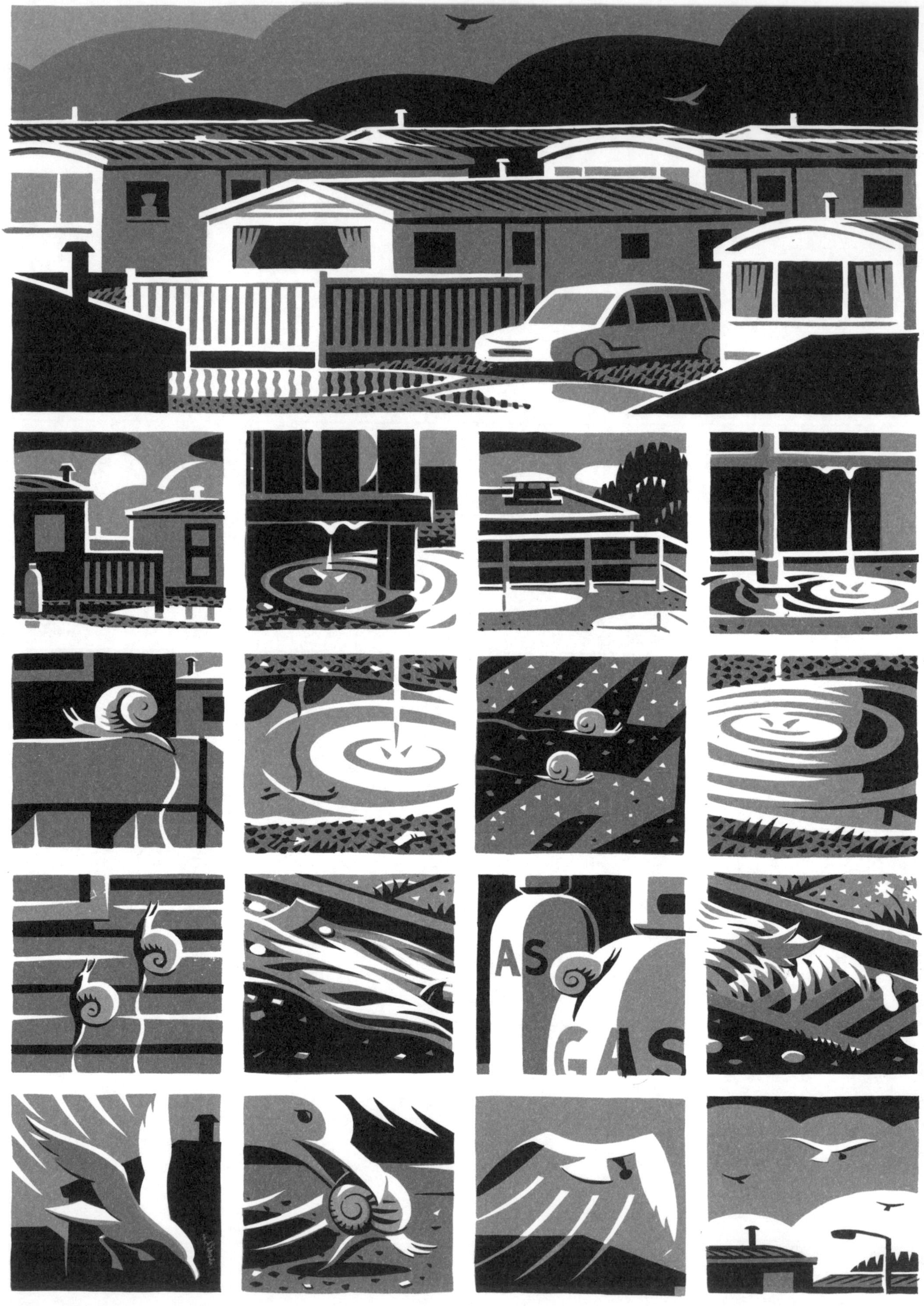
AS
GAS

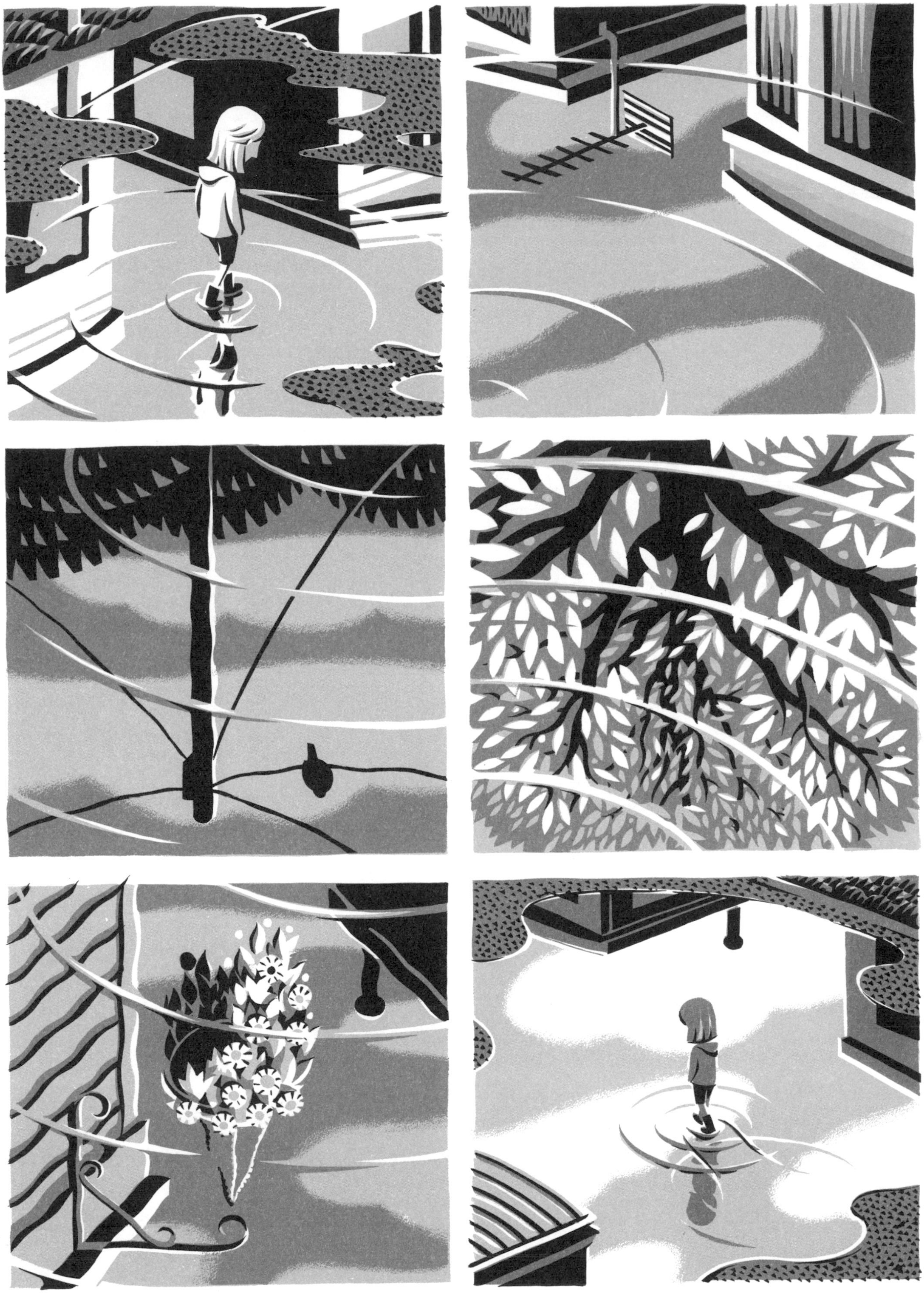

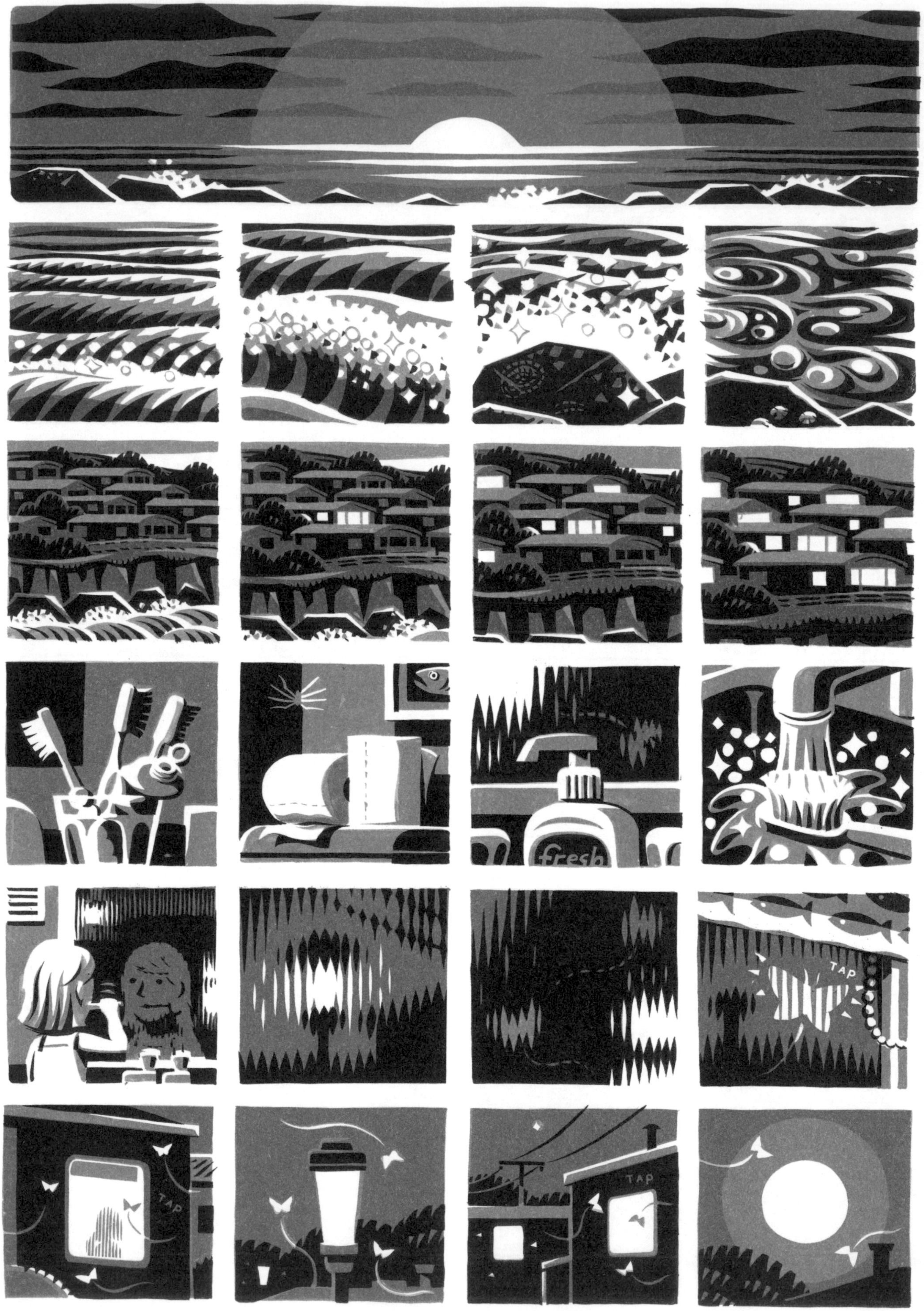
fresh
TAP
TAP
TAP

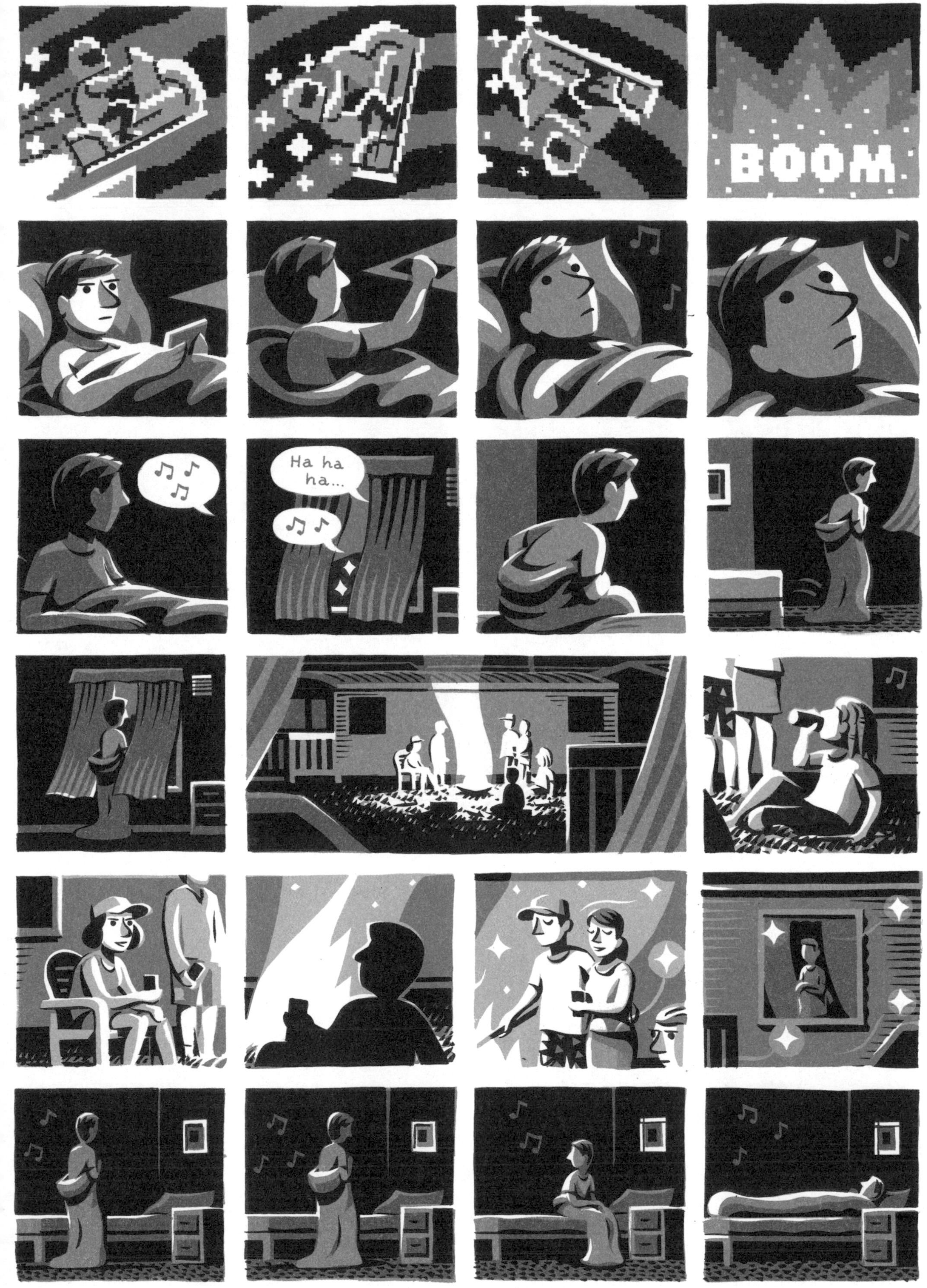
BOOM
Ha ha ha...

The Waves

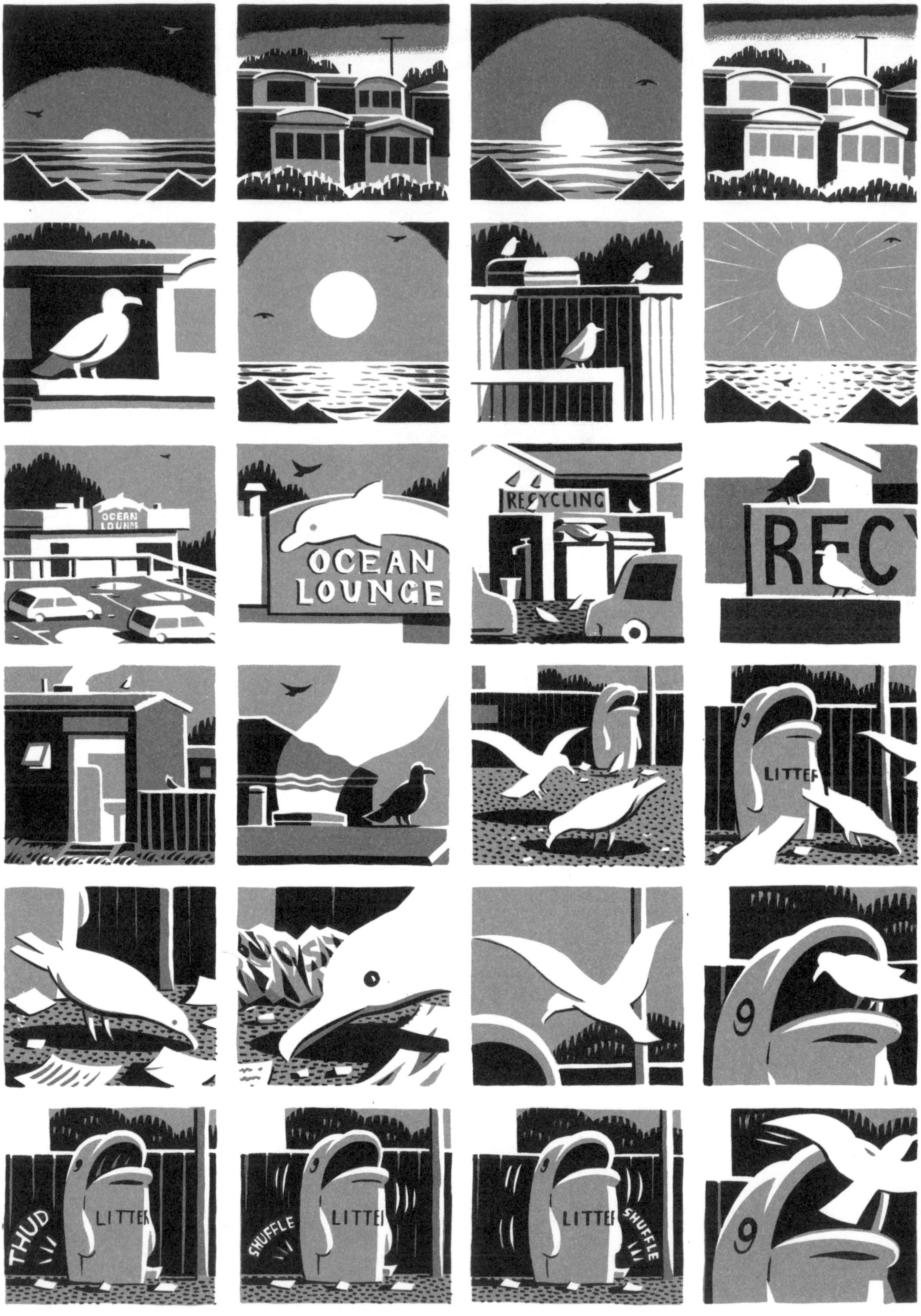

OCEAN LOUNGE
OCEAN LOUNGE
RECYCLING
RECY
LITTER
THUD
LITTER
SHUFFLE
LITTER
LITTER
SHUFFLE

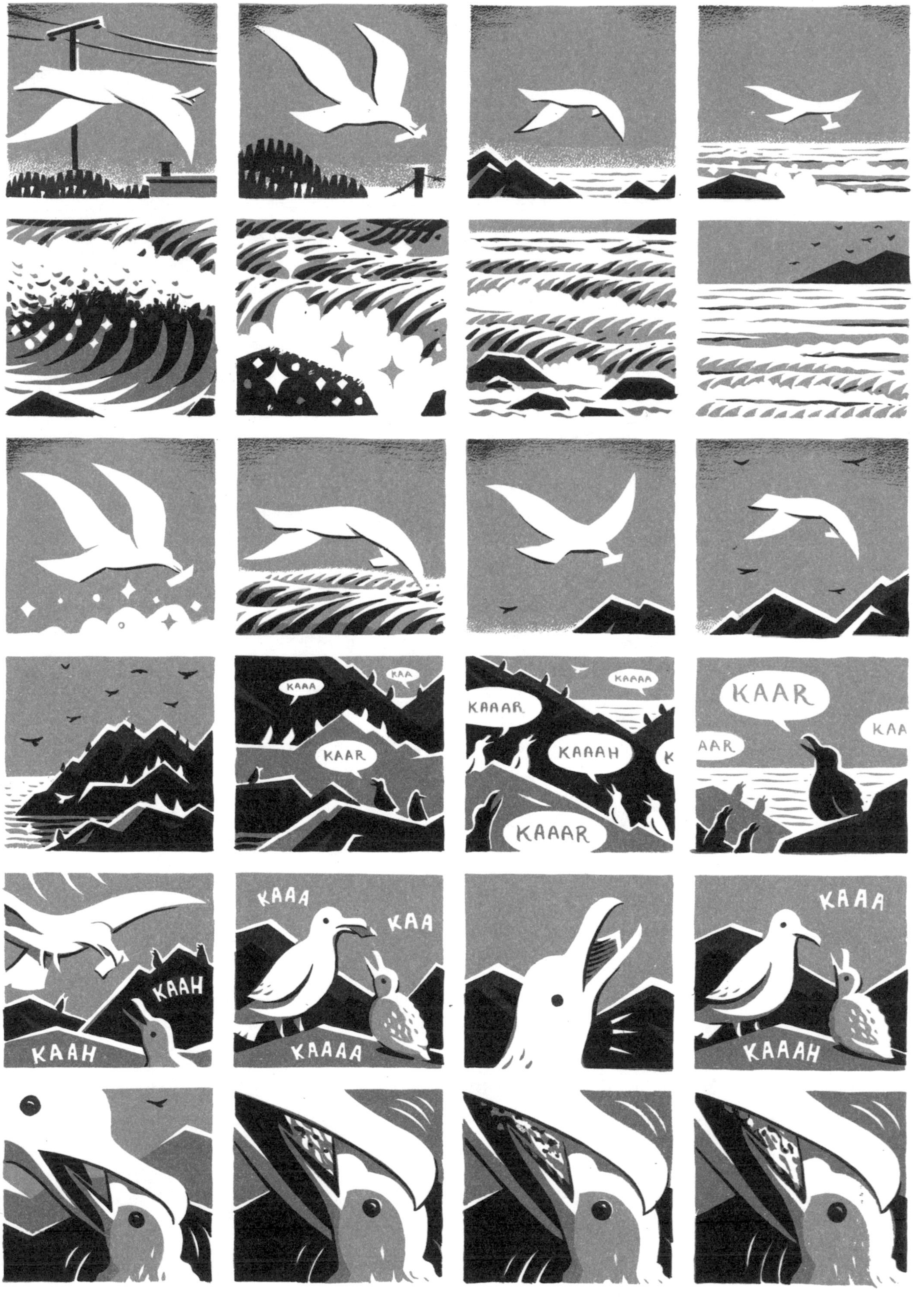
KAAA
KAA
KAAR
KAAAR
KAAAA
KAAAH
K
KAAAR
KAAR
AAR
KAA
KAAH
KAAH
KAAA
KAA
KAAAA
KAAA
KAAAH

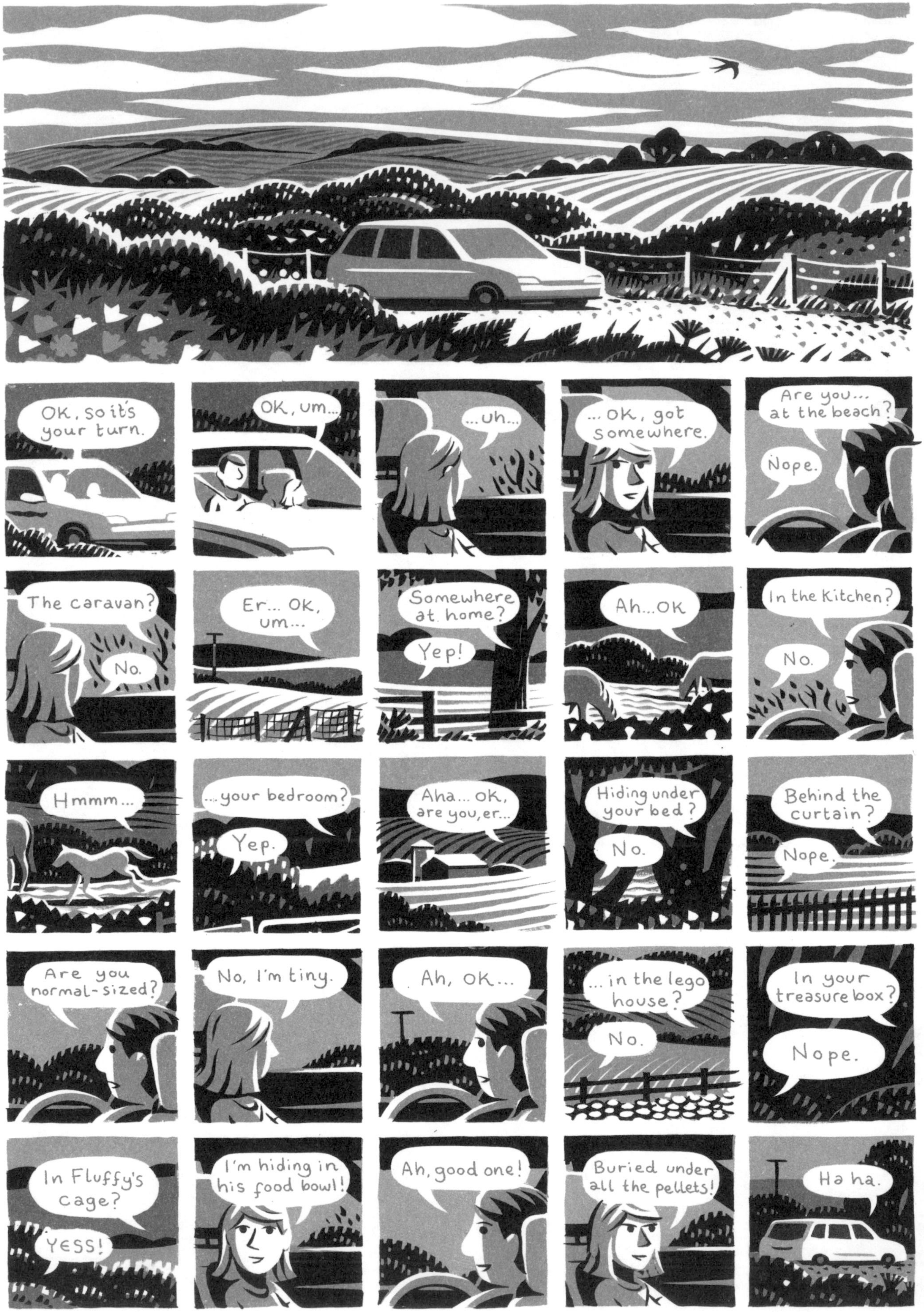
OK, so it's your turn.
OK, um...
...uh...
...OK, got somewhere.
Are you... at the beach?
Nope.
The caravan?
No.
Er... OK, um...
Somewhere at home?
Yep!
Ah...OK
In the Kitchen?
No.
Hmmm...
...your bedroom?
Yep.
Aha... OK, are you, er...
Hiding under your bed?
No.
Behind the curtain?
Nope.
Are you normal-sized?
No, I'm tiny.
Ah, OK...
...in the lego house?
No.
In your treasure box?
Nope.
In Fluffy's cage?
YESS!
I'm hiding in his food bowl!
Ah, good one!
Buried under all the pellets!
Ha ha.

  How come Andy's allowed to stay behind?

  He's just being...

 ...difficult.

  Great-aunt Lizzie's lovely though!

 You'll like her a lot!

  We used to visit her every summer!

  She'd give me painting lessons in her little studio!

  Oh, you know the little painting by the telephone...

 ...that's one of hers!

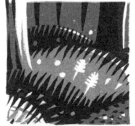  You know, the sailboat and the stormy sky?

  Yeah, but...

 ...Why couldn't I stay behind WITH him.

 You let me stay with him at HOME.

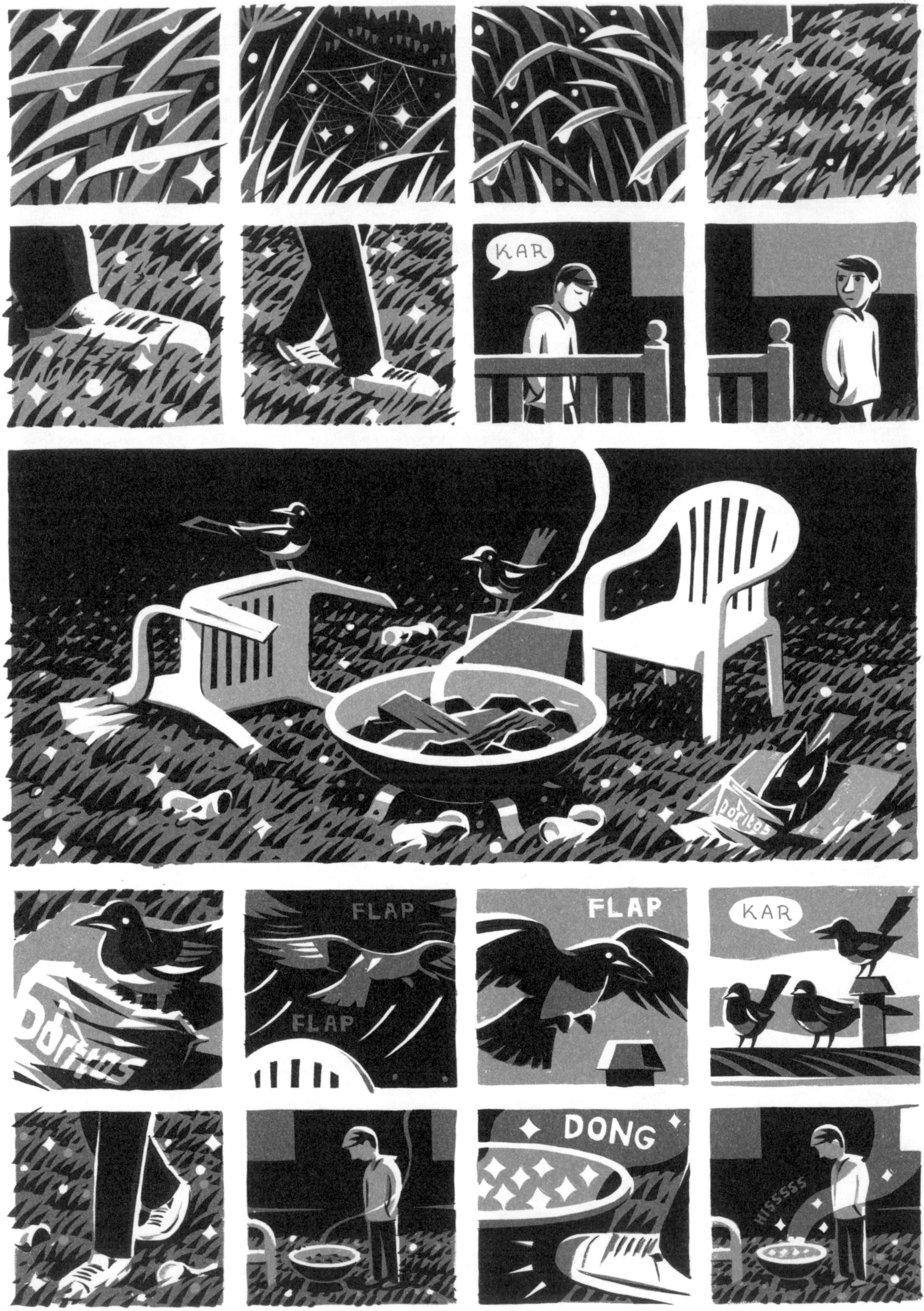
KAR
FLAP
FLAP
FLAP
KAR
DONG
HISSSSS

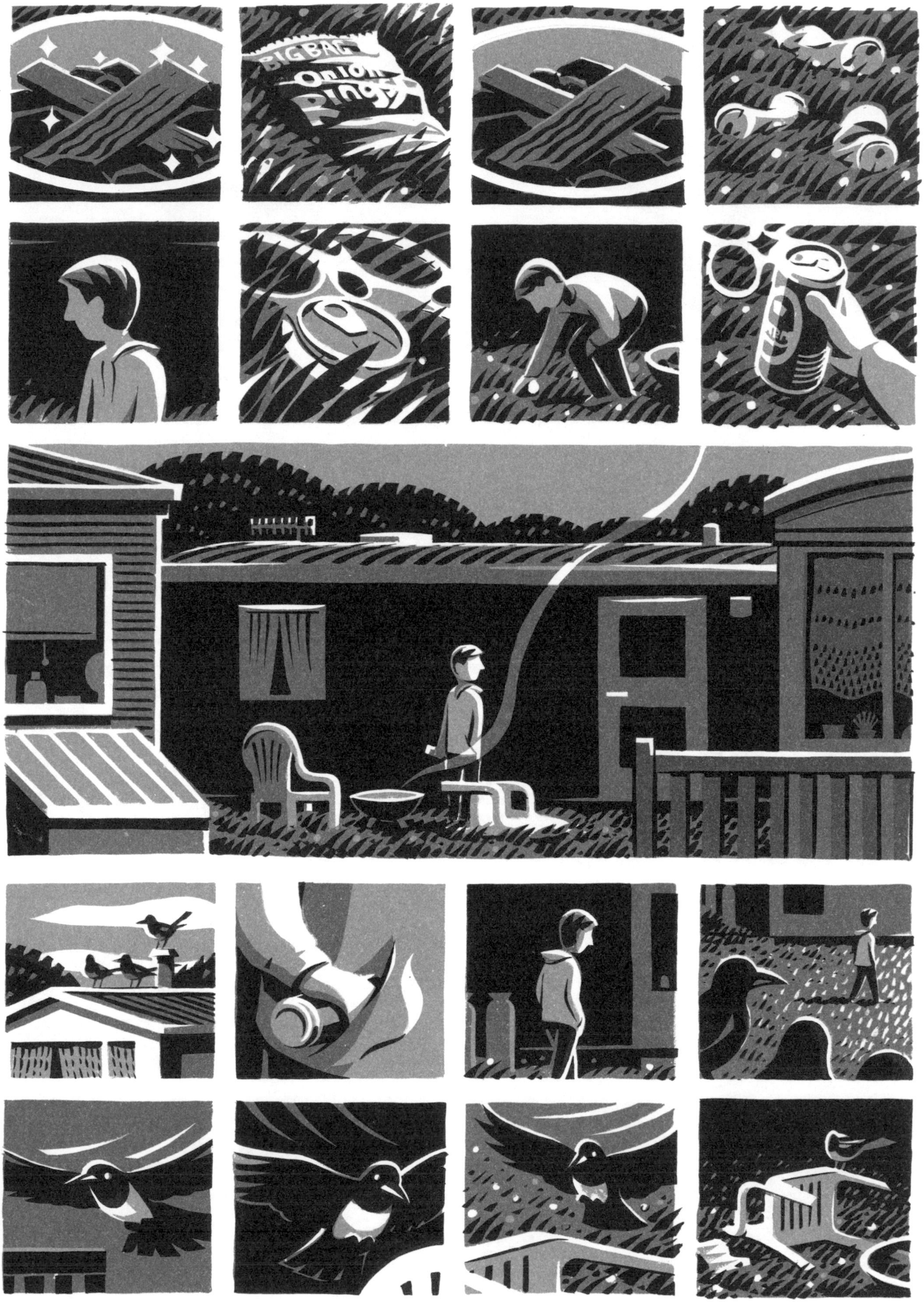
BIG BAG
ONION RINGS

DING DONG
KLAK KLAK
Hello, love!
Hellooo!
Lovely to see you!
Hello darling!
Come on in then, come on in.
Lets go thr to the Kitch
I'l put t ettle on must
Oh, no need to take your shoes off love...
...ha ha, it's not Buckingham Palace!

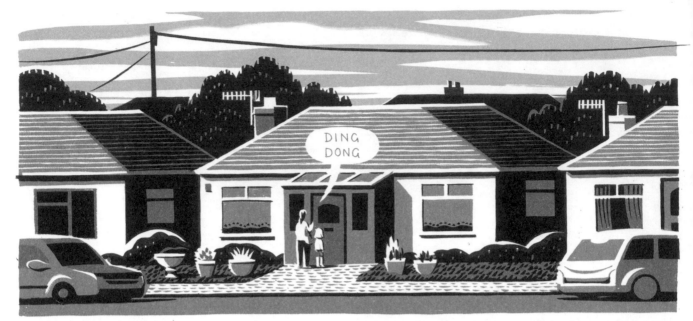

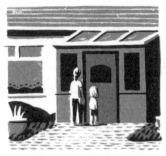

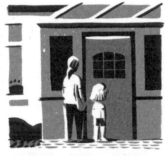

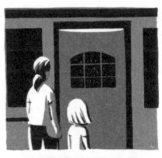

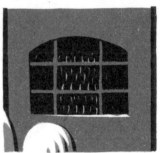

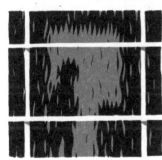

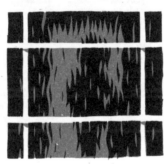

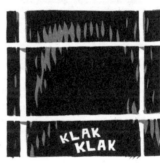

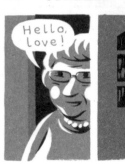

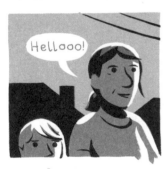

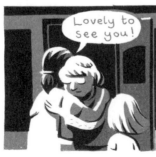

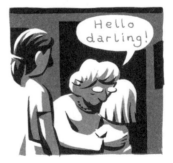

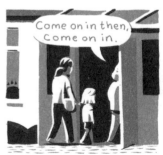

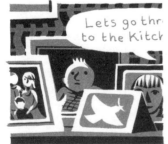

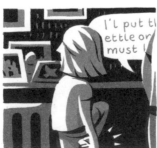

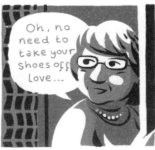

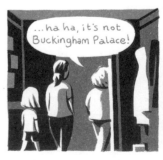

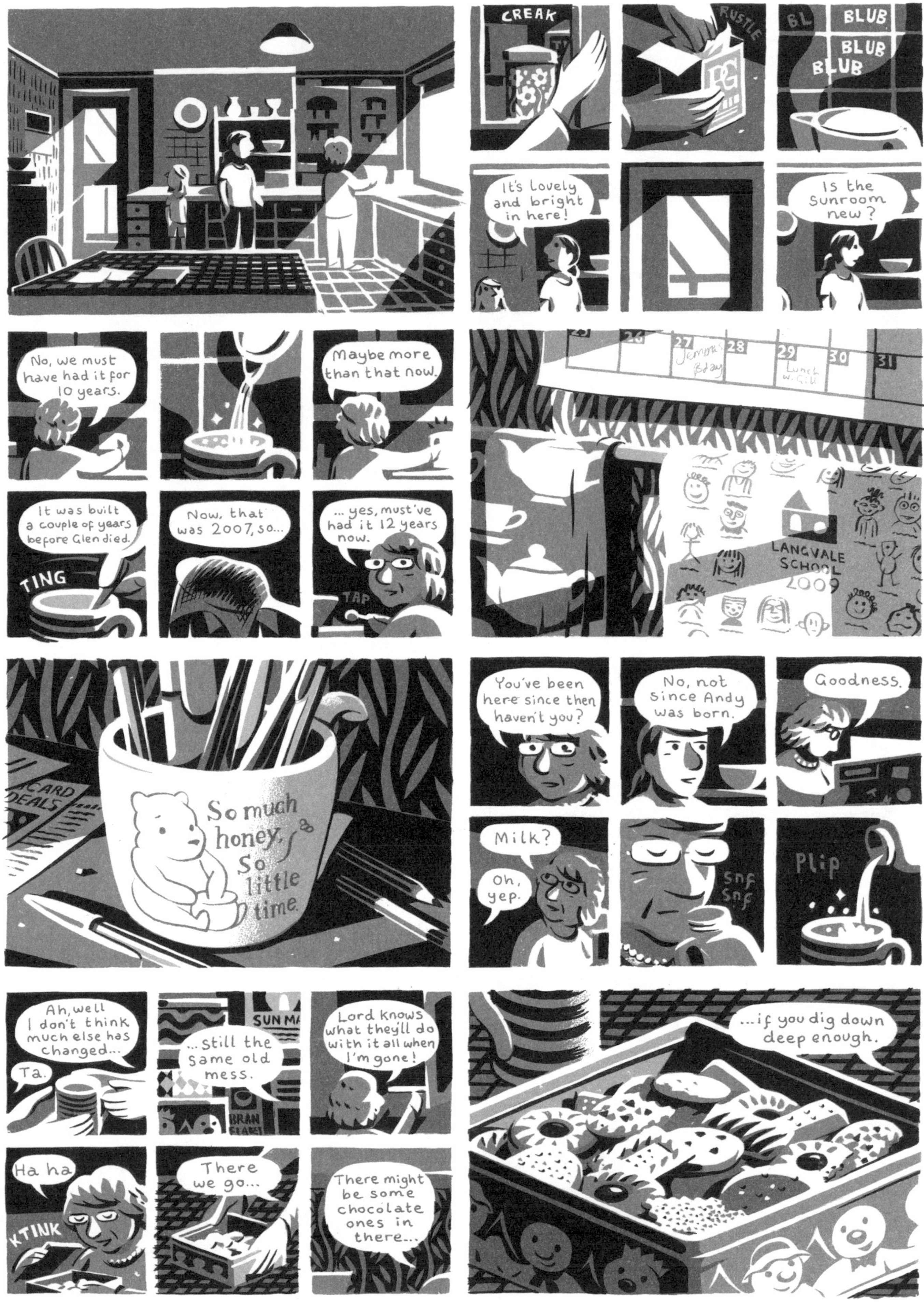
CREAK
RUSTLE
BL
BLUB
BLUB
BLUB
It's lovely and bright in here!
Is the sunroom new?
No, we must have had it for 10 years.
Maybe more than that now.
It was built a couple of years before Glen died.
TING
Now, that was 2007, so...
...yes, must've had it 12 years now.
TAP
26
27
28
29
30
31
Lunch w. Gill
LANGVALE SCHOOL 2009
CARD DEALS
So much honey, So little time.
You've been here since then haven't you?
No, not since Andy was born.
Goodness.
Milk?
Oh, yep.
snf snf
Plip
Ah, well I don't think much else has changed...
Ta.
...still the same old mess.
SUN MA
BRAN
Lord knows what they'll do with it all when I'm gone!
Ha ha
KTINK
There we go...
There might be some chocolate ones in there...
...if you dig down deep enough.

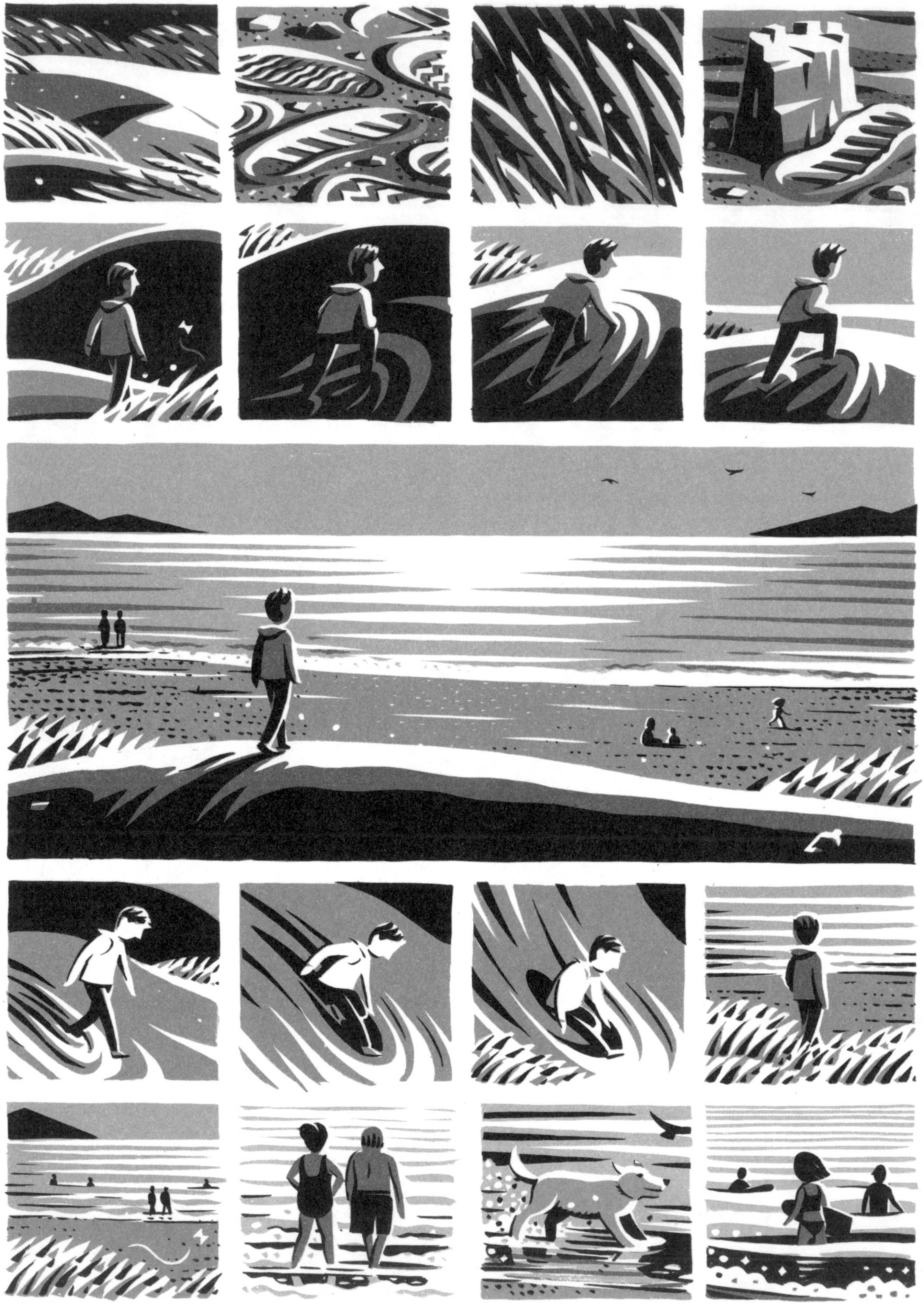

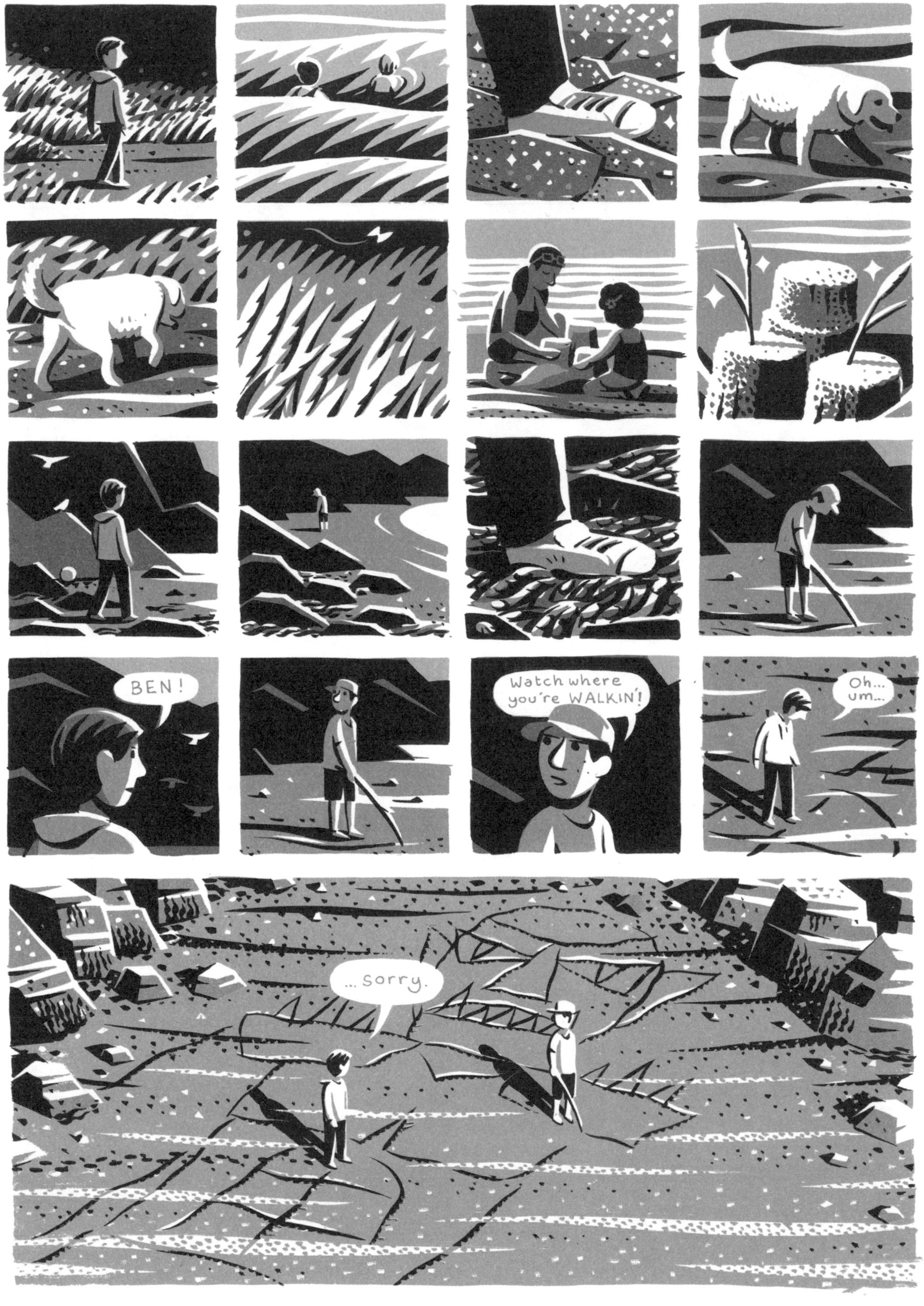
BEN!
Watch where you're WALKIN'!
Oh... um...
...sorry.

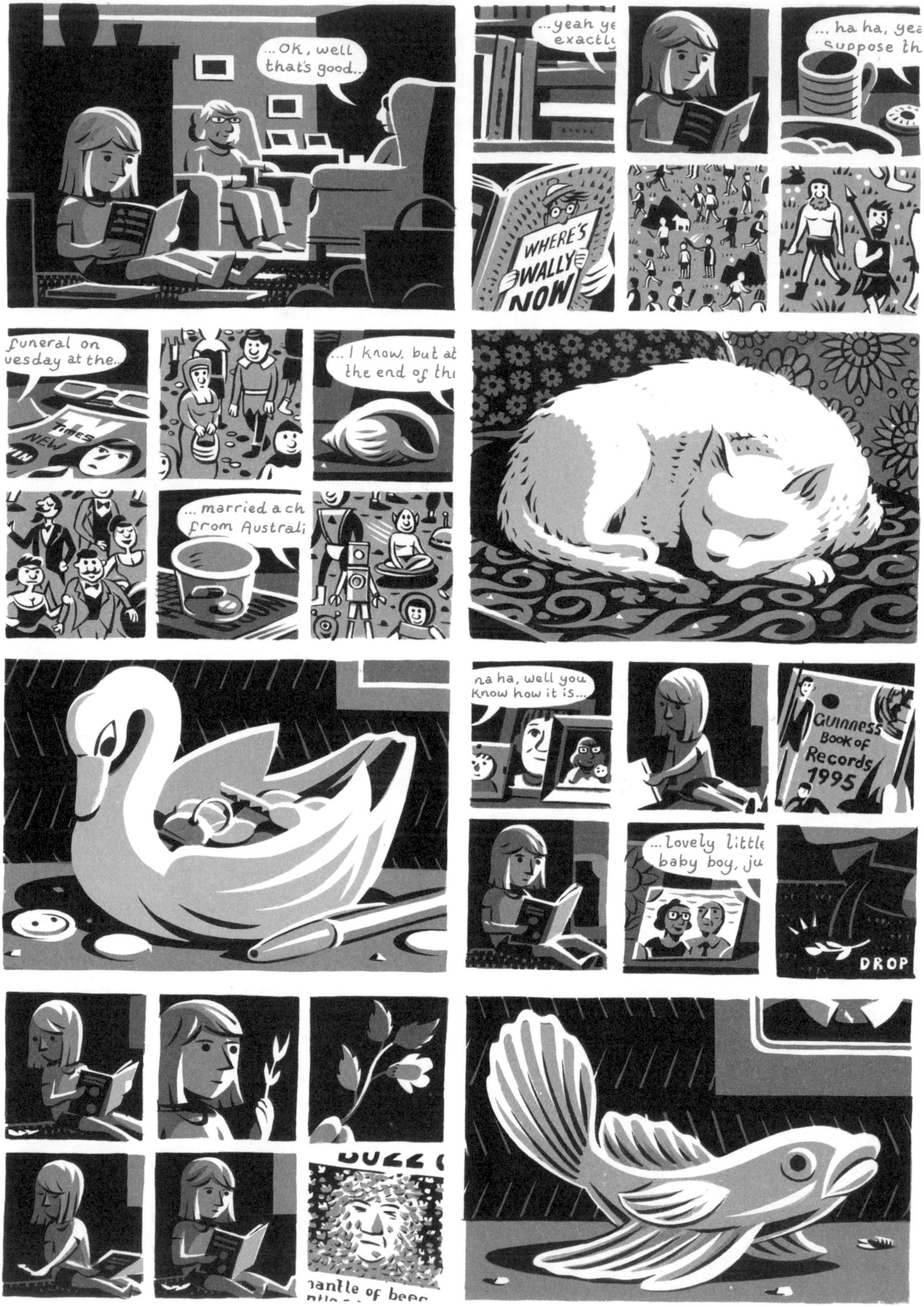
...OK, well that's good...
...yeah ye exactly
...ha ha, yea suppose th
WHERE'S WALLY NOW
funeral on uesday at the...
TIMES NEW
...I know, but at the end of th
...married a ch from Australi
na ha, well you know how it is...
GUINNESS Book of Records 1995
...Lovely little baby boy, ju
DROP
nantle of beer

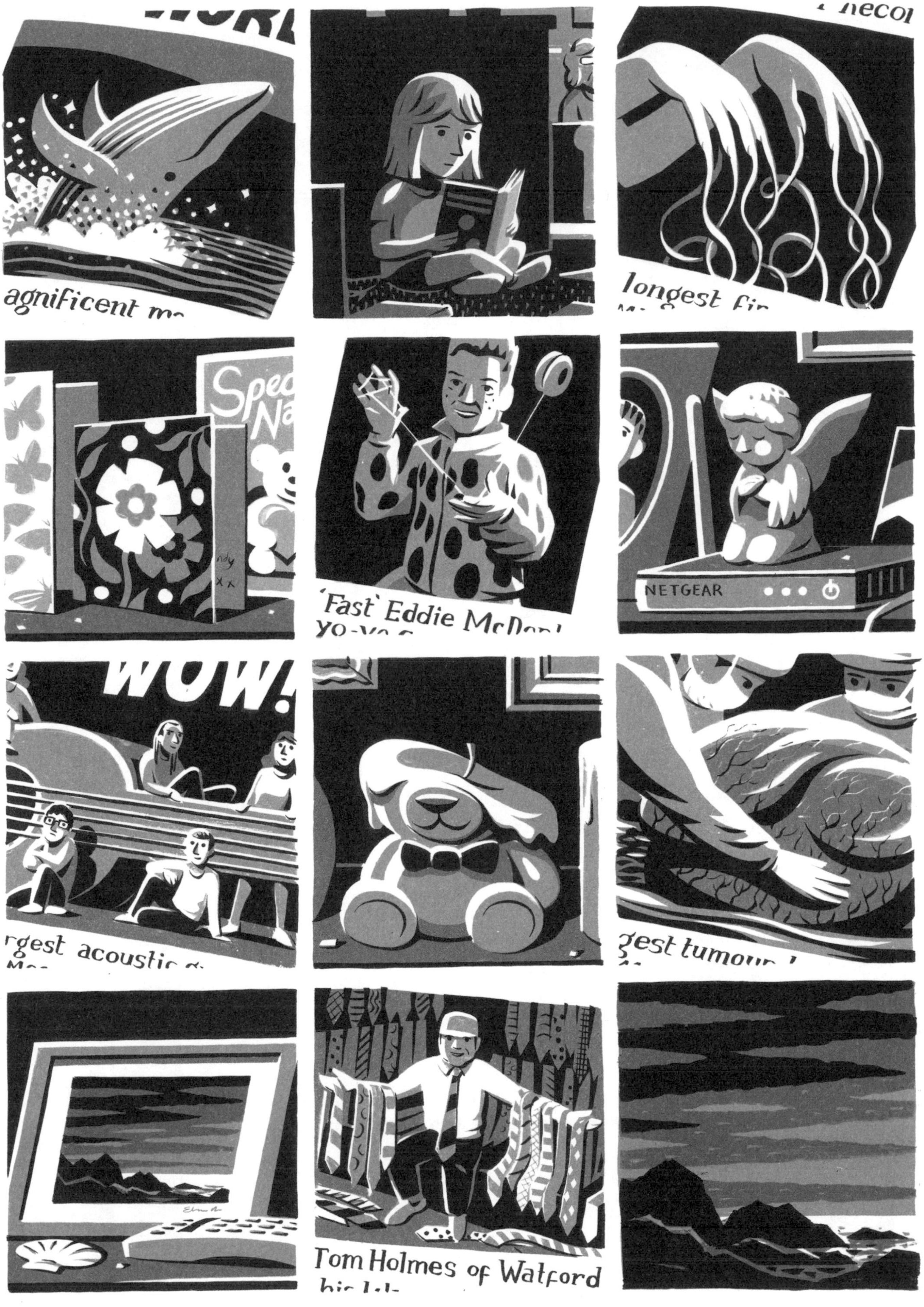
agnificent
longest
'Fast' Eddie McDon
NETGEAR
WOW!
rgest acoustic
gest tumour
Tom Holmes of Watford

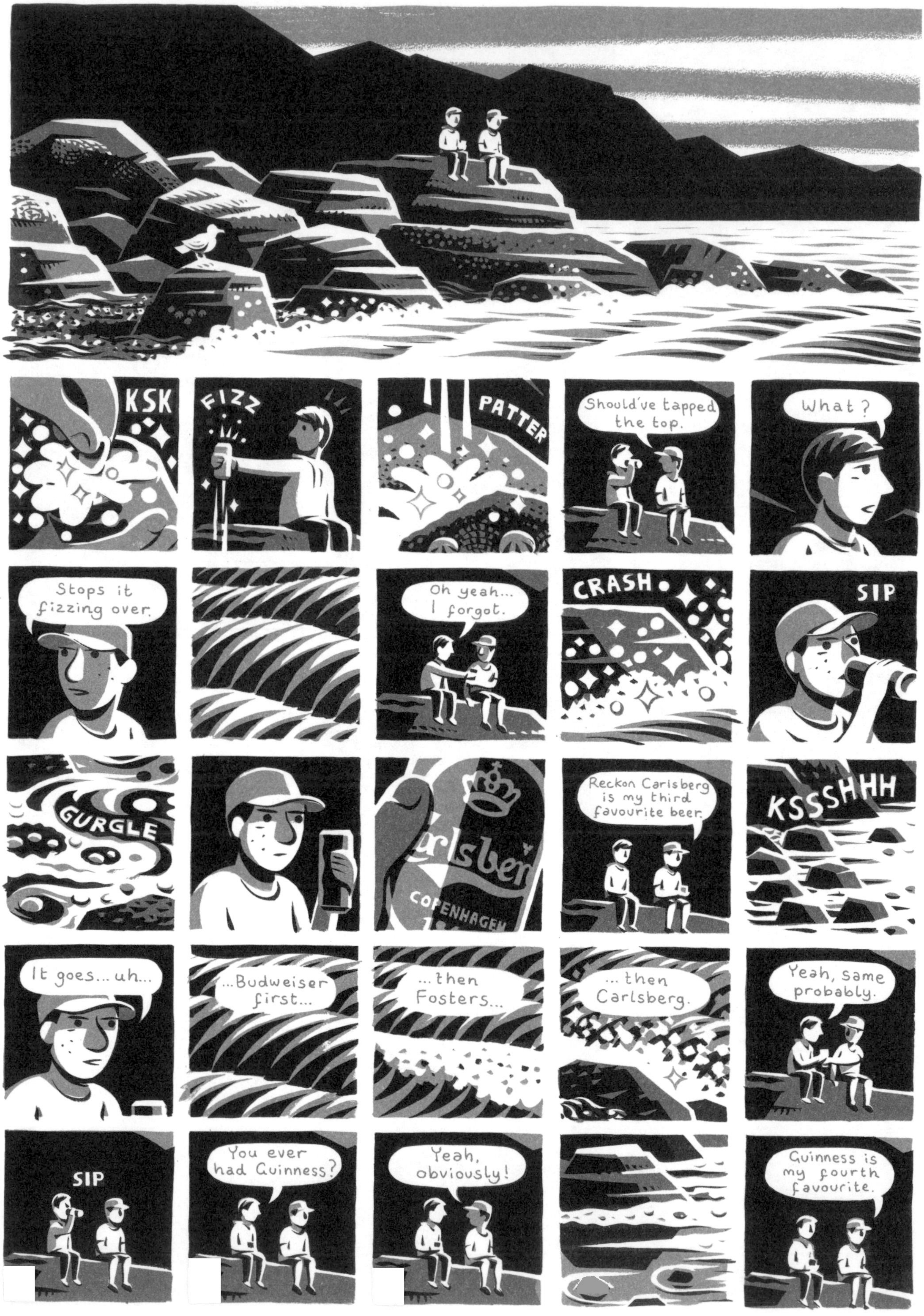
KSK
FIZZ
PATTER
Should've tapped the top.
What?
Stops it fizzing over.
Oh yeah... I forgot.
CRASH
SIP
GURGLE
Reckon Carlsberg is my third favourite beer.
KSSSHHH
It goes... uh...
...Budweiser first...
...then Fosters...
...then Carlsberg.
Yeah, same probably.
SIP
You ever had Guinness?
Yeah, obviously!
Guinness is my fourth favourite.

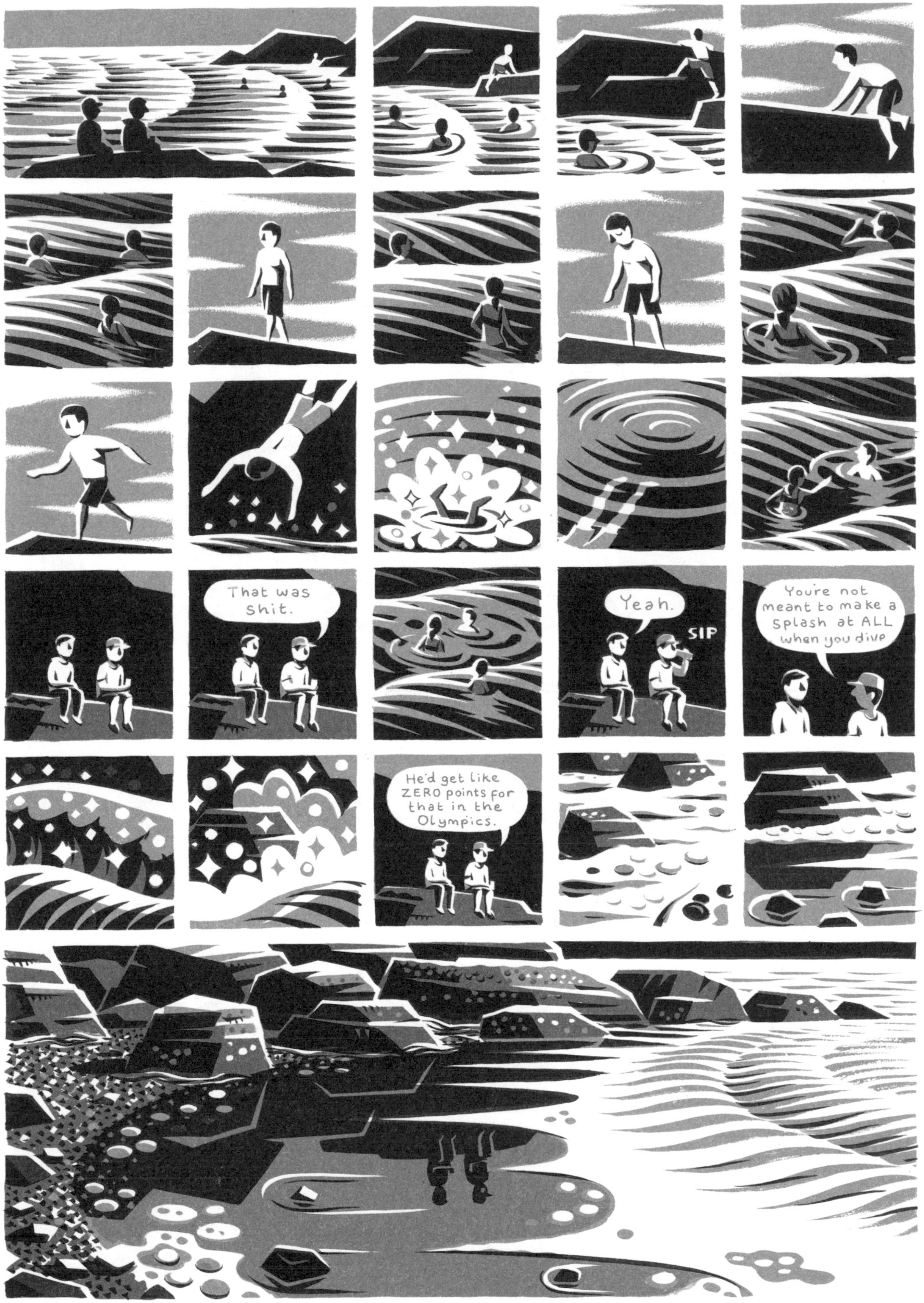
That was shit.
Yeah.
SIP
You're not meant to make a splash at ALL when you dive
He'd get like ZERO points for that in the Olympics.

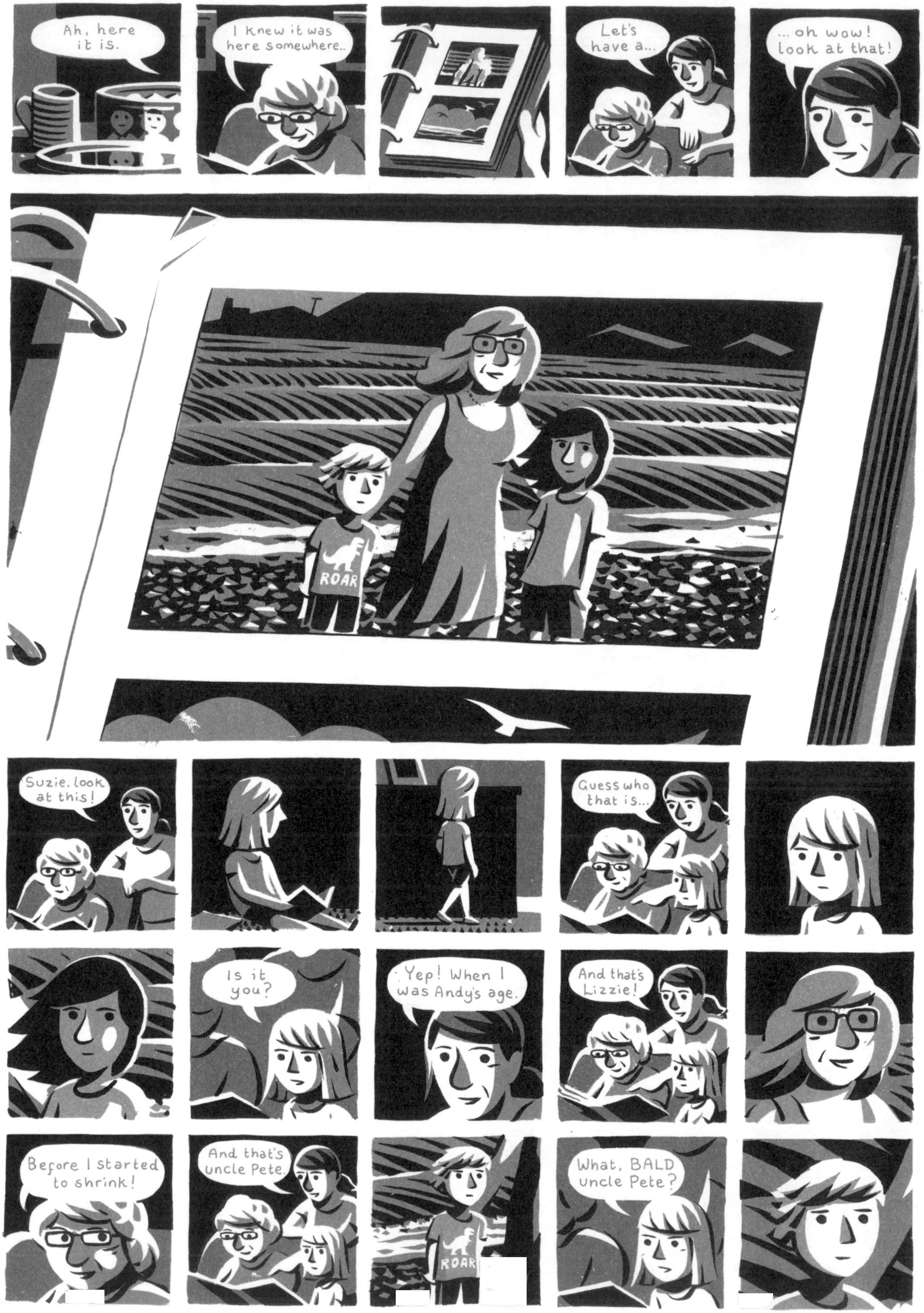
Ah, here it is.
I knew it was here somewhere..
Let's have a...
... oh wow! look at that!
ROAR
Suzie, look at this!
Guess who that is...
Is it you?
Yep! When I was Andy's age.
And that's Lizzie!
Before I started to shrink!
And that's uncle Pete.
ROAR
What, BALD uncle Pete?

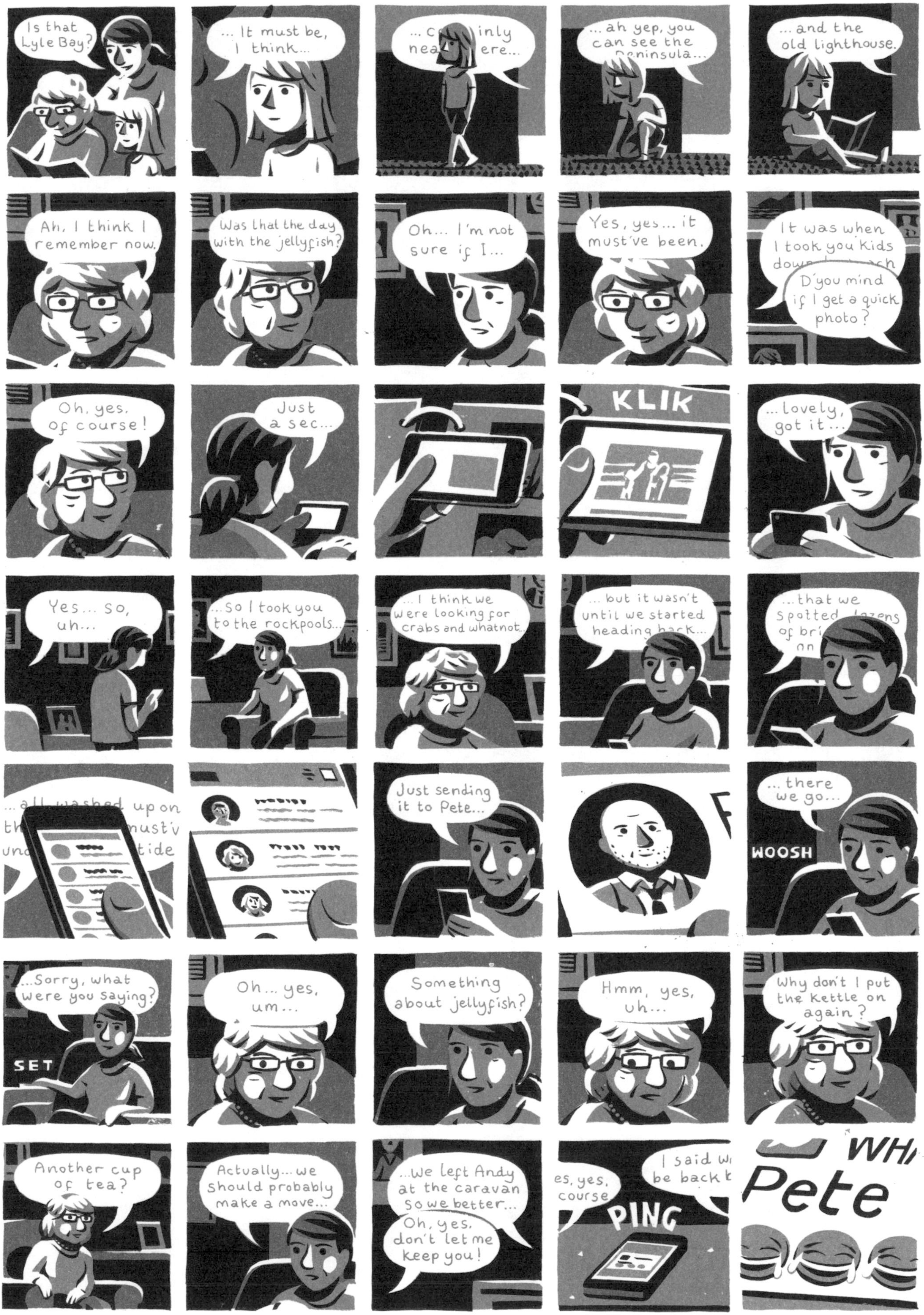
Is that Lyle Bay?
... It must be, I think...
... c inly nea ere...
... ah yep, you can see the
... and the old lighthouse.
Ah, I think I remember now.
Was that the day with the jellyfish?
Oh... I'm not sure if I...
Yes, yes... it must've been.
It was when I took you kids
D'you mind if I get a quick photo?
Oh, yes, of course!
Just a sec...
KLIK
... lovely, got it...
Yes... so, uh...
... so I took you to the rockpools...
... I think we were looking for crabs and whatnot...
... but it wasn't until we started heading back...
... that we spotted
Just sending it to Pete...
... there we go...
WOOSH
... Sorry, what were you saying?
SET
Oh... yes, um...
Something about jellyfish?
Hmm, yes, uh...
Why don't I put the kettle on again?
Another cup of tea?
Actually... we should probably make a move...
... We left Andy at the caravan so we better...
Oh, yes, don't let me keep you!
es, yes, course
I said
be back
PING
Pete

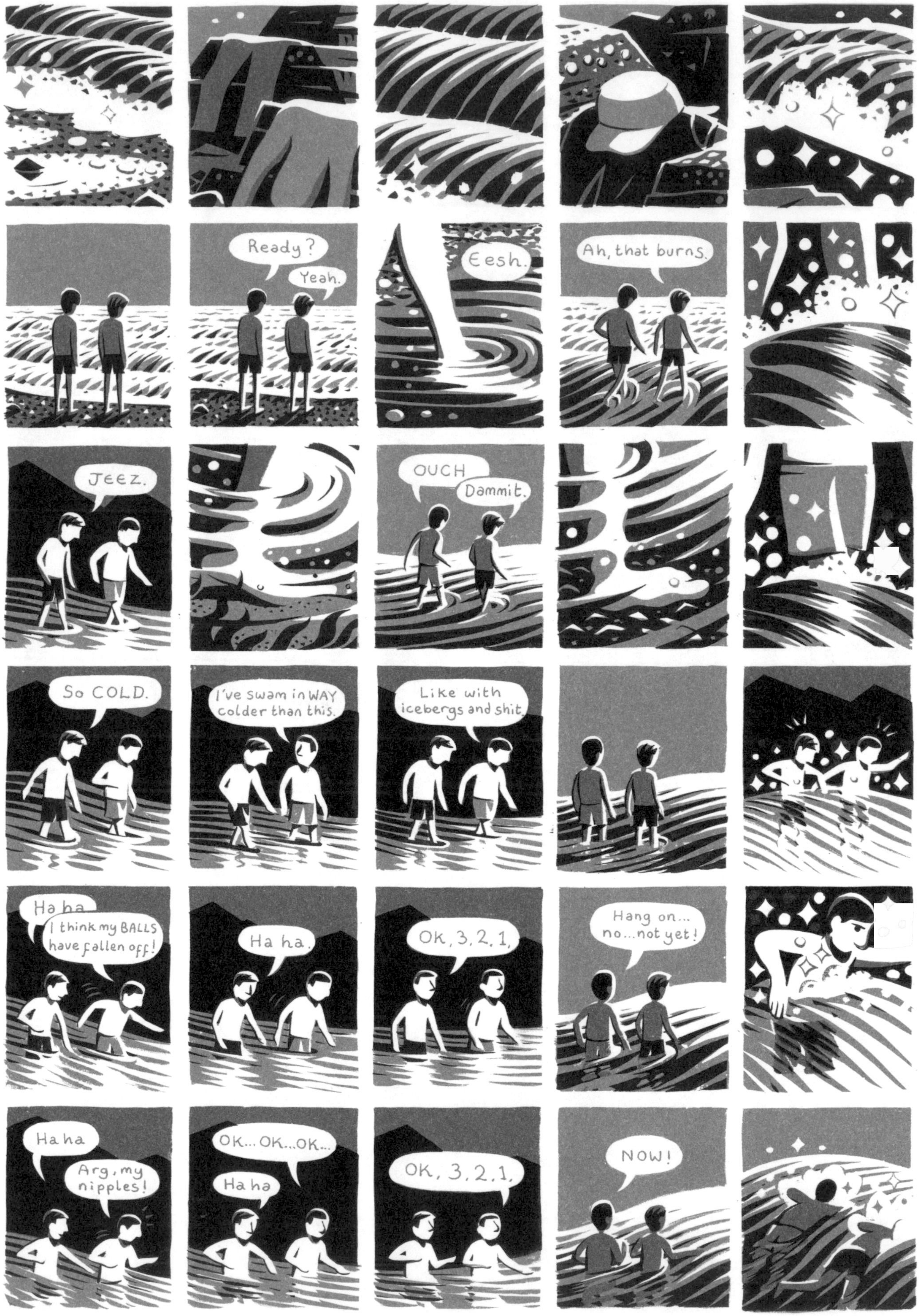
Ready?
Yeah.
Eesh.
Ah, that burns.
JEEZ.
OUCH
Dammit.
So COLD.
I've swam in WAY colder than this.
Like with icebergs and shit.
Ha ha
I think my BALLS have fallen off!
Ha ha.
OK, 3, 2, 1,
Hang on... no... not yet!
Ha ha
Arg, my nipples!
OK... OK... OK...
Ha ha
OK, 3, 2, 1,
NOW!

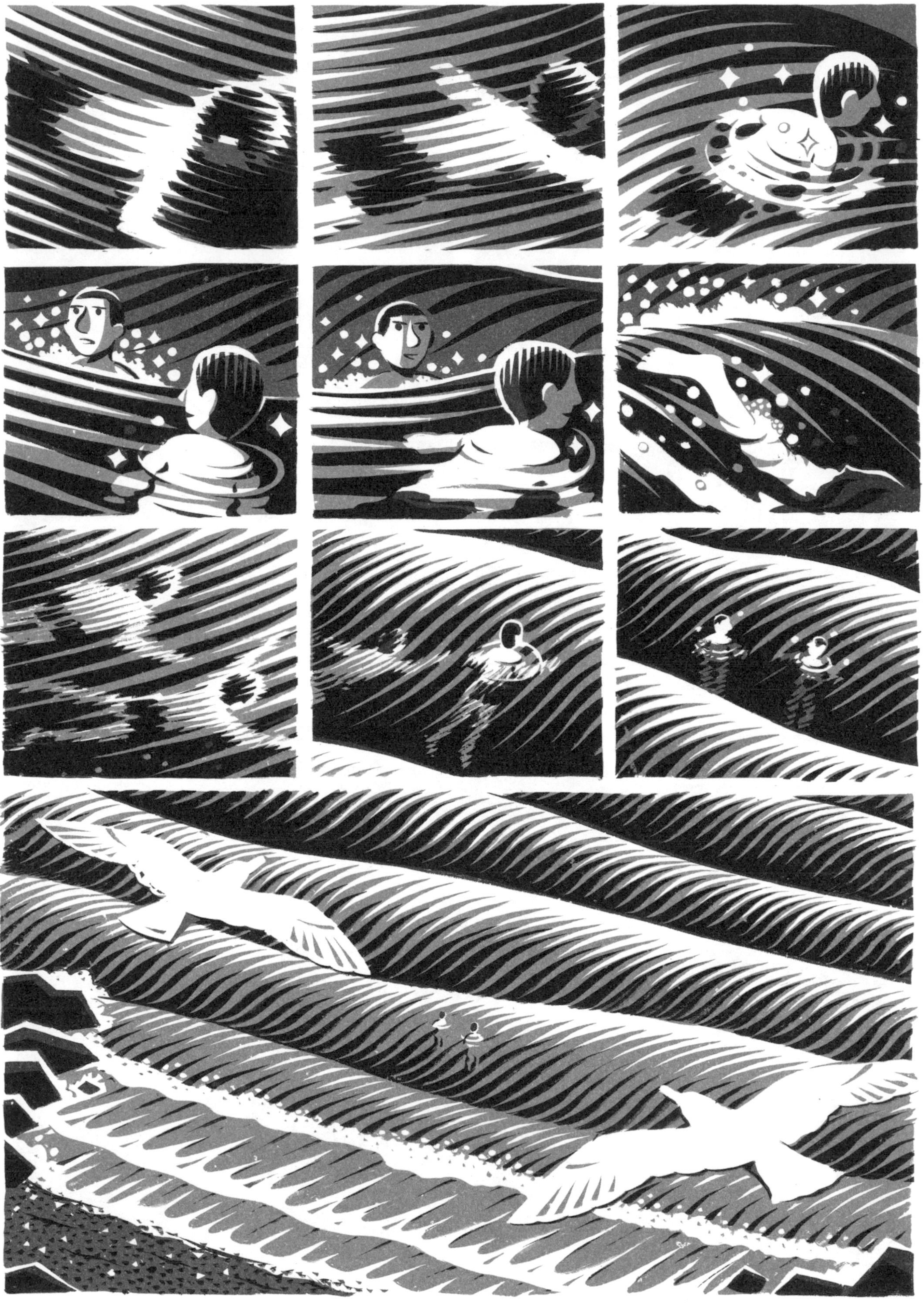

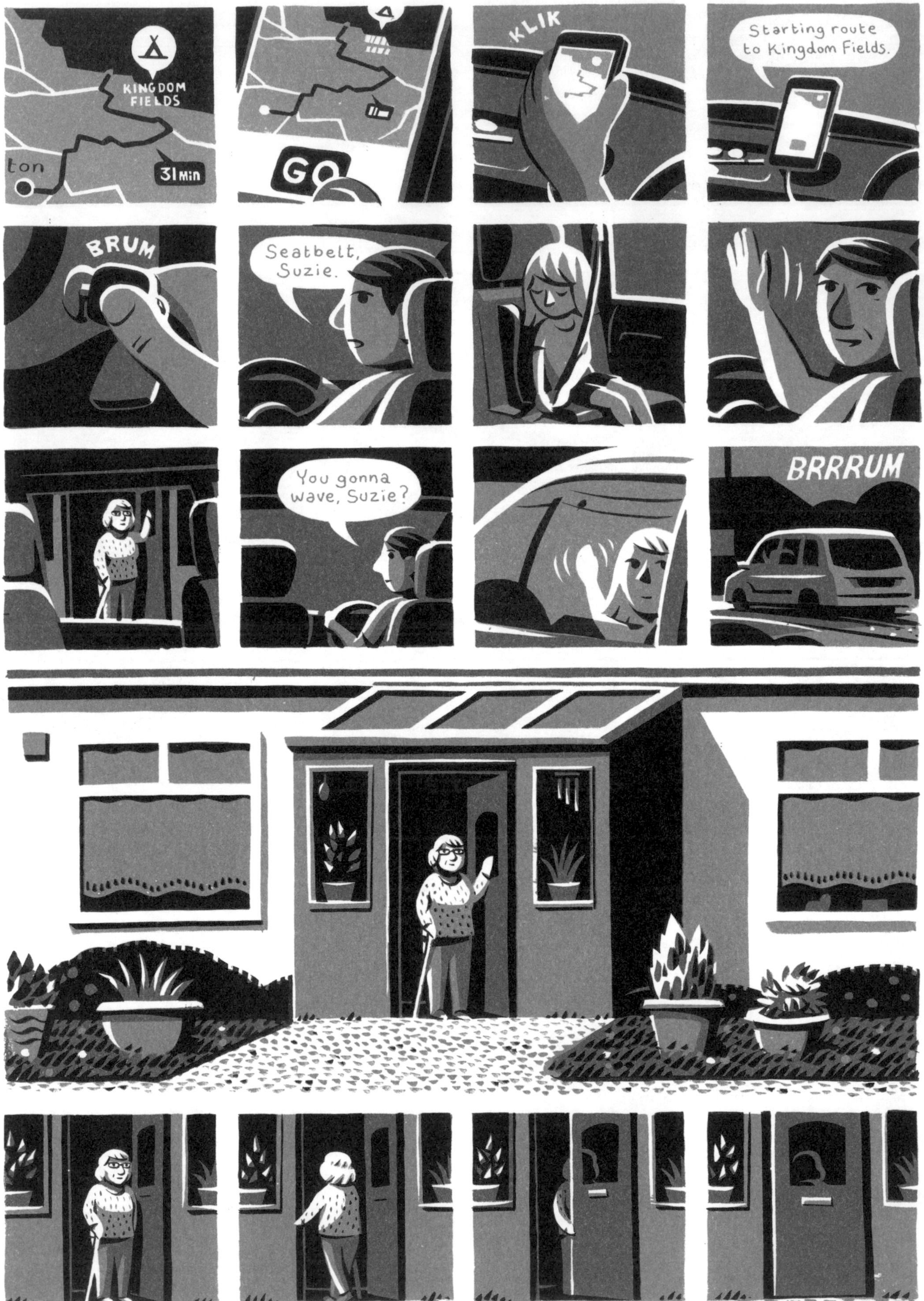
KINGDOM FIELDS
ton
31 min
GO
KLIK
Starting route to Kingdom Fields.
BRUM
Seatbelt, Suzie.
You gonna wave, Suzie?
BRRRUM

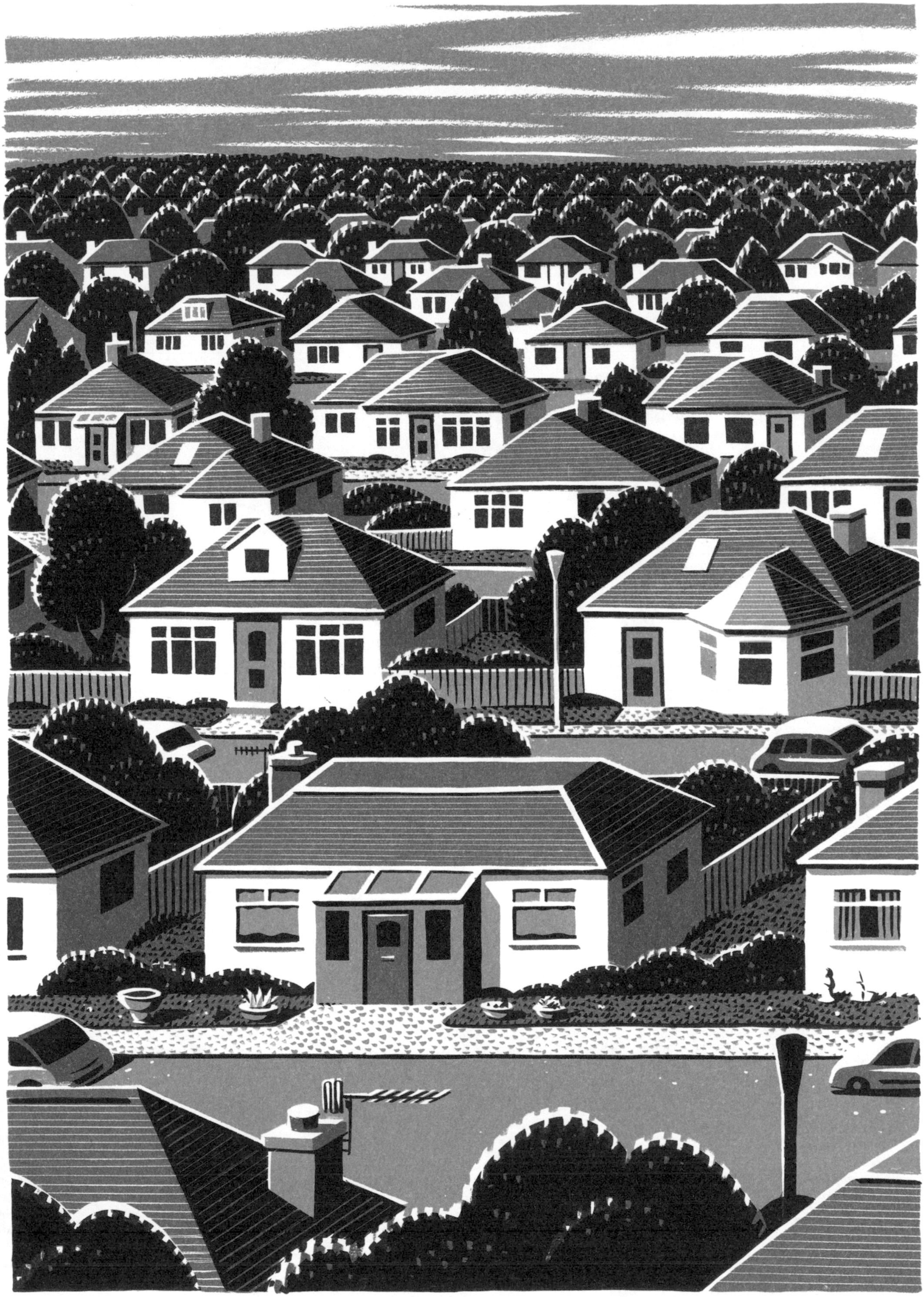

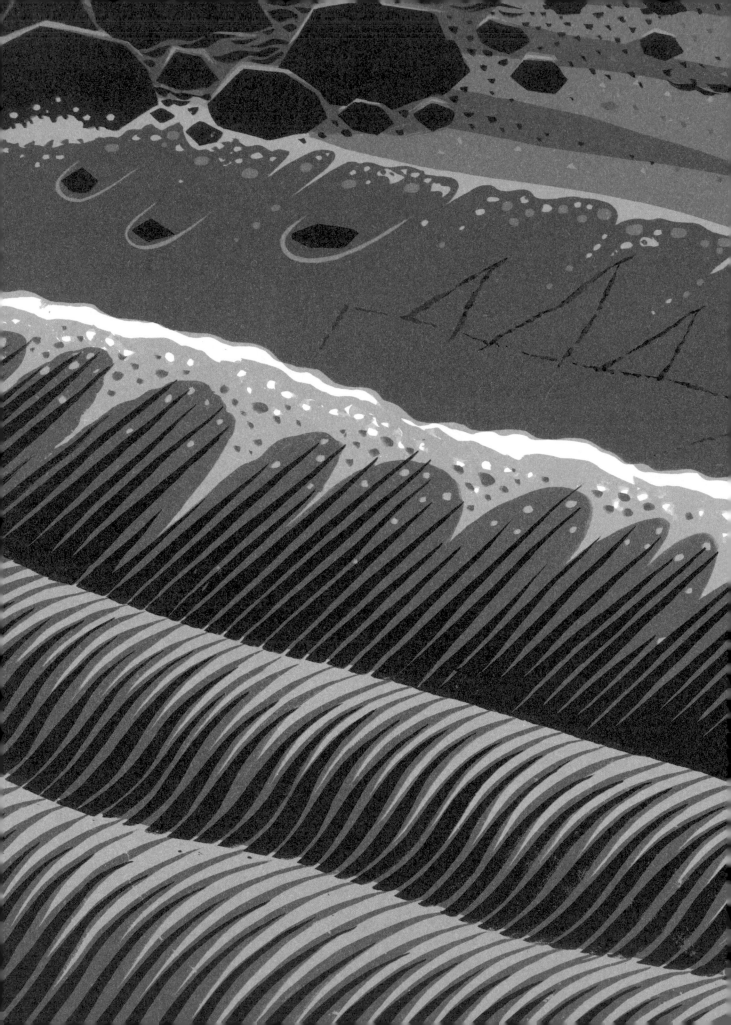

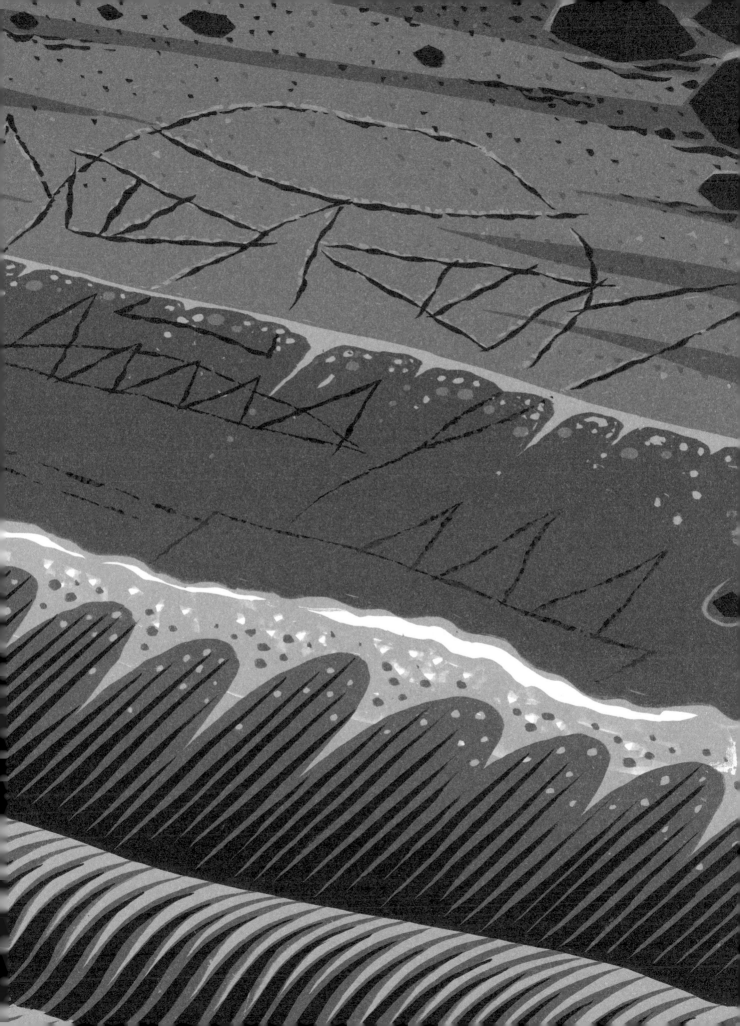

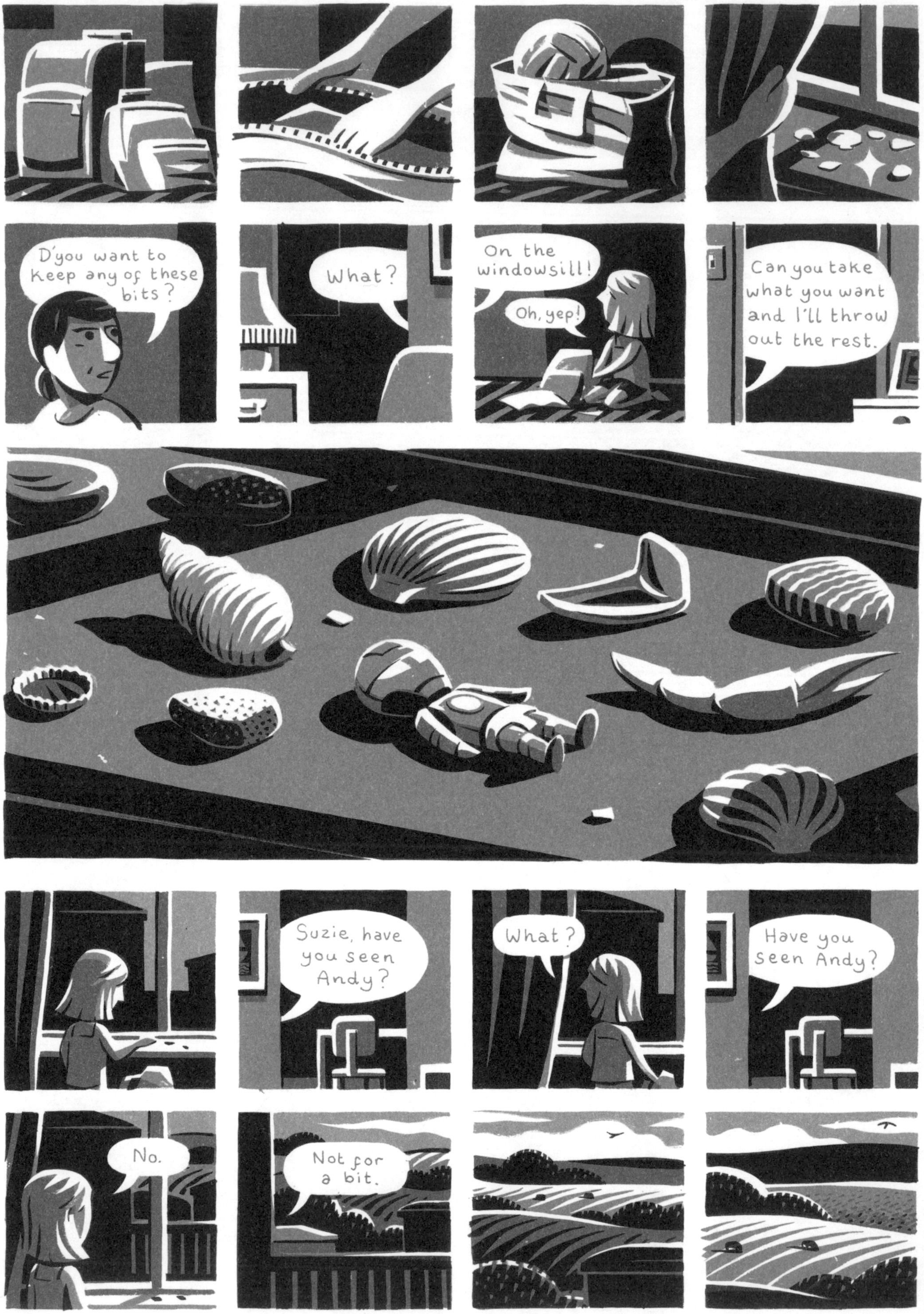
D'you want to keep any of these bits?
What?
On the windowsill!
Oh, yep!
Can you take what you want and I'll throw out the rest.
Suzie, have you seen Andy?
What?
Have you seen Andy?
No.
Not for a bit.

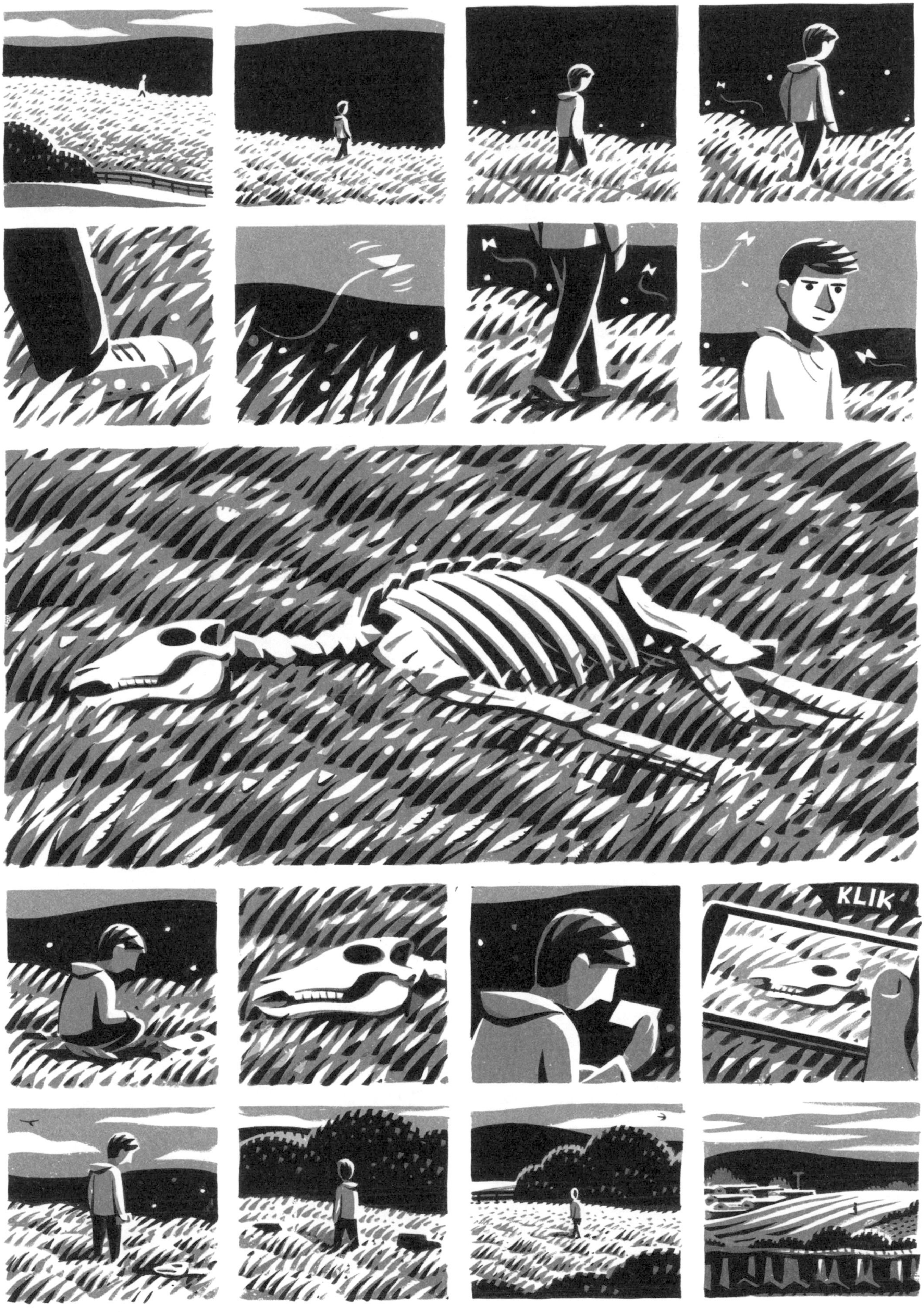
KLIK

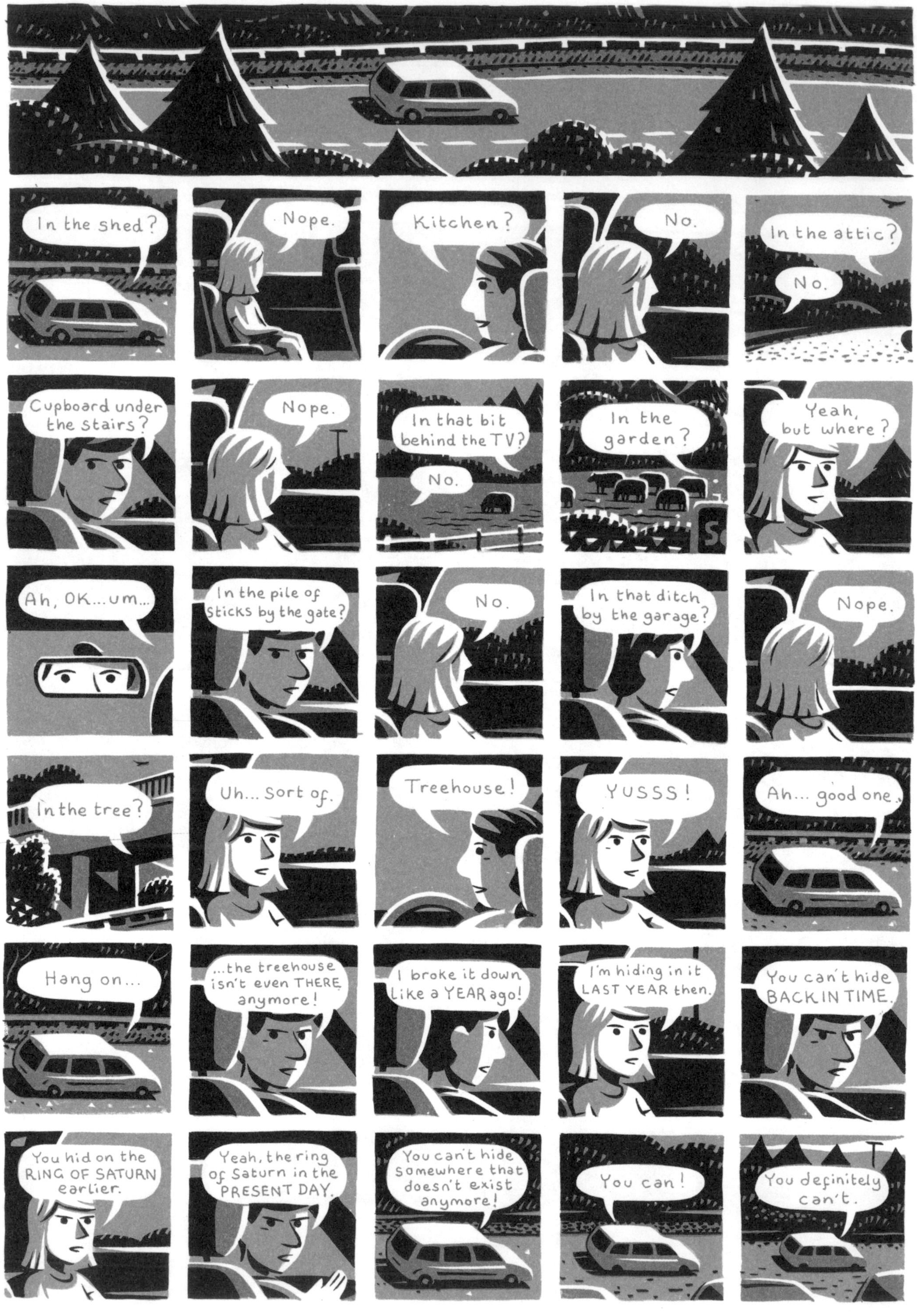
In the shed?
Nope.
Kitchen?
No.
In the attic?
No.
Cupboard under the stairs?
Nope.
In that bit behind the TV?
No.
In the garden?
Yeah, but where?
Ah, OK...um...
In the pile of sticks by the gate?
No.
In that ditch by the garage?
Nope.
In the tree?
Uh... Sort of.
Treehouse!
YUSSS!
Ah... good one.
Hang on...
...the treehouse isn't even THERE anymore!
I broke it down like a YEAR ago!
I'm hiding in it LAST YEAR then.
You can't hide BACK IN TIME.
You hid on the RING OF SATURN earlier.
Yeah, the ring of Saturn in the PRESENT DAY.
You can't hide somewhere that doesn't exist anymore!
You can!
You definitely can't.

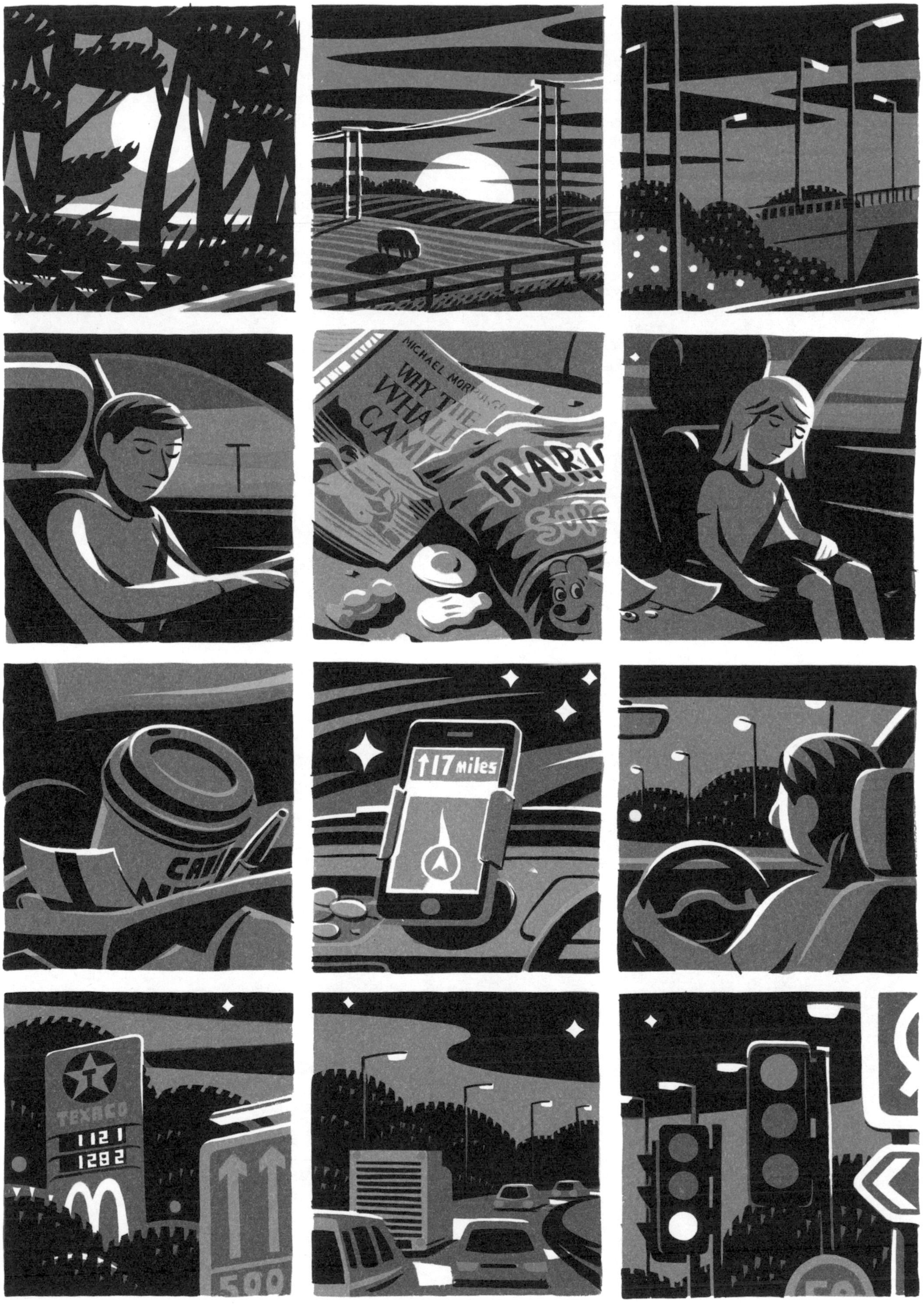
WHY THE
17 miles
TEXACO
1121
1282

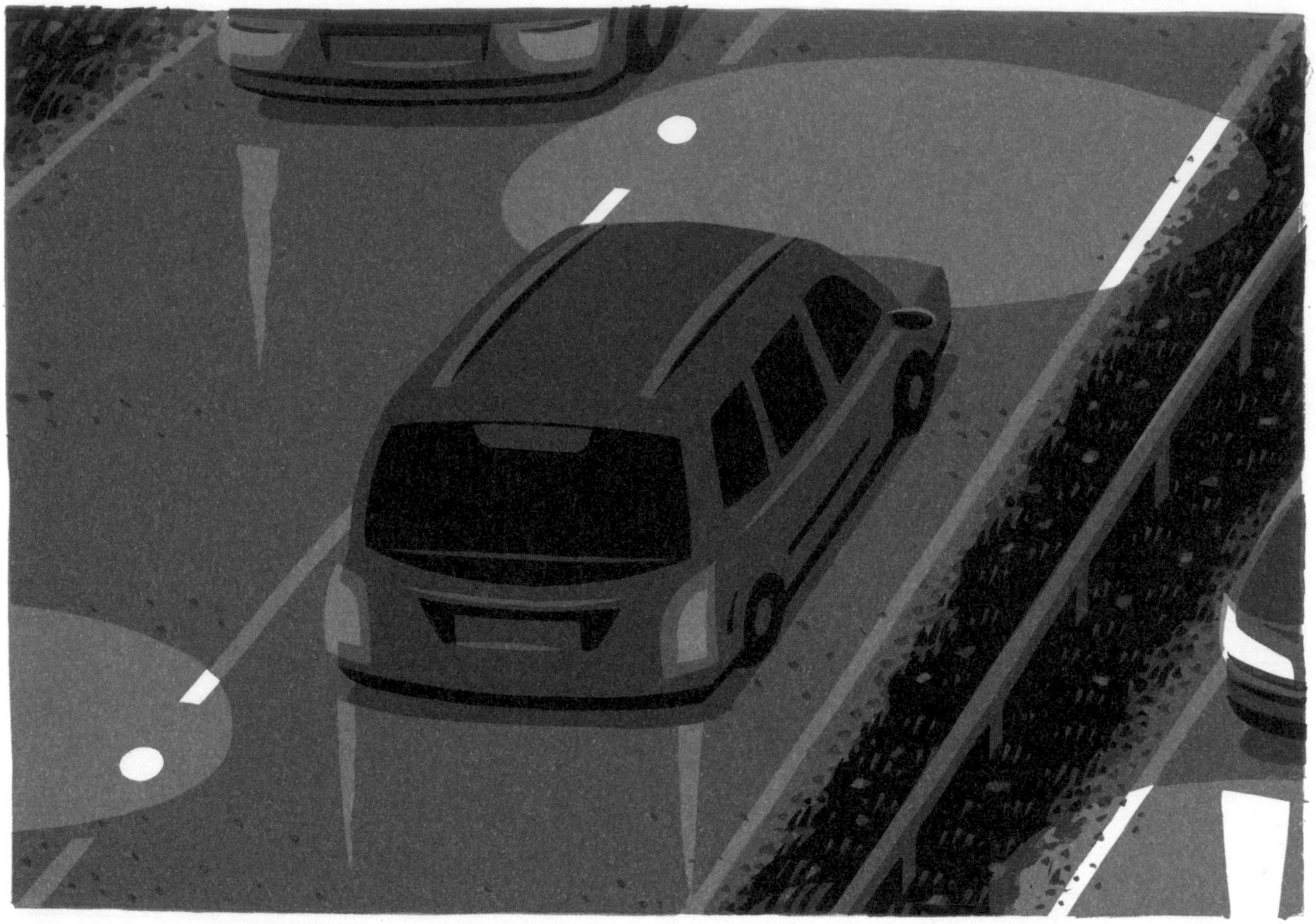

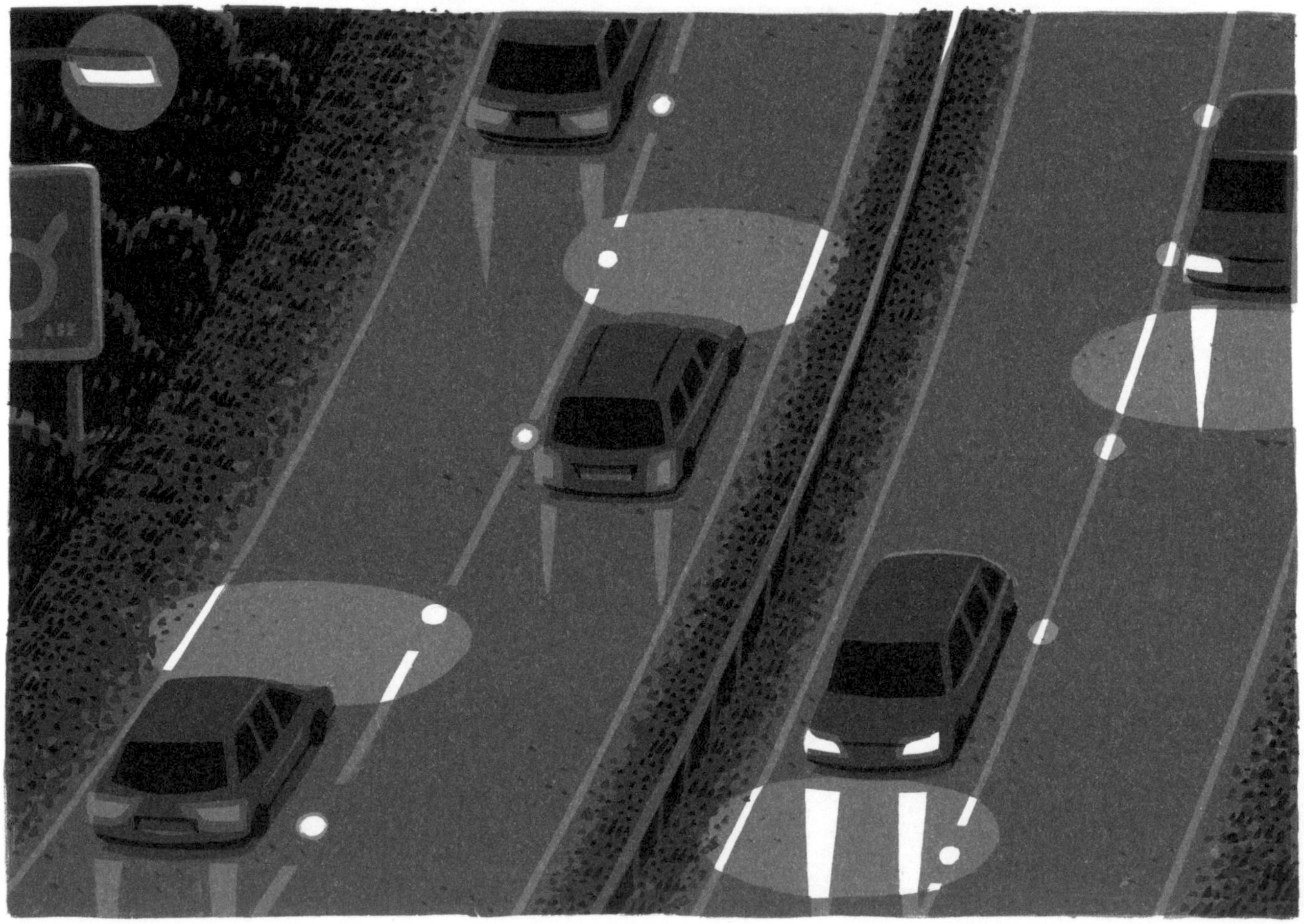

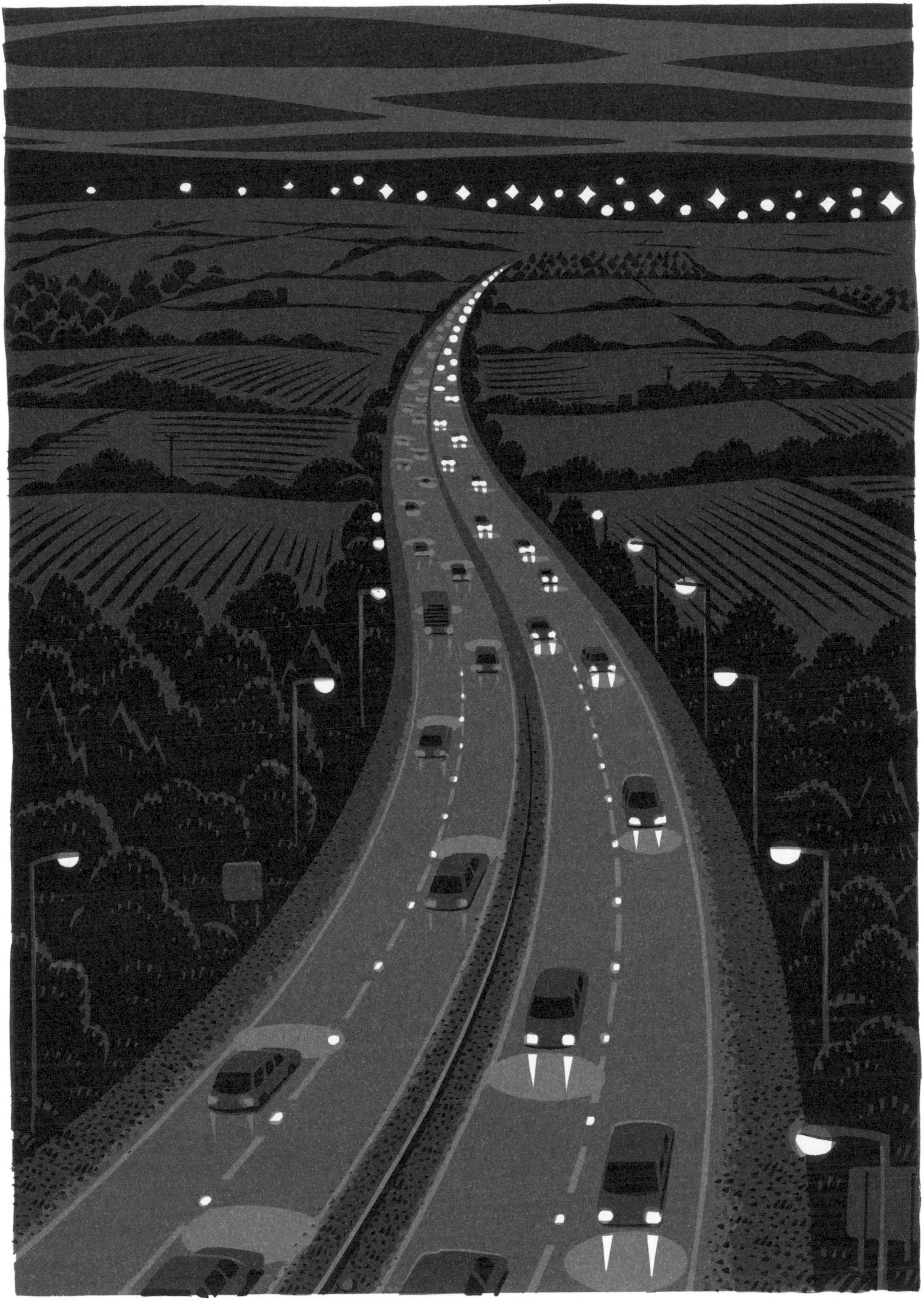

Thanks to Amy van Luijk, Bjorn Rune Lie, Matthew McNaught, Tim McNaught,
Luke Pearson, Chloe Emiabata, Jon Hill, Eleanor Hardiman, my colleagues
at the UWE Print centre, Nobrow, and my family.

Jon McNaught was born in 1985. He lives
in Bristol where he draws comics, and works
as an illustrator, printmaking instructor and
occasional teacher. He is also a regular cover
artist for the London Review of Books.

•

His previous books with Nobrow are *Birchfield
Close*, *Pebble Island* and *Dockwood* (Winner of the
Angouleme 'Prix Révélation' award in 2012).

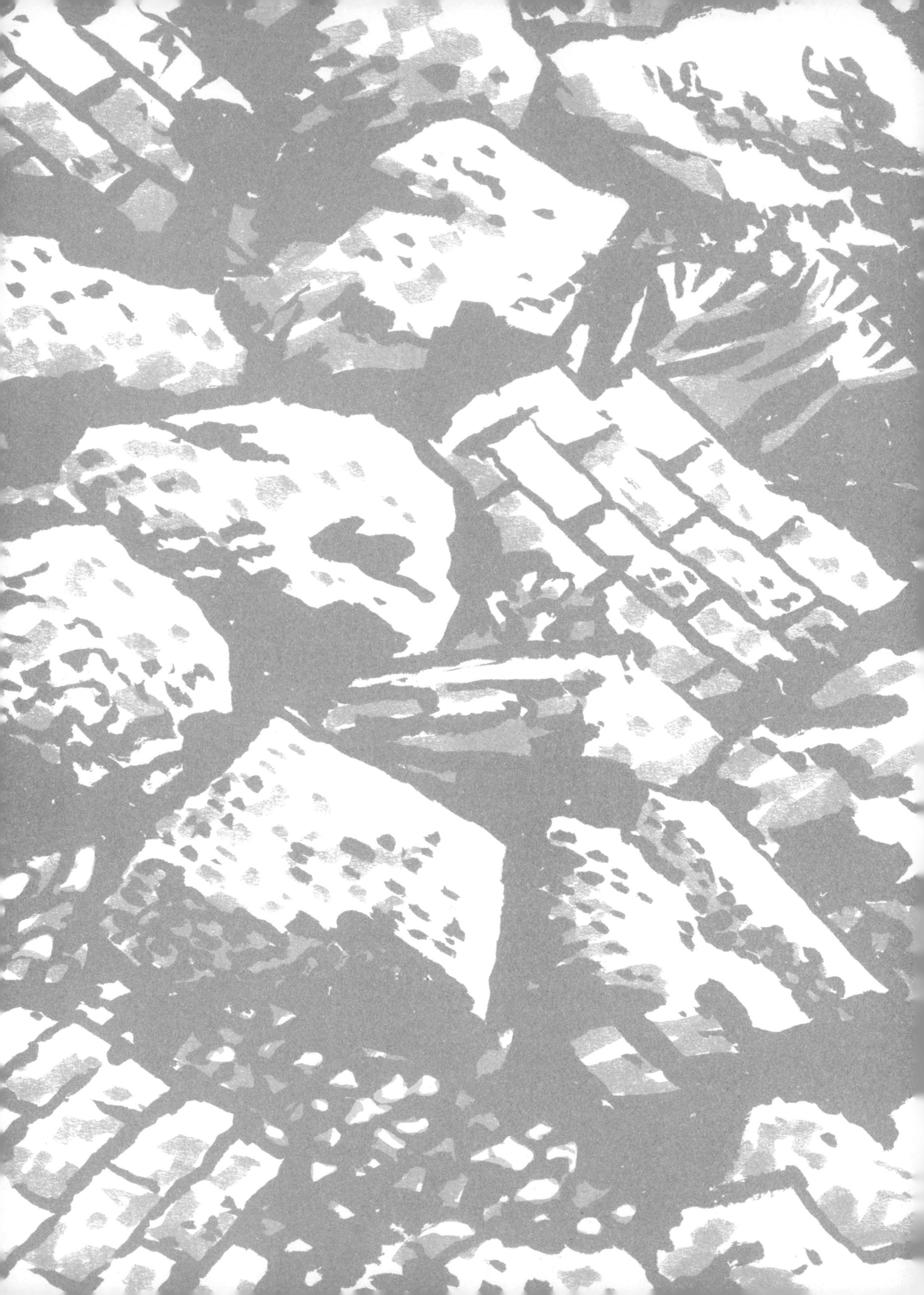